1

I DON'T DARE LOOK at the pregnancy test.

Not yet. First, I must set up the tripod, adjusting its legs so that it's the correct height, snapping my phone into the clutch, positioning it perfectly.

I want my reaction to be genuine if it's good news. I remind myself to think positive thoughts: *Worries create wrinkles! Smile instead!*

I wouldn't normally film in our bathroom. It's a private space, and Graham would be embarrassed, but this is different. *Special.* Besides, our bathroom is beautiful. It's new enough that I stop to admire it after washing my hands or, apparently, peeing on a stick.

We redid the downstairs bathroom after we closed on the house, and I told Graham it would be worth the price tag. The sink is made from hundred-year-old reclaimed wood; a porcelain bowl sits atop of it, as if waiting to be filled with colorful fruit, fragrant and shiny. The walls are white wood, and fluffy eggshell-colored towels are neatly displayed on floating shelves. The towels are still warm; I did the laundry earlier today, carefully folding everything. The bathroom smells of lavender, from the oil diffuser on the counter, and eucalyptus, from the rib-boned bundle that hangs from the showerhead, tender green heads resting against the subway tiles.

The plastic test is flat on the sink's counter, sitting on top of a lace doily I crocheted last year. I recorded a time-lapse video of me making the doily, flaxen hair spilling loosely over sun-kissed shoulders, my face fresh and filter-free; it got over a million views.

Standing behind the tripod that holds my phone, I place both my hands on my flat belly, imagining it swelling, imagining the photos I will take, imagining baking barefoot in the kitchen, flour dusting my glowing skin.

Manifest this, I repeat to myself. *Manifest.*

Graham would tell me to pray, but that's more his wheel-house than mine.

I move around the tripod, ducking out of the bathroom to check my reflection in the hall mirror. The one in the bathroom is too close to the pregnancy test. I don't want to be tempted to glance down before I'm ready.

I examine my face in the mirror. Pinch my cheeks, bringing color to them. My eyes are wide and hopeful. Almost desperate. That won't do. I lean closer to my reflection and think of sad things like dogs in pounds and old men waiting for the bus in the rain. Dewy tears collect along the rims of my eyes, making them look more hazel and less brown. Perfect.

Now I am ready.

Stepping back into the bathroom, I hit record on my phone and hop into the camera's frame, smiling.

"Hi, friends! It's me, Camille. If you've been following me for a while, you know how important this is. So I wanted to share it all live." Technically, that is a lie. There's no way I would actually live stream my pregnancy results. I want to tell Graham first. And what if it's bad news?

TRAD WIFE

SARATOGA SCHAEFER

bantam

TRANSWORLD PUBLISHERS

UK | USA | Canada | Ireland | Australia
India | New Zealand | South Africa

Transworld is part of the Penguin Random House group of companies
whose addresses can be found at global.penguinrandomhouse.com.

Penguin Random House UK, One Embassy Gardens,
8 Viaduct Gardens, London SW11 7BW

penguin.co.uk

Penguin
Random House
UK

First published in Great Britain in 2026 by Bantam,
an imprint of Transworld Publishers

001

Copyright © Saratoga Schaefer 2025

The moral right of the author has been asserted.

Printed and bound in Great Britain by Clays Ltd, Elcograf S.p.A.

The authorized representative in the EEA is Penguin Random House Ireland,
Morrison Chambers, 32 Nassau Street, Dublin D02 YH68.

A CIP catalogue record for this book is available from the British Library.

ISBNs:

9780857509413 hb
9780857509420 tpb

Penguin Random House is committed to a sustainable future
for our business, our readers and our planet. This book is made
from Forest Stewardship Council® certified paper.

For Cricket,
my little demon.

Above all, love each other deeply, because love covers over a multitude of sins.

—1 Peter 4:8

I

First Trimester

Happy thoughts only! I correct myself, hoping the agitation doesn't show on my features. Graham is always saying I look far less cherubic when I'm upset. *It* will *be positive!*

"OK, here we go, the results from my pregnancy test!" I chirp, staring into the camera lens. "I'm so excited. I already know we're going to have a little girl; I can *feel* it . . ."

I lean over, lift the test up, cast my teary eyes down, a celebration already forming on my naturally exfoliated lips.

The plastic trembles and my sight blurs for a moment before I refocus, swallowing hard, words tumbling down the back of my throat like rancid pomegranate seeds.

Tearing a piece of toilet paper from the roll, I wind it around the test, dropping it in the trash. I have to remember to take the garbage out before Graham gets home in an hour. And I should have started dinner already. I'll have to make a few canapés so he has something to tide him over.

All our food must be handmade, cooked from scratch. Dinner will take a while. I was going to do a pork roast with sautéed vegetables; I haven't even washed the veggies yet. I was avoiding them, ashamed I had to buy the zucchini and peppers from the nearby farm instead of yanking them from my own garden like I did at our old house. I haven't had enough time to set up a new plot here yet. But I can whip up some bruschetta—we have leftover sourdough from the batch I made this weekend and local tomatoes and basil. There's fresh-squeezed lemonade in our fridge. We aren't big drinkers, but maybe I'll add vodka to Graham's lemonade tonight. He'll put on a game and relax on the ivory sectional while I cook, thinking I planned it that way.

At least I had the forethought to not tell him I was testing today. If I don't say anything, he'll have no idea.

I take down the tripod quickly, deleting the truncated video from my phone and swiping away the tears, real ones, this time, clinging to my expertly applied mascara. I'm smudging my "makeup-free" look and I'll have to retouch it before Graham comes home, but I can't help it.

I really thought things would be different here, in the new house. It's only been a month, but I had hoped the change in location would make everything better. Instead, here I am again with a negative test and an empty womb.

I need a baby. I promised our family. I promised my husband. I promised my followers.

Looking at my reddening face in the gold-trimmed bathroom mirror, I picture slamming a fist into the glass, watching shards drive into my knuckles and wrist, scowling as blood runs down my arm, staining my beautiful taupe linen dress.

Instead, I shake my head, golden locks swaying, dab at my eyes, and smile.

CHAPTER

2

G RAHAM IS GOING to be late. Again. Second time this week. He texts me twenty minutes after he is due home—the phone screen lights up as my fingers drip with balsamic.

Grabbing drinks with the sales team. Be home later. Don't worry about dinner.

When I was little, my mother would tell me that every time I felt like frowning, I should smile instead. It's one of the few memories I have of her.

"It takes more muscles to frown, Camille," she would say. "Avoid those wrinkles on your forehead. Change the negative into a positive and smile!"

When my mother died, my father continued her tradition, warning me off creases and crinkles by telling me to stay calm and serene.

Early on in our relationship, Graham asked why I smiled so much. I didn't tell him the truth. I said smiling was part of who I was.

Graham and I met when I was twenty and he was twenty-five. We were both at a farmers market—he noticed my hand-woven basket filled with fresh fruit and vegetables and came over to chat, asking if I liked to cook, if I had made the basket myself. We planned a coffee date, an enraptured expression on Graham's face when I showed up with loose hair and a long, linen dress.

"So, Camille, what do you do?" he asked over lattes and scones.

"Oh, well, I'm not in school anymore, so I'm working at a wholesale growing center. I help grow and harvest plants and flowers, then we send them to retailers and local florists." Graham's expression glazed over, his eyes skimming the rest of the coffee shop. Hurriedly, I added, "But I'd love to have a family one day. I lost my mother when I was young, and I've always dreamed of giving my child what I didn't have."

This Graham liked. He perked up, gaze swiveling back to my face. "I'm so sorry to hear that, Camille. That must have been hard for you. Do you want to talk about it?"

His kindness in that moment endeared him to me even more, and he spent the rest of the date holding my hand across the table, stroking a thumb against my knuckles.

A picnic in the park followed the success of our coffee date, then we made it official. We married a year after we first met. Very romantic. Photos of our wedding day, me with soft curls and a lace dress, him in a smart blue suit, dark hair slicked back, decorate our walls.

Shortly after we wed, I noticed a new type of content pop up online: attractive women in beautiful kitchens, baking bread from scratch, collecting eggs from their chickens, doting upon angelic children who politely smiled for the camera. Their ruggedly good-looking husbands bought them aprons and handwoven wool blankets as gifts. I saw their lifestyle, and I wanted it. With Graham's blessing, I started posting photos and videos of our life with a pretty, rustic aesthetic that people—mostly women—flocked to.

I made sure to always smile, showing gratitude and keeping those pesky wrinkles at bay.

I smile now as I rinse off my hands in the farm sink. I grin as I use a moss-green dish towel to dry off. I keep my lips curled as I put plastic wrap over the bruschetta and slip it into the huge stainless fridge.

The kitchen smells of pork, slowly roasting. The vegetables sit dripping on the butcher block counter. I haven't gotten around to cutting them yet.

Learning to cook, and cook well, took me a while. Years, really. It wasn't natural for me like it is for some of the women online, making meals from scratch easily and calmly. But perhaps that's because my home education started earlier, under more dire circumstances. When my mother passed, it was only me and my father, so I became the lady of the house. I was eight. Father was an attorney, always busy, always hungry when he returned home. Adopting my mother's recipe books, I painstakingly learned to cook for him, but I didn't get any good at it until I reached my teens. Cleaning the house was easier. Keeping things tidy and organized was my forte.

The first time I cooked a perfect steak, my father sighed, lips twitching. "Finally. No more sneaking takeout after you go to bed. Excellent work, Camille. You're your mother's daughter."

That approval meant more to me than anything else in the world. I latched on to it, craved it. Smeared it around my lips and licked it up like ice cream.

No worries, babe, I text back to Graham when I'm calmer and my smile has faded slightly. *I'll see you later. I'll leave leftovers in the fridge for you in case you get hungry.*

He's been doing this more and more often since we moved. Staying out late. Coming home looking peculiar, like a stranger wearing a mask of his face. We haven't had sex in weeks. I think of the pregnancy test. I had hoped his dip in amorousness was because he knew, on some level, that I was growing our child. As if his manly, evolutionary instinct had kicked in and recognized the pheromones of his mate. But I know now that can't be true.

The roast still has thirty-five minutes in the vintage oven Graham bought for us when we first moved in, upon my request. I have some time. Unwinding the ties from around my neck and waist, I drape my apron across the back of a wooden stool at the marble breakfast bar and move around the muted, minimalistic space.

Our new home is a farmhouse-style two-story that we—well, I—decorated to be quietly rustic, with wooden accent furniture and white walls. The color palette for everything is neutral tones—beige, champaign, pearl, sand. Where I wanted pops of color, I used a light apricot, which shows itself in throw pillows and candlestick holders. I had researched other accounts like mine, pausing on videos and zooming in on homes in the background, eager to imitate the gorgeous aesthetic I was never able to recreate in our other house. Our old place was cramped, too small for the farmhouse minimalist style that's popular within my online niche. But, with Graham's help, I made this place into the ideal home. Both for us and for social media.

I don't stop to admire the open-concept living room today. The smell of meat permeates the first floor as I open a charmingly carved pine box that sits on the glass coffee table. I dip a hand inside, digging around the loose change until I find what I'm looking for: a penny, shiny and coppery. I don't keep ugly coins. If they look green or battered, I toss them in the church collection basket along with whatever crisp bills Graham has in his wallet that week.

Holding the penny loosely in my hand, I move through the living room until I come to the sliding glass door at the back of the house, floating out onto the concrete slab that will eventually become a patio and into the backyard. Which is really just a giant field.

A lot of girls like me have a real farm, but we're not at that point yet. I don't even have a chicken coop—we get our eggs and meat from the Calloways, our neighbors up the road. I'll need to work on that; the least I can do is get the herb and vegetable garden started soon.

We have no fence. We have no boundaries. Our land is sizable and unbound—we are the only house in sight. I stride over the gently sloping grassy lawn, walking straight into the wheat field, turning the penny in my palm, feeling it grow warm with the heat from my skin.

The ankle-length linen dress I'm wearing *shush*es against my shins as I walk, bare feet parting the green blades as I go. The late-summer sun is beginning to sink below the faraway tree line, casting mellow liquid gold over the wheat. The field moves as one being in the breeze, and my breath catches as I am reminded again that this is mine now. Well, Graham's, technically. But part of my life. My home.

The wheat comes up to my shoulders. I discovered early on that walking in the field made me feel like I was swimming in a sea of straw. When Graham caught me wandering into the wheat the first time, he cautioned against it, citing ticks and snakes. Chastised, I avoided the field for a few days before I was drawn back to it. Now I only visit when Graham isn't home, letting my palms drift against the wheat heads, my feet crunching through the fallen stalks.

The setting sun bathes my face and the penny grows hotter in my hand. I try to swallow the lump forming in my throat, but it makes my eyes water more.

I wander through the field, heading toward the back of the property, where a thick line of ancient trees announces the arrival of the forest. I am consumed by the wheat, and I glance over my shoulder to catch a glimpse of our house's eaves rising above the thicket.

Everything is quiet inside the field; I am aware of crickets chirping and birds whizzing by overhead, traveling to their nests ahead of the sinking sun, but there is a silence within the wheat all the same. The inside of my head quiets the most, easing away thoughts of the pregnancy test, the pork roast, Graham.

At the edge of the field, the wheat drops away, getting shorter and sparser, creating a bare strip of land right before the trunks of the trees erupt from the ground, signaling the darkness of the forest.

I haven't dared to go into the woods; I always stay in the liminal space between the wheat and the forest. The trees sprawling before me are thick and close together—the light is dim and watery, like the bottom of a brackish pond. I can't see much more from here except gnarled roots and underbrush lashed together.

Walking in the field is one thing, but there are probably animals lurking among the trees that I don't want to come upon. Bears, maybe. Or foxes with needle-sharp teeth. Owls that will rip my hair out for their nests.

The other reason I don't like the forest is because it hums. A low, almost inaudible vibration that steals into my body and settles on my bones. But I keep coming back to this part of our property, every chance I get, because this is where the old well is, crouching several yards away from the forest's hemline.

I approach the well now, weeds flattened around it from where I've trampled them, rocky wall eroding slightly, the tattered remnants of a wooden bucket leaning sadly against its side. The whole thing will have to be boarded up when I eventually have a baby, but for now, I keep its existence to myself. I haven't told Graham.

I discovered the well a week ago, and at first, it frightened me. It smells sweet and sharp, like rotting flowers, and it reminds me of a person, hunched over, waiting to spring to their feet. But now I need it.

Before the car accident, my mother and I used to take walks to Mr. Jasper's yard down the block from our ranch house. He had a little wishing well in the front yard. There was no water at the bottom, no hole—it was for show only, but my mother and I would still toss pennies in there, wishing.

"What did you wish for?" I would always ask her.

"If I tell you, it won't come true," she would reply, smiling.

And every night after visiting the wishing well, while she was tucking me into bed, she would whisper in my ear, "I wished for you to be happy."

This well doesn't have the little awning over the top that Mr. Jasper's well did. Maybe it used to, but it rotted away. The rocky rim comes up to my hips, and the frayed end of a rope drapes against its lip.

I peer over the edge, looking down.

It's pure darkness. The penny is sweaty in my hand.

The sun's rays turn red, growing longer and darker as it begins to slip from my sight, offering no light to examine the bottom of the well with.

I slide my phone from my dress's pocket and tap on the flashlight app, lifting the light over the lip of the well. The phone's beam shines into the darkness and immediately disappears.

I pull my hand back, skin prickling. Is my phone broken?

I tap the flashlight off and on. Try again. The same thing happens—it's like the well has consumed the light, chewing off the ends of the beam so it can't reach the bottom.

My heart flutters. The quietness in my head dissipates, and I start thinking of the roast in the oven. Of my to-do list, all the things I still need to finish before Graham comes home. What am I doing out here with this musty old well in front of a decrepit forest?

The lighting is nice, though. I quickly step back from the well, turning off the flashlight and positioning the phone for a selfie. I hide my hand with the penny. I stare shyly at the camera, as if I've just noticed it, admiring the golden hour glow on my flawless skin. The well is visible in the background. It gives the photo a charming look—my followers might like to hear about it. This could end up being a marvelous content plan: I can throw the penny in, make my wish, and when it comes true, I'll post the photo and story. It will definitely go viral.

After snapping several dozen photos with slightly different angles and facial expressions, I put the phone back in my pocket and hesitate, staring at the well.

I came here for this, to do this, but now that I'm looking at the yawning opening that eats up light, I am apprehensive.

The pork roast, I remind myself.

Yes. I have things to do.

I step forward again, gazing down into the inkiness of the hole. I press the penny against my lips, kissing it, feeling the hot metal ridge against my mouth.

"I wish for a baby," I whisper, and before I can second-guess myself, I release the penny, letting it fall into the darkness.

I lean forward, hands resting against the rough ring of rocks around the edge of the well, listening for a splash. Or even a clink if the well is dry. But there is nothing. A cool breeze caresses my face, but it doesn't come from the woods or the field—it comes up from the well, and it carries a mildewy, earthy scent. The breeze is accompanied by a whooshing sigh. My mouth goes dry, and my hands tremble, gripping on to the lip of the well so hard that they begin to cramp.

The darkness below shifts. There's no other way to describe it—the hole is becoming even murkier, swirling, moving around within itself. A scraping noise comes from far below me, soft at first, then more insistent. Like a bird rubbing its beak against the metal bars of a cage.

My breath comes short and fast, and I want to pull my hands away, turn back to the house, but I can't seem to move. My feet are rooted down, a tree that has fused itself to the stones of the well. I can only blink, rolling my eyes back and forth, my brain seeking images within the black hole. The bottom of the well beckons me; the sighing breeze, the rhythmic scraping, the smell of wet soil getting stronger and stronger.

Goose bumps collect on my arms. I can't look away. The shadows in the well are like liquid, and there's something moving underneath the surface of them, pulling itself upward, toward the dying light of the day.

My phone chimes, breaking my trance.

I release the lip of the well, gasping, stumbling back, nearly tripping over the skirt of my dress. Automatically, I check my phone, noting Graham's text: *See you soon, love.*

Soon? He said he would be late.

When I look back at the well, the sun has set. The sky is an indigo blanket above me, the sleepy shine of early stars showing their faces. The temperature has dropped, and I shiver in my white linen, staring at the well. It's too dark to see it clearly now.

Where did the time go? How long was I out here?

"Oh no, the roast," I murmur.

I turn my back on the well, ignoring the tightness in my chest as I do. I run through the field, following the beckoning lights of our house in the distance, the absence of the penny pressing into my hand.

CHAPTER

3

I AM LEANING AGAINST the counter in the kitchen, scrolling through Mara Shoemaker's Instagram page, when Graham's car crunches outside on the gravel driveway. Inhaling deeply, I glance up from my phone screen. Hopefully I got the acrid smell of charred pig out of the house—I opened all the windows and lit some incense after returning from the well and throwing out the ruined pork roast. I opted to whip up a simple pasta salad instead, using the veggies as a side. Then I turned to Mara's social media, needing to forget the strange way time had slid away when I was out in the field, the things I thought I saw in the well.

Mara Shoemaker is my favorite influencer, queen of the niche we both belong to—traditional women who focus on taking care of our families and tending the house, living a natural and healthy life.

Mara was on her way to becoming a potential Hollywood star before she switched to influencing. She was a semi-known household name from her Micastra commercials; people loved the way she sang her line, "Now my heart burns only for you," to her handsome costar-turned-boyfriend.

Micastra built an ad campaign around her, the Heartburn Girl, with her short dark bob and appealingly soft features. People were actually turning on their TVs to sing along to her catchy and charming commercials, and there were rumors she was being circled for a sitcom pilot. But then she got serious with the man she met on the set of that first commercial, Jake Shoemaker, and married him. Mara hung up her promising acting career and focused on starting a family instead.

I don't personally know Mara; she has millions of followers and I only have forty thousand on my Instagram and seventy thousand on my TikTok, but that's to be expected. Mara has a publicity background, plus she and her husband have eight children. I have none. My content is sorely lacking something important, and one of the reasons I'm not seeing much online growth is because I don't have any children to share with the world.

The clunk of the garage door opening echoes from the front of the house, and my gaze drops back down to my phone screen.

I have a few minutes—Graham will park the car and grab a beer from the mini-fridge I set up for him in the garage before kicking off his shoes and plodding through the hallway to meet me in the kitchen. I can finish watching Mara's latest video. It's her evening routine, with exact time stamps and quick cuts.

Mara, with sun-drenched skin and dark braided hair, wears a white linen skirt that I know for a fact costs $275 and a blue blouse. Her makeup is fresh and minimal, and even though she tells her followers she gets up at five in the morning to start her day, there are no bags or shadows under her eyes. She ignores the camera in her newest video, instead leading her eight children inside the house, helping each one hang up their backpack and cardigan on assigned hooks near the front door.

They move through the house in a series of smash cuts—washing their hands, taking a bath (Mara strategically positions the camera here so that all you can see of the children are bubbles and chubby cheeks), getting into loungewear, sitting quietly in their playroom so Mara can start dinner. Mara's slender, unblemished, tanned arms come into frame as she chops vegetables, seasons meat, deftly cuts homemade bread. Even her cutlery and glassware are intimately selected—cucumber water is drizzled into heavy mason jars; bamboo utensils and place mats complete the look.

Mara sits down at her spotless table to eat with her family, her square-jawed husband Jake swooping in the frame at the last second to drop a kiss on her forehead.

I wonder how she gets some of these camera angles—it's like there's a tripod on her highest shelves or dangling from the ceiling. Maybe her past life in the film and TV industry helped her organize a fancy setup, but I suspect Mara and Jake have generational wealth too.

The video ends with Mara collecting her family's dishes and handwashing them in their farmhouse sink. She glances up, finally acknowledging the camera, and smiles.

Mara's home is immaculate. Gorgeous. It's all white lines and slick pine floors, white wooden furniture, beautiful open shelving, high ceilings with mahogany beams—her world is a Pinterest board come to life. I've tried to style much of our home after hers, but she is unrivaled.

I want it so badly I can taste blood in my mouth. Real blood—I've bitten my tongue.

"Hello, Camille."

I swallow the blood at the sound of Graham's voice. I smile at my husband with my lips closed in case there are any lines of red trapped between my teeth.

"Welcome home," I murmur as he sweeps into the kitchen, looking dapper in his white button-down and blue jacket. Then again, Graham could look dapper in anything. He's not quite as handsome as Mara's godly husband, but he's close—cropped dark hair, a short, trimmed beard that smells of licorice, and thick arms that can wrap you up and make you feel miniscule.

Graham drops a kiss on my cheek; he has to bend slightly to do so. "You look beautiful today."

Graham says this to me almost every day, but I still cherish it. It's validating—like when I was younger and my father complimented my cooking or noticed what a good job I did folding his laundry.

A coal of warmth nestles in my stomach as I kiss Graham back. "Thank you, darling."

I wish I had good news to tell him. I wish I could share the test with him so we could commiserate together. But Graham doesn't like bad news. He's a positive person; I can't bring him down with my complaints and worries. Besides, I'm feeling off-kilter, unsettled by what happened earlier by the well. It was all in my imagination, obviously, but I don't want my sour mood to ruin my husband's day.

"What's that?" Graham asks, looking down.

My phone is still out, paused on Mara's smiling face. I show him, turning the phone screen toward him and unpausing the video so he can see Mara, on a loop now, puttering through her perfect life.

I say, "She's incredible." Graham nods sagely. He is aware of my admiration of Mara, my desire to emulate her impeccable life. "I want this to be us."

"Me too, honey." Graham squeezes my shoulder.

I don't have to say it's about the children. He knows.

I start to bite down on my tongue again and stop myself at the last second. I look up at Graham coyly, tucking a perfumed strand of blonde hair behind my ear. "Should we try tonight?"

My husband sighs, heavy, burdened, like a dog in front of a fireplace. "Oh, Camille, not today. I'm sorry. I'm so exhausted. Rain check?"

"Sure," I say quickly, choking down the rejection. This has happened more and more often lately. Graham is always kind about it. Acts as if he's genuinely disappointed. But then he'll stay out late or play golf with his buddies on the weekend instead of making time for romance like he used to. It's probably my fault. I'm the one who wanted to move so far from his friends and job, after all. "I'm sorry. I shouldn't have asked the second you came through the door. Here, sit down. Relax. Do you want a beer? Some dinner?"

"I already ate," Graham says carelessly, his eyes trailing over my face, but in a way that seems almost objective. Like I'm a car making a coughing noise he can't figure out. "You OK? Your eyes look a little red."

"I'm fine," I say, smiling again at him. "I missed you, that's all. Come on, go sit in the living room. Watch the game." What game? I never know. It's late summer; what sport is played in late summer? Football? "I'll make you a plate."

"No thanks. I told you I'm not hungry," Graham says, gaze sliding away from me. "A beer would be good, though. Thanks, babe."

He drifts away, already slipping past our interaction as if he is a leaf in a river. Meanwhile, I latch on to a log in the current, holding on for dear life as I tiptoe over to the fridge and get him an icy-cold bottle of beer.

*　*　*

I think of Mara as I clean up the kitchen, zipping back and forth from the living room to get Graham beers or offer him food.

Mara is luckier than most—she realized her true calling, being a mother and wife, in her mid-twenties, and immediately began popping out babies to make up for lost time. From her social media, it seems like she has no qualms or regrets about leaving her potential rise to stardom in Hollywood behind.

My mother was the same way. She was a systems analyst before she was pregnant with me, but when I was born, she quit. I don't remember much of her, since she died when I was young, but I do remember her telling me often that it was the best decision she ever made, that there was nothing more important than being a good wife and mother. And her thesis was backed up by evidence—my father said he was madly in love with her, and we were a happy, healthy family unit. Right up until the day a truck blew through a stop sign and ended her life.

I wish I had known right away, like Mara and my mother, but at least I met Graham when I did.

We decided early on that he, a senior technology adviser, would be the breadwinner while I took care of everything else. I embraced my role as a traditional woman, a traditional wife. I started following other girls like me, posting content to cater to the algorithm. I gained ten thousand followers in the first year of our marriage. But now my growth has plateaued, and it's clear what I'm missing—a child. When Graham was promoted to CTO, I told him it was time to expand. We sold our old place in the suburbs and moved out to the country, into my dream home.

When I come back into the living room for the fourth time to check on him, Graham bristles. "Honey, can you give me a moment? I'd like some private time. Why don't you go upstairs to your craft room? Do some knitting or something?"

The game he's watching, which turns out to be baseball, blares as he pointedly picks up the remote and increases the volume. My cheeks grow hot and I offer a smile—not a frown, never a frown—and nod.

I've been clingy lately. I can't help it—he's been distant since we moved. Graham clearly misses being closer to his office in the outskirts of the suburbs. Misses his friends. Am I not enough? This was supposed to be a good thing. A fresh start in the countryside; a house to fill with children.

I suspect Graham is pulling away because he thinks I can't do it. My husband doesn't believe in birth control, and the first few years of our marriage he would withdraw, aim elsewhere. That stopped over a year ago, but still no baby. I haven't seen a doctor, too afraid of what Graham's reaction might be if it turns out I can't have children at all. There's usually a conception rate of 30 percent after the first month of trying for healthy couples, and women my age have a very high chance of getting pregnant within a year. But it hasn't happened yet for us.

And it could be him, a voice in the back of my head points out before I chase it away. *It's true,* the voice mutters, almost petulantly. *I read a chapter about male infertility three weeks ago.*

It isn't Graham's fault. It couldn't be. That's not how this is supposed to work.

I turn off the lights in the kitchen and pad away from the hub of light and sound in the living room that Graham has sequestered himself in.

Our house has a simple layout: The kitchen gracefully transforms into the wide living room, which takes up the whole back end of the house and leads to the sliding glass door that opens to the yard, the fields. The front of the house holds a hallway, Graham's home office, which is rarely used, and a bathroom and laundry room near the flight of stairs that leads to the three bedrooms and one bath on the second floor.

I take the stairs quickly, eager to return to the comfort of my phone, speeding through the upstairs hallway, ignoring the engagement photos lovingly framed on the walls.

Filled with our belongings, the house feels welcoming, but we've only been here a month. I'm still getting used to navigating the new space. My eyes dart into each room as I pass them on my way to our bedroom at the back of the house. One room is filled with crafts—sewing and knitting supplies, candle-making kits, and other quaint hobbies I picked up from scrolling through social media and copying the women with larger accounts than mine.

The next room features a crib with a beige mobile dangling from the ceiling above it. There's a matching beige dresser. Brown flower decals are stuck to the white walls. A round, wooden mirror reflects the wicker baskets on the other side of the room, stuffed with beautiful, handmade toys. All within my preferred neutral color palette.

The nursery was the first thing I set up in the new house. Like I could will a baby into existence simply by being overprepared for it.

I reach our bedroom, complete with an en suite bathroom. Swiping open my photo app, I collapse onto our king-size bed with its tight hospital corners and latte-colored comforter. I have dozens of photos of the nursery on my phone, filtered, edited, ready to be posted once I have good news. Sometimes when I feel sad, I look at the photos and begin drafting captions for them in my Notes app. That always cheers me up—thinking of the likes and comments I'll get. The videos I'll be able to take of tiny hands and little beige outfits.

As I scroll, looking for my nursery photos, I spot the shots I took earlier at the well, and pause. I swipe through the selfies. Most of them I deem unusable for various reasons—my face looks wide, my lips are too thin at that angle, you can see a flyaway—but one makes me hesitate for reasons other than critiquing my physical appearance.

It's the well, visible behind my right shoulder. It's slightly blurry, since I'm in the foreground of the photo, reddish-gold sunlight dappling my face. I pinch the screen, zooming in on the well.

Something is coming out of it.

It's as if the darkness inside the well is spilling out from the lip, dripping over the edge and reaching for the ground. Or reaching for me. The longer I stare, the more the darkness forms into an actual shape. Not just shadows overflowing, but what looks like a long, searching arm, melting over the stones of the well, pulling itself up.

I STARE AT THE photo for several minutes, zooming in, zooming out, trying to discern if what I'm seeing is real or a terrible exposure issue gone wrong. The armlike shape is in none of the other photos, and eventually I decide it's a trick of the light, the setting sun's rays mangling the background so that it looks eerie and odd.

I delete the photo, which slows down my pattering heartbeat, and go back to Instagram, scrolling through Mara's posts, letting her curated aesthetic and charmingly posed children rub a cooling salve on my nerves.

When I hear Graham's footsteps on the stairs, I shove my phone away—Graham doesn't like me to be on it too long; he says it rots my brain—and dart into the bathroom to get ready for bed. I'm applying lavender-scented lotion to my smooth legs, one foot up on the clawfoot tub, when Graham's snores come from the other room.

He didn't say good-night. He didn't even brush his teeth. I sigh, rubbing cream into my golden, toned calf. Graham does this sometimes when he's had more than three drinks.

I fight away the disgust that creeps up my throat at the thought of his beer-filmed teeth, his molars hoarding food crumbs from whatever he ate tonight without me. He's my husband and I love him. Even when he does things I wouldn't do. Or things that make me not want to touch him.

I am very lucky to have Graham. I try to remind myself of that often.

Every day after our first date, Graham would text me once in the morning and once at night, saying how beautiful I was and how he couldn't stop thinking about me. He extolled my virtues often and ardently: *I can't believe I met someone like you. You're different from other girls. You're special.*

I brimmed with joy from the compliments, heart fluttering the whole time. Three weeks later, he took me to the nicest restaurant in town and disappeared for ten minutes during the meal. When the waiter brought out dessert, a gluten-free torte, the words *I love you, Camille* were written in frosting across its chocolate face.

I didn't think about it. I didn't pause to assess the time frame or the fact that we had only been on a handful of dates. This was true romance. I beamed at Graham across the table, instantly responding, "I love you too."

It didn't matter that Graham was my first real relationship— I'd been too busy taking care of my father in high school to date. My father hoped I would find a good man one day, and he got his wish with Graham. We were meant to be.

When I finish my nighttime routine, I slip back into the bedroom. Graham has turned all the lights off, leaving me to blunder through the darkness, my eyes not yet adjusted after being in our bright and spotless bathroom. The room is still unfamiliar enough to me that I have to feel my way along the wall, fingertips brushing against the white pine dresser, trailing over the door handle to the walk-in closet. Slowly, I begin to make out the moonlight bleeding over the floorboards, the rustling white flap of the sheer curtains in the breeze entering through the open windows. The massive shape of the bed rises before me, punctuated by my husband's guttural snores.

I crawl onto my side of the mattress, feeling a chill in the air even though fall is still several weeks away. We'll have to start shutting the windows at night soon.

Everything is unpacked—I got everything decorated and put away in record time—but this will be our first winter in a new home. I can't help feeling anxious about it. Especially because I want to be pregnant for it. I want a summer baby.

Once my eyes have adjusted, I stare at Graham to make sure he is asleep, watching the rise and fall of his broad, shirtless chest. I'm struck by a sudden desire to score my nails across his skin, drawing pink lines across his pecs and nipples. I shake my head, alarmed.

You're tired. Read. And sleep.

I remove the secret book I have stashed under a pile of *Country Living* magazines in my bedside drawer. It's not that Graham wouldn't approve, although he might have something to say about the name, which I admit was off-putting to me at first too. *The Flesh of Fear* sounds lurid, but it's really about the physiological fear response in humans and other mammals. No, I hide the book because sometimes I crave . . . privacy. Something that is mine alone. It's wrong—not the way a good, traditional woman should be—but I can't help it.

Clipping a tiny book light onto the back cover, I adjust the beam so it shines down on the pages, allowing me to read the text without waking Graham.

One of the most fascinating characteristics of the human skin is its ability to flex. Within the skin are arrector pili muscles, located inside hair follicles. These largely involuntary muscles

can contract when faced with cold or certain emotions, such
as fear or arousal, causing the hair on the skin to become
erect. Colloquially, this is known as "getting goose bumps."

My eyes get heavy as I continue reading, beginning to drift
off. This isn't new information, and its familiarity soothes me.
Thoughts of my arrector pili muscles, taut and on guard at the
well earlier, dance in my mind. I'm dimly aware of the book
slumping forward on my chest.

Everything goes dark for a moment, and then I jolt awake,
eyes flying open. Trying to move, I find I'm frozen to the bed,
and Graham's sleeping form has vanished. I am alone, buried in
blankets, staring up at the ceiling, which shifts in shadow.
Moonlight moves, illuminating a giant, half-lidded eye watching me from the faux rafters.

Everything in my body feels like it's made of syrup. Slow.
Melted. Sedated.

The eye blinks—the wet squelch of white jelly, a click as the
eyelashes thread downward as if they're made of metal and not
keratin. There are massive feathered wings reaching from the
corners of the eye, tips disappearing into the shadows at the
edges of the room.

The wings begin to rotate, spinning around the eye, which
doesn't move, centered on its own axis, unperturbed by the
feathered arms around it.

My throat is stuffed with cotton. I want to move, hide my
face, but I can't. I try to smile. Like my mother taught me. My
mouth is rigid and laced shut like a corset.

All at once, the wings cease their circles and freeze. The eye
opens wide; it has no irises. Only an inkblot of a pupil.

A voice comes from nowhere and everywhere—both in my
bones and outside my head; too loud and too soft. I can't

understand it at first. It speaks in a way I can't fathom. There's a clicking sound as the eye blinks rapidly and then settles.

The next time the voice speaks, I can follow its words, but only by tracing them on my own skin. It's as if someone's mouth is pressing against my body, speaking directly into my being.

Why do you want a baby?

I must be sleeping. This must be a dream. I try to wake myself up, try to jerk out of this nightmare. When that doesn't work, I imagine licking my lips, freeing my tongue, screaming for help. My mouth doesn't move. Not even a twitch.

Why do you want a baby?

The voice is starting to hurt; its words are like electric currents that burrow into my marrow. I don't want it to ask again, and I can't open my mouth, so I try to answer in my head.

Because I have so much love to give. I want to share my life with a child. I want to start a family with my loving husband.

It's what I've said online, over and over.

WHY DO YOU WANT A BABY?

A whimper trapped against my throat vibrates my uvula as I try to articulate the pain that has suddenly invaded my body, but I still can't say anything.

WHY DO YOU—

I need something to take care of! I think as loudly as I can, frantic, hoping to cast my inner voice up toward the eye. The other speaker falls silent, and I sense it waiting. Fearing it starting up again, I continue. *I've always been a caretaker. My father. Now my husband. But something is changing with us. He's . . . he's pulling away. I feel it. If we had a baby . . . I could have someone else to take care of. Someone who wouldn't leave me. I would always have someone to watch over. Someone to love.*

A baby is also expected. I have a husband. A home. The natural progression is a child. Then another. That is my job as a wife. A housekeeper, a nurturer, a homemaker, a mother. This is what it means to be a good woman—it was how my mother was, and her mother. It was what my father expected, what Graham loved about me. He said I was a rare breed these days, that he loved my values and femininity. But it isn't enough, because he's slipping away. A baby would tether him back to me, but more importantly, a baby would give me purpose again. Not to mention necessary and important content for the burgeoning influencer I've become.

You shall have a baby, the voice announces, interrupting my stream of consciousness.

What? I ask in my head, frozen, hope lodged in my lungs.

You shall have a baby, the voice repeats into my skin, and the eye above me tears up, damp, shiny. Forming in the center of the black pupil is a copper coin. A penny.

A drop of liquid, molten and metallic, hisses from the eye and lands squarely on my face, the pain so rampant and intense that everything around me shatters, waking me up instantly.

Gasping, I scramble upright, sweat clinging to my brow and armpits, my blonde hair sticking to my shoulders. *The Flesh of Fear* falls off my chest and thumps to the floor. Raggedly inhaling, I turn to see Graham, sound asleep. His hairy arm is flung over his face as if to block out the sight of me. His snoring is even louder now—something I couldn't hear in the dream at all.

"Don't you care?" I whisper. "I had the worst nightmare."

His snores are uninterrupted.

I glance at the ceiling. There's nothing there, just shifting patterns of moonlight gently dancing from the breeze pushing through the white curtains and the half-open window.

My hands tremble as I reach over to the nightstand and sip from the glass of water I keep there. Warm liquid laps against my lips. It tastes metallic and thick. A dense odor comes from the cup. I look down at the dark fluid.

Dark?

Before I can swallow, I spit it back into the container, gagging, finally recognizing the salty, tangy taste.

Blood.

Even shaking, choking down vomit, I don't dare drop the glass. The carpet in our bedroom is white. It would be ruined.

Carefully, I put the glass back on the nightstand, trying to extricate myself from the down comforter, stomach churning. Graham hasn't moved; his snores are as deep as they were moments earlier. Dry heaving, I grab the cord of the lamp on the end table, wincing as warm yellow light blasts through the bedroom.

When my eyes have adjusted, I stare at the glass, the rollicking in my stomach refusing to subside despite what I see. I can taste the blood. Smell its scent.

But the glass is filled, nearly to the brim, with crystal-clear water.

CHAPTER

5

THE NEXT MORNING, I resolve to pretend that life is like social media—perfect, filtered, fine. Yesterday was an anomaly. Bad news leading to a bad dream. Nothing more.

I make Graham's coffee the way he likes it, black with a sprinkle of cinnamon, and he pecks my lips when he comes downstairs, only a little bit perfunctory.

I smile all through breakfast, which is fresh fruit from the farmers market, creamy scrambled eggs, and lightly toasted rye bread with smears of hand-churned butter. I nearly gave myself tennis elbow making it, but it was worth it. Butter is my favorite.

"You look chipper this morning," Graham says, eyeing my outfit as I rise from the breakfast bar to clear his empty plate.

"It's going to be a great day," I sing, swaying as I carry dishes around the counter so Graham can admire my dress as I go. It's sunflower colored with a scoop neck and an A-line silhouette that flows down to my shins. The dress brings out my tan skin, complementing my golden locks. The ridges of my collarbone are warmed by the sunlight inviting itself in through the big bay windows in the kitchen. I look youthful and cheery—like a farm maiden.

It's all on purpose. Graham likes it when I remind him of simple country girls. It helps him forget that I grew up in a dingy, dark city, catering to my father until I was able to move to a quieter, family-oriented area a few hours north.

"You look good," Graham observes, and my heart leaps.

I get "You look beautiful" every day, no matter Graham's mood, but he only tells me I look "good" when he's feeling amorous. As if he's so turned on his brain can't find any stronger adjectives.

"Thank you. I hoped you would like it," I say, leaning against the sink, twisting a strand of hair around my finger as I set his dishes down one-handed.

He doesn't move, watches me appraisingly. As I turn to the sink, releasing my hair, I ache to feel Graham's hands on my hips, spinning me around so he can lean into a kiss, pressing his body against mine.

Graham's stool scrapes behind me and to the right as he leaves the breakfast bar, and I tense, looking out the window at the rippling golden fields, the only view we have.

He is close, I can tell. His hands. His body. Our baby. It feels so real, so predetermined, that I can already sense my skin responding to a touch that hasn't yet come.

Arrector pili muscles.

Graham moves into my peripheral vision and ducks low, kissing my cheek roughly. It's not the sultry embrace I was imagining, and my pulse flattens.

"I'm sorry, babe," Graham says, adjusting the collar on the shirt I starched and pressed for him. "Gonna be late again tonight. You know it's that time of year."

Is it?

"But I—"

"I love you, Camille," he says, as if that ends things. And it does.

"I love you too."

He leaves, and my lower half throbs, the promise of a child drying up slowly but inexorably, like a puddle on the pavement in July.

The door to the garage, accessible via Graham's home office, slams. The car purrs as Graham backs out on to the crunchy gravel. I dart over to the window in his office to watch him drive away down the flat and barren road, a paved line that shoots between swaths of corn and wheat before curving off in either direction. Here we are surrounded by vast sky and golden land. Ours is the only house visible on this stretch of road. I watch for several minutes after Graham has disappeared, but no other cars pass by.

I haven't left the country since we moved. It's been easier to order organic, local ingredients directly to the house. A few times I have walked down the dusty road to the Calloways' farm to pick up fresh eggs, milk, and flour. But mostly, I am alone.

A crow lands in our front yard, poking its obsidian beak into the soft lawn. Its feathers are iridescent, and I wonder what they look like from above when it's flying.

My whole life, I've doted on others. Mostly my father and Graham. I love it: the gratitude I receive, the compliments when I do a good job, the tangible evidence that I am loved and useful. There is only one thing I've ever asked for—sure, I recommend certain pricey things to have in the home, but those are to make *Graham's* life better, to make it so that I can be the perfect wife.

All I've asked for in return is a child. I've waited so long and gotten nothing for my patience.

Outside, the crow croaks out a call and flaps its wings, lifting off. It disappears over the top of the house, cawing until I can't hear it anymore.

Pulling away from the window, I return to the kitchen, the nightmare from last night coming back to me in bursts. The spinning eye, the wings, the disembodied voice: *You shall have a baby.*

What a stupid fucking dream.

I leave the dishes in the sink for now, grab a pair of scissors from a drawer, and charge into the living room, stepping through the sliding glass door and into the brisk morning. It's late summer, so the days start out cooler before becoming hot and sticky midday. Outside, I inhale the fresh air, such a different quality than what we got in the suburbs, and kneel by the side of the house.

I haven't had a chance to plant or tend to a full garden, but there are some black-eyed Susans in full bloom near the foundation of the house. I snip the stalks of flowers until I have enough to bundle in my arms, then go back inside to put them in an asymmetrical ceramic vase. I position the flowers carefully, stepping back every so often to examine them from farther away as I rearrange them to my liking. Satisfied, I wrap a blue ribbon around their stalks and nod.

I place the beige vase on our coffee table, right in the splash of morning sunlight streaming in through the sliding glass door. When I take a photo, the effect is dreamy, worthy of a Pinterest board, especially when I apply the filter I use on all my photos.

I post the flowers with the caption *Look what my darling husband got me today! For no reason at all! I'm so #blessed to have such a strong and beautiful marriage.*

Almost immediately, the likes and comments start rolling in, and I take a moment to sift through them, smiling, before I start the rest of my chores for the day.

Girl, you are living the LIFE!

God bless you both!

When are you having a baby!! You two are perfect together!

Oooo flowers?? Did he get good news from you?? ;)

My shoulders sag slightly. I wish Graham and I *were* celebrating something today. Instead, I "like" all the comments, adding winking emojis or prayer hands when appropriate. These women are my peers, after all. I can't ignore them. Some I might even consider my friends. They'll be the first to know when I finally get pregnant. After Graham, obviously.

A baby will fix everything. And besides, can't Graham see that the world expects it?

*   *   *

An hour after Graham leaves, the doorbell rings. It violently lurches me from my laundry folding. I don't think I've ever heard the doorbell before, and it buzzes again as if someone has stepped on a wasp.

"That will have to be changed," I mutter as I set down Graham's underwear. "Something more melodic. Whimsical. Mara Shoemaker probably doesn't even have a doorbell. We should get a door knocker. Something wooden. Much more aesthetic."

Stop talking to yourself, I scold. *That's not very ladylike.*

The doorbell rings again, and I jump, rushing from the laundry room tucked under the stairs and hurrying over to the entryway, if only to not hear that dreaded sound for the fourth time.

Our front door is white with a chunky bronze knob and four frosted panels of glass. I absolutely hate it. I tried my hardest to get Graham to replace it when we moved in, but he balked. The door, for some reason, was where he decided to make his stand.

"I like it," he said. "And we're not replacing something that works perfectly fine. Come on, Camille. I bought you the eight-thousand-dollar couch and let you decorate the whole place. We redid the downstairs bathroom. If you dislike the door so much, save up some of your monthly allowance for a while and get it replaced then."

But I need my monthly allowance for the latest clothes, the correct kitchen appliances, and the very expensive makeup that girls like me wear but pretend not to. I have to live with the ugly frosted door, for now.

A shape moves outside, dark against the panels. I press an eye against the peephole, my muscles relaxing when I see a slender woman on our little porch. She's holding a pie.

I brush my hair back from my eyes, straighten my dress, and unlock the door, smiling widely right as the woman's finger hovers over the doorbell again.

Good Lord, would she have kept ringing the bell? What if we weren't home?

"Hi," I chirrup. "Can I help you?"

"Oh my God, hi!" the woman says, her voice bulging with enthusiasm. She's wearing dark-blue jeans and a blue-and-white-striped button-down. Her dark curly hair spills from a side ponytail and rests against her left breast. Strands of hair stick to her shirt, waving gently in the breeze as if greeting me. Her mouth encompasses most of her face, smiling, lips covered in pink gloss. Her eyelashes are long and sweeping, and I'm pretty sure she's not wearing mascara. That's all natural, even though she looks quite a bit older than me. She's probably in her thirties. There's a vaguely familiar smell about her that I can't put my finger on. Something fruity and mineral.

"Hi?" I say again, after a moment passes as the both of us check each other out, doing quick scans of hair, clothes, and facial expressions to see if we might get along.

"Gosh, where are my manners! I'm Renee Colt. I live across the way. The blue house down the road?" When I nod in recognition, she brings the pie up closer to our faces; Renee is almost exactly my height. Her pink gloss is smeared, as if she missed her lips putting it on. "I made you a pie. Homemade! I hope you like apple."

"That's so kind of you," I say, perking up at the pride in her voice when she tells me she made the pie herself. "I do a lot of baking and cooking too." I pause, then open the front door wider. "I'm Camille Deming. Come in, come in."

"Oh, thank you!" The porch is barely large enough for one person and a potted plant, and Renee steps in gratefully, chattering as I lead her through the hallway and into the kitchen. "Is your husband home? I'd love to meet him too! It's so nice to have another young couple nearby."

"Graham's at work," I tell her. "He's a chief technology officer for one of the top software firms in the country." My chest swells with pride.

"How fun!" Renee squeaks. "I'm sorry I didn't come over earlier. But when *we* moved in, the neighbors came over right away and I was like *Hey, gimme a minute to settle in*, you know? You guys got unpacked super fast, though. Wow, look at it in here! You've done a great job with the place!"

"Thank you. I consider myself a bit of an interior decorator." I smile, taking the pie from her, peeling back the layer of plastic wrap and inhaling the spiced aroma, wondering if she made the whole thing from scratch like I would have.

"Wow, nice rock!" Renee exclaims, catching sight of my wedding ring. It dwarfs her own by several carats. "And interior decorating, nice! Is that your job?"

I wince, replace the wrap on the pie, and slide it onto the counter. I hate this question, the *What do you do?* question that people always ask. Graham's friends know the deal—they think he's lucky. I heard them talking once, during a Super Bowl party at our old place. I was bringing them fresh beers and snacks, hovering in the doorway behind them, holding a plate of organic chicken wings I'd seasoned and grilled myself.

"You've got it made, dude," Brandon, Graham's old frat brother, said. "You don't have to do anything! She cooks, cleans, looks hot as shit."

"Yeah, but I pay for everything," Graham replied.

"Small price," Brandon said, bumping his fist against Graham's shoulder. "Come on. You're living the dream."

"Happy wife, happy life," Graham said, laughing.

But people who don't know me, don't know Graham, sometimes give me weird looks. Say things like "You don't . . . do . . . *anything*?" As if being a wife isn't a full-time job that requires early mornings and late nights and tons of skills. Other women especially take issue with it. Except, of course, my online friends. We have the same values, the same priorities. But in real life, it's easier to stay away from other women.

Will Renee look down her nose at me? Tell me she's a doctor or a lawyer and I'm wasting my life being a housewife?

"I do this," I say, gesturing to the house. "I stay at home. Graham does very well, so I take care of everything here."

To my surprise, Renee's eyes light up. "I'm an SAHM!" She sees the cock of my head and clarifies: "Stay-at-home mom. My kids are five and two. You got any?"

A twinge flutters in my gut. "Not yet. Hopefully soon."

Renee looks me up and down again. "How old are you?"

"Twenty-four."

"Oh, hon, you've got years to have a baby! I didn't have my first until I was twenty-eight. I'm thirty-three now, and let me tell you, having two kids under five is not a picnic."

Renee smiles, and blood drips through her teeth, pooling on her bottom lip, as if she's got a mouthful of viscera and it's leaking through the cracks in her enamel.

I blink, furiously, quickly, and the bloodstained image in front of me disappears, replaced by Renee, looking politely confused, her pink lip gloss smudged around her mouth.

"Are you OK, dear? You got very pale. Let's sit down."

I let Renee guide me over to the sectional in the living room, my hands clammy. I keep glancing at her mouth, which is wide and plump, but there are no bloodstains on her teeth, no hint of red. Did I have a hallucination?

"Have you eaten today?" Renee asks gently. I'm still staring at her, so she says, "Sorry, I'm jumping into mommy mode."

She smooths out my hair, and the loamy scent of whatever strange perfume she's wearing rears up again. I'm suddenly struck by how invasive this whole thing is. Renee, already asking me about babies and my age, touching my body, coming into my house, settling herself comfortably on our couch like she's known me forever. I want her to leave, but I've had limited interactions with women who aren't dating Graham's friends or who aren't my counterparts online. I'm not sure how to kick her out.

"Want me to get you a slice of the pie?" Renee asks.

"No, I'm OK, thanks. I must have overdone it on my workout," I lie, my brain scrambling for a plausible excuse. The woman's mouth clearly isn't filled with blood. Just lots of words. And lip gloss.

"Oh, I do that all the time!" Renee exclaims, withdrawing her hand from my hair, successfully distracted. Her voice is too loud for this house. It clashes with my prim furniture and stylish decor. "Do you like running? We could go on runs together. Run club!"

I don't know how to answer Renee. Outdoor walks and light yoga are part of my daily exercise routine. A few years ago, Graham caught me trying a strength-training workout. He took my hand, gently paused the video, looking at me with concern.

"Darling, you're perfect. God made you this way, and your body is beautiful. You don't need that."

He led me away from the garage, which doubled as a workout area in our old house, stripping off my sweaty tights in the kitchen, tenderly making love to me on the counter. Each time he thrust into me, he whispered in my ear, making the hair on the back of my neck lift up like it was trying to get closer to him: "Don't change. Don't change. Don't change."

I didn't do any of my exercises for a week after that, until Graham noticed and said, "Honey, why aren't you doing your walks? You need to move your body—it's good for you."

"I thought you said I didn't need that," I replied.

He laughed. "You don't need high-intensity workouts. What do you need big biceps for, Camille? You're a girl. But you should still do your yoga and cardio. It's important to stay healthy and in shape."

"Oh, OK."

I returned to my programs, shuttering away the thrill I had gotten from the lunges and lifts, the surprising power that coursed through my veins as I struggled through the movements. Graham was right—why would I need huge, masculine muscles anyway? That's what he was there for.

"Earth to Camille!" Renee's voice, which is starting to sound grating, drags my attention back to her. "Where'd you go? You look a bit peaked. Sure you don't need water or something?"

"I'm fine," I insist.

I'm taken aback by her energy, her assertiveness. I hoped we could be friends, but she's not modest and even-tempered like I am. She reminds me of a puppy being house-trained, eager to learn but far too committed to chaos to be any good at it. Still, Renee stays at home, cares for her kids. She bakes. Maybe it's worth forging a relationship.

"So, running," she prods me.

"Sometimes I run," I say cautiously. "Once a week I go for a longer walk, and occasionally I'll take a Pilates class. But I haven't gotten a chance to get a real schedule going here yet. Since we just moved."

"Yeah, I get it," Renee agrees. "When you're feeling up to it, let's go on a jog together! It'll have to be after the kids start school, though. Millie begins kindergarten in a few weeks; she's so excited! And Henry is about to start preschool soon. I'll have a lot more free time then." Her voice softens. "I miss them so much."

"Well, they're not in school yet, right?" I say. "You still have time with them."

Renee brightens, grinning again. There's a stiffness to it, like it's a painted backdrop being propped up on a stage. "Damn right!"

"Who's with them now?" I ask, peering around her as if her children will burst into the room.

Renee sighs, washing a wave of her fruity scent over my face. "Henry has a cold, and he passed it to Millie, and now they're both feeling yucky. Zach stayed home from work today to take care of them. And I used this as an excuse to get away from all the noise!"

I can't help glancing at the kitchen, where the pie sits. I wonder how many germs are crawling around on it. How many I snorted up earlier when I smelled it. Maybe I won't serve it to Graham for dessert tonight like I planned.

"It's nice to meet another homemaker," I say, deciding it's time to get this woman out of our house. "But I should get back to my chores. Thank you so much for the pie."

"Oh, sorry, didn't mean to intrude!" Renee says, in a way that makes me think she *did* mean to intrude. "I'm so glad someone else moved in who I can talk to! It's nice to have someone close by. This area is so remote! And you seem nice. The last couple were elderly and barely left the house. And your *style*. My goodness, Camille, you are so fashionable! And your home is gorgeous."

A murmur of warmth grows in my belly at her words. My shoulders relax. Maybe she isn't so bad. She's . . . enthusiastic. There's nothing wrong with that. "Well, thank you," I reply, offering a smile. "I couldn't do it without Graham, though. He always takes care of everything. I didn't even have to use my allowance on any of this; he bought it all for us!" I sweep my arms, gesturing to the decor, the kitchen appliances, the matching furniture.

Renee's smile flickers. "Allowance?"

"Yes. Doesn't your husband give you money every month to buy clothes and home necessities?"

The other woman raises a brow, a shadow in her eyes. "Um, no. We have a shared account. I have some money saved up too. How did you and Graham meet again?"

I never told her in the first place, but I don't like the change in her tone. I must not be explaining this well. She doesn't seem to understand how romantic and supportive Graham is. I try again: "Farmers market. When we started dating, I was working for a growing center who supplied floral shops, but Graham promised to take care of me. He said if I quit, he would handle everything so we could spend more time together. He bought me a rare orchid and sent it to me with a note saying the only thing I needed to grow now was our love."

I expect an *Aww* or a glimmer of jealousy, but Renee's reaction is muted. She folds her lips, then clears her throat. "I see."

A heavy iron door slams shut over my heart. I abruptly rise to my feet. I was wrong; this woman doesn't get it. She needs to leave my home. "Thanks for stopping by. Let me walk you out," I say.

"Ah, right. I won't keep you. It was lovely to meet you!" Renee has infused a lightness into her voice that doesn't land, and I ignore it.

I guide Renee back through the kitchen and toward the ugly front door.

I'm about to usher her out when she stops, turns, her face suddenly slack and serious. "One more thing, Camille," she says.

"Yes?"

"Don't go near the woods."

I pause, my throat cold and contracted as if I've swallowed a snowball. It's such a non sequitur that I fumble to respond, forgetting I was offended by her lacking reaction after my story about Graham. "What do you mean?"

Renee shakes her head, dark eyes solemn. "The woods aren't safe. Don't go near them." Then she shrugs, tries to smile. "You know. Bears and other critters. You could get lost! Best to steer clear."

She pats my shoulder, not noticing how icy my skin has become, and gives me a wave, closing the door behind her as if she's locking me in a prison cell.

CHAPTER

6

AFTER MY CHORES, I snap photos—the laundry room with all its neat labels and folded towels; the carved wooden vase filled with hand-picked wheat I dried myself; a knitting project, beige, of course, dangling from the ends of bamboo needles.

I apply a carefully curated Lightroom filter over all the images and draft some captions, making sure to come across as quaint and grateful. I schedule the posts out across the next few days, then post clips of my morning routine, modeled after Mara's recent video. It gets a couple hundred views right away. It's not enough, though. I won't see record-breaking views or numbers until I have a child.

Last year, a woman slid into my DMs to tell me how stupid I was for centering my life around a family that didn't exist yet. She called me sheltered and foolish. I blocked her without responding. She didn't know me—who was she to judge? I may be sheltered, but I'm not stupid.

A baby solidifies my place online *and* within my marriage. It's an absolute necessity.

I'm back in the kitchen, about to start chopping vegetables for dinner, when the doorbell buzzes again, making me grit my teeth. It's a truly awful sound, and I can only imagine Renee is back, jabbing the ringer.

Smoothing away a scowl, I drop the knife on the butcher block counter and peep my head out from the kitchen entryway, gazing at the hated door.

A shape is silhouetted against the frosted glass; there's a dark splotch visible at shoulder height, as if the person outside is leaning against the front door, bored. But whoever is out there is not Renee—their size is wrong. The proportions are off too, as if whoever is standing on my doorstep has stepped through a fun house mirror and come out the other side still retaining some of the qualities reflected in it.

The hair on my arms stands up, dotting my skin with rows of pimply bumps. My first instinct is to rub my forearms aggressively—goose bumps aren't becoming. The passage from *The Flesh of Fear* repeats in my mind: *These largely involuntary muscles can contract when faced with cold or certain emotions, such as fear or arousal . . .*

My arrector pili muscles are activated.

I shiver and drop my hands to my side, fingertips working the fabric of my yellow dress as if to rub holes through the sturdy, stiff material. Deliberately stepping into the hallway, I hesitate going to the door this time, unable to tear my eyes away from the shape at the glass. It's disconcerting, like someone has propped up a scarecrow and let it rest against the house.

The ephemeral shape of an arm reaches across the middle panels of frosted glass, and the doorbell blares again. Though I expected it, saw it coming, I still jump, a gasp escaping from the back of my throat.

Stop being silly, I chastise myself. *Go use the peephole. See who it is. Maybe Graham got a delivery. Maybe it's flowers for you!*

Graham used to do that, when we first moved in together, years ago. I'd stay at his place all day, setting about making his bachelor-pad house a real home, and occasionally the doorbell would ring and there would be a giant bouquet of roses or wild-flowers with a love note about how much he appreciated me.

Graham hasn't bought me flowers in a long time, but maybe the new house and his moment of desire this morning inspired him.

Cheered by this prospect, I release the hem of my dress, ignoring the goose bumps littering my skin, and move toward the front door, lightly stepping down the hallway. I pass framed photos of Graham and me on our wedding day, where his friends and family outnumber me and my father's family ten to one; the walnut console table featuring a vase filled with decorative twigs and a magnolia-scented candle; the stylish bamboo shoe rack near the door.

The shadow grows darker as I approach, as if it's pressing harder into the glass the closer I come. I stop a few feet away, my hand already automatically reaching out for the knob.

Something is wrong. I can feel it. My body trembles, and images of terrible things happening to a woman alone in her house threaten to swarm inside my head. The shadow in front of the glass shifts and pulls away, as if they are stepping back to allow me to get a good look at them through the peephole.

Stop being crazy!

Using whatever momentum I have left, I lurch toward the door, letting my brow rest against the cold glass so I can stare through the fish-eye hole.

The porch is empty.

An unfamiliar gurgle frees itself from my throat as I step back, eyes whipping across the paneled door. There are no shadows. No shape visible outside. But I *saw* something. I know I did.

I lean forward and look through the peephole again, scan-ning the porch, the edges of the house, the paved path that leads up to the front door. It's all normal: the patchy grass on our front lawn, the hint of the gravel driveway off to the side. The road—flat, black, empty—stretches in front of the property like a steamrolled rat snake. Beyond the road are more wheat fields. There are no neighbors nearby. Renee's house is the closest, but that's a ten- to fifteen-minute walk at least.

I could pop my head outside, look around for a delivery truck or a bundle of flowers on the welcome mat, but the temperature has dropped in my body and the idea of opening the door right now makes me want to cry.

I backstep, warily watching the paneled glass. An intense stillness has fallen over the house: the pause at the top of an inhale before the rush of release.

The air in the house feels musty, even hot. As if I've left the windows open too long and the last vestiges of summer have crawled their way inside, digging claws into the floorboards so they won't be peeled away by the encroachment of fall.

A *shush*ing sound echoes from deeper in the house. It's familiar, but I can't put my finger on it. A bead of sweat collects near the nape of my neck and drips down my spine, dampening the zipper of my yellow dress.

The *shush*ing comes again, and this time I can pinpoint its location—the back of the house. Near the living room.

The sliding glass door opening, and now closing.

My jaw locks, and for a moment, I can't swallow; I gasp on nothing, choking on dry air, slapping a palm against my sternum in an attempt to force a gulp. A whimpering cough racks my throat, and my neck bobs like a seagull as I finally inhale.

The smell of damp stones and forgotten soil creeps through the house. It's like I'm standing inside an ancient crypt—yet there's a humidity that clings to my lungs and makes the odor more overpowering, more swamp-like.

Footsteps. They are slow, clunking, as if someone wearing heavy work boots is dragging their body through the living room, approaching the kitchen. If they continue this way, they will appear near the fridge. They will see me, rigid and taut, in the hallway.

I open my mouth to call out. To cry for Graham, hoping it's him, knowing it's not. A dead whisper leaks from my lips instead. The power of speech has escaped me, making a retreat that feels nearly permanent.

The footsteps grow louder and louder as my body vibrates with anticipation. A shadow flickers in the kitchen, and then the steps abruptly stop.

I can't take it anymore. I dart into the doorway of the kitchen, one hand gripping the frame's molding so that my knees don't fold and send me sprawling to the tiled floor.

The kitchen is empty. The living room, visible beyond it, is empty too.

I move forward, breath soft and flighty, scanning the rooms. Looking for anything out of place. The sliding glass door is undisturbed and locked the way I left it, even though I could have sworn I heard it opening and closing.

Something is wrong with me, I think, squeezing my eyes closed. Ever since the well. I'm seeing and hearing things that aren't here.

Cracking my eyes open, I glance around one more time. Nothing.

It's the stress, I decide. It can't be anything else. I know about mental illnesses and mood disorders. I can't have any of those. I simply cannot. That would mean I am not the perfect wife. That would mean I risk passing on something to my future child. Graham wouldn't stand for that, and neither would I.

Stress, I think firmly.

I ignore the scent of soil and mildew that lingers. I don't think about the creaking coming from the stairs. I pretend to not fear the iron taste in my mouth, reminiscent of the blood I drank from my bedside table last night.

Instead, I open my phone and scroll through Mara's idyllic videos until I'm calm enough to start chopping vegetables for dinner.

CHAPTER

7

I HAVE THE DREAM about the eye on my ceiling every night for
the next six days.

It affects my waking life. My sleep, interrupted and restless,
suffers, and I start getting up at three or four in the morning,
beginning my chores early to avoid the tossing and turning.
What's worse is the creaking in the house when I'm home alone—
the smell of damp stone permeates the first floor, and the shad-
owy figure appears on my doorstep two more times, ringing the
bell and disappearing when I approach the peephole, trembling.

There are flickers of movement around the house during the
day when Graham is at work—shadows darting by the big windows as if something is running around the house in circles; soft
scuffling from rooms I'm not standing in; shapes hovering at the
edge of my vision that disappear when I spin around to catch them.

I can't tell if I'm losing my mind from lack of sleep or if I'm
being haunted by something that wasn't in the house when we
first moved in.

The eye keeps me company every night, asking me over and
over why I want a baby. I always give the same answer I did on
the first night it appeared.

On the fourth day, a memory clicks into place while slug-
gishly washing dishes after serving Graham dinner: a conversation we had years ago.

"Do you believe in angels?" I asked once, when we were visiting my mother's grave.

"Definitely," Graham said. "I married you."

I smiled, kissed him. "No, I mean, like a real angel."

He seized my hand and brushed his lips across my knuckles.
"I do, yes."

"I like to think of my mother as an angel."

"You know, angels aren't always what we expect."

I pulled away. "What do you mean?"

"Angels come in many forms, darling," Graham explained,
his voice taking on that pleased, teacherly quality it always did
when he found out I didn't know something. "Yes, they can look
like people. But the Bible has many different descriptions of
them. A wheel with eyes. A creature with four faces. A person
with six wings and beryl skin. Some say angels are so terrifying
to look at that humans can't comprehend them."

"Why would you say that?" I exclaimed, stepping away from
him, glancing down at my mother's grave, her polished tomb-
stone glinting in the sunlight. "My mother isn't a wheel with
eyes!"

Graham's face darkened at my tone, then smoothed out.
"No, you're right. I'm sorry, beautiful, I got carried away. You
know how interesting I find the Bible. I didn't mean anything
by it."

"OK," I said, taking the hand he offered me in a conciliatory
gesture. I winced as his grip immediately tightened once my fingers were enveloped inside his. "I'm just sensitive about my
mother."

"I'm sure she's looking down at you right now," Graham said
confidently. "With beautiful white wings."

I'm not as religious as Graham, but I appreciate the rules—these things are bad; these things are good. I like that there are instructions on how to be a decent person and an admirable woman. Before we moved, we went to church every week because Graham was raised a devout Catholic, something I couldn't relate to. My parents had taken me to church when I was little, but when my mother died, it was difficult to make time for it between staying on top of schoolwork and housework.

Yet I believe in God. How can I not? Faith has essentially been grandfathered into my life due to my marriage, even though a small, secret part of me finds it a tad inaccessible. I've always been drawn to data, evidence. I tell myself there is proof of God: Yes, my mother died young and I had to grow up without her, but I was given a supportive father and a handsome husband instead. I want for nothing—except a baby. And now, after tossing a penny into a wishing well, things are changing.

Maybe I got it wrong. Maybe I'm not being haunted. What if my prayer at the wishing well was heard?

Graham said angels can come in many different forms.

"Do angels ever appear to people in dreams?" I ask Graham before bed one night, trying to ignore the way he turns his body away from me on the mattress, keeping his phone tilted so that I can't see what he's doing.

Graham pauses, giving me a curious look over his shoulder, phone forgotten for a moment. "Well, yes. In the Bible, sure. And I've heard of people getting visions or messages from angels in their dreams sometimes. Why?"

"No reason," I reply. "It popped into my head."

Graham's response is helpful, but it's not a confirmation. I need more data points to compare. Something more objective than my husband's potentially biased opinion.

I look up renderings of biblical angels, examining them on my phone, zooming in. They aren't exact, but there are enough similarities that I begin to think my theory could hold weight. I study passages from the Bible, flipping through Graham's copy when he's at work. I scour theology forums, reading through different accounts and interpretations. The combination of these different sources satisfies me enough to home in on a central thesis: My dreams are plagued not by a ghost or monster but by an angel, one that asks me over and over again why I want a baby and then tells me I *will* have one before I wake up in a cold sweat.

Hoping it's a sign to try again with Graham, I make overtures toward him when we're relaxing on the white couch one night after I've cleaned up dinner. Graham kisses me, pets my breasts, but instead of making love, he draws my head down to his jeans, unzipping his fly. I don't know how to tell him *No, we won't get pregnant this way. We don't need it to be in my* mouth.

He's my husband. I love him. It's what he wants, and it's been so long since we've been intimate. I do it, telling myself it's fulfilling enough when he groans how good I am, how perfect I am.

We don't make a baby that night, and when I go to bed, the eye greets me again, a small copper coin suspended in its dark pupil.

I haven't been able to go back to the wishing well since tossing my penny inside; in fact, I've struggled to leave the house, not wanting to run into whatever has been lurking around the wheat fields and creeping in through the sliding glass door I check dutifully every day. It's always locked, yet I catch glimpses of something gray and limbed moving through the downstairs rooms when I'm home alone.

But the need to understand is strong. One morning, I grab a coil of rope from our garage, left over from the previous owners, and head back to the well. I fasten the decrepit bucket to the end of my rope, which is sturdy and strong, unlike the rotting one dangling from the well's mouth. Lowering the bucket into the shifting gloom makes my shoulders tense and my feet sweat, but I ease it down, occasionally scraping it against the shaft on its descent.

When the bucket hits bottom, I'll mark the length on the rope and be able to measure—

There's a sharp tug, and the rope burns through my palms, nearly jerking me into the opening. Gasping, I plant my feet, leaning back. The well is silent, but a snapping sensation echoes up the line and suddenly I'm on my rear on the ground, the rope considerably lighter than it was a second ago.

I scramble to my feet, rapidly raising the rope, bristles brushing against my burning hands. The end of the rope frees itself from the well's opening, frayed and ragged.

The bucket is gone.

There must be a logical explanation, I think. The bucket caught on a rock or something. I should try again. See if the same thing happens. Oh, I could try a few more tests and—

I bear down on the thought until it snaps and crumbles. Not everything in the world has an explanation. Why am I fighting against this so hard? This need to qualify what's happening, the desire to study it and analyze it, is not who I am anymore. I shouldn't be out here, dangling things into an old well. I should be inside, preparing my husband's dinner and accepting the potential gift that is being offered to me.

Back in the house, I hide the rope in the garage and lock all the doors. No more tests, no more evidence. I have to just *believe.* Between my sleep deprivation, the glimmering hope that somehow, miraculously, something has heard my prayers, and the constant presence of the eye in my dreams, it's easy to come to a conclusion.

An angel. I've been found by an angel. One offering its services to make my greatest wish come true. Is it ideal? No, but everyone says God works in mysterious ways. Who am I to question that?

Graham himself said that angels could come to people in dreams.

Thursday evening, a little over a week since throwing the penny in the well, I float around the kitchen, trying to stay focused on my chores. I'm prepping Graham's dinner, but I keep finding new things to add to my to-do list. For example, we're running low on bread. I'll have to bake a new batch soon, and I'm pleased to see my timeline has lined up with Mara's—her newest Instagram story says *Bread-making party this weekend with all my girlies!*

She's tagged several other large accounts that she often collaborates with. I try to squash the heat of jealousy that rises underneath the eggshell-colored dress I'm wearing and wafts toward my neck, warming my face. Mara lives in Utah somewhere; I am hundreds of miles away from her, but I ache for the connection anyway.

I've always said all I need is Graham and, eventually, my children. But I do get lonely sometimes. Whenever I mention it to Graham, he hugs me and says I should chat with my online friends more.

"They seem so supportive!" he says.

"You're right," I reply, not knowing how to explain to him what I can barely understand myself—that there is something missing in those interactions that leaves me feeling hollow and small. Would my online friends still like me if they knew about my past? Will they still follow me if it turns out I can't have a baby?

I glance up from the new batch of likes and comments that have come through after I posted a video of my immaculately chopped onions and zucchini. There's a wooden spoon in the shot, strategically placed alongside a handmade cutting board that cost Graham $200.

The sun is setting, sending rosy fingers through the kitchen window, bathing a sink full of dishes that I absolutely must do before Graham gets home. Whenever that will be.

He hasn't answered my texts yet. He must be busy at work.

I've already eaten—a summer squash soup with a sprig of mint delicately placed atop the surface and one of the remaining pieces of bread smeared with a thick square of hand-churned butter. Graham would likely be aghast if he knew how much butter I secretly eat, and I should be better about conserving it, since I make it myself and it takes forever, but I can't help it.

Butter reminds me of early-morning pancakes with my mother—a rich, creamy spread of yellow on any food makes my taste buds sigh in delight. Every so often, I'll eat a little pat all on its own, relishing the sweet, silky texture as it melts on my tongue.

Putting my phone away, I rinse out the dishes, using a natural sea wool sponge to scour away the residue from pots and pans. We have a dishwasher, but I prefer to hand-wash everything. It makes it feel more real. Like I'm doing my job better. Mara is the same way, and it gives me comfort to know I'm doing the right thing.

Upstairs, barely audible over the splash of the running water, a floorboard creaks.

It's been happening more and more frequently lately.

I begin to hum, to drown out any other unwanted noises—a church hymn I can't remember the name of that we used to sing with our old congregation. I keep humming as the sun dips behind the forest out back, its final tendrils of light waving goodbye as I use a hand-stitched dish towel to dry everything. By the time I place the damp dishes on the bamboo rack near the sink, the sky is indigo and my throat is vibrating from humming so long.

I look around for more distractions. I sweep the floor, even though it's near spotless. I move into the living room and straighten the coffee table books, checking the sliding glass door to make sure it's locked (it is) and drawing the curtains across the windows. I don't usually do this—there's no one out here to look inside—but I've started to hunker down in the last week, wary of the complete darkness of country evenings.

I sit on the couch, waiting for Graham to text or for his car to crunch in the driveway. My phone stays silent as it gets later and later. I do laundry. I check my social media. I knit rows upon rows of a new winter scarf for my husband.

Upstairs, the floorboards groan.

By 9:15, I can't stall any longer. I have to get to bed at a reasonable hour in order to wake up with the sun and start my day. Tomorrow is Friday—one more day until the weekend, and then I'll get Graham to myself again. Maybe we'll be able to have sex and this time, finally, it'll take.

There is nothing upstairs, I tell myself as I flick off the lights in the living room and kitchen, leaving only the hall light on so Graham doesn't walk into a wall when he finally gets home.

As I stand at the foot of the stairs, looking up into the darkness of the second floor, an overwhelmingly claustrophobic sensation sweeps over my chest. I picture a rat sniffing at a trap it can smell but not see, apprehensively waiting for the *snap* that signifies the arrival of death.

Trembling, I hit the switch at the bottom of the stairs, next to the photo of Graham and me on our honeymoon in Italy. The upstairs explodes into focus as the light illuminates the painted white slats of the railing, the soft gray carpeting on the steps, and the rickety, narrow table at the top that supports pearled prayer hands Graham's mother gave him.

Everything is quiet and unmoving, so I begin to climb the staircase, one hand dragging against the banister, the other lifting my dress up around my hip so I won't trip on its length. The upstairs hallway branches off at the top of the staircase, the craft room and the nursery along one side, our bedroom at the very end, near the back of the house.

My eyes slide into each room's open doorway as I pass, bare feet tapping across the finished floors. The craft room, nearest the stairs, is dark and transformed into a series of looming shadows, but nothing moves inside, and I pass it by.

I grit my teeth as I glance into the nursery, which is dimly illuminated by the night-light plugged into the wall—a little brown bear, glowing faintly, who casts rounded shapes on the floor and yellows the edge of the crib. The nursery is a pain in my chest, a burr in my hair that won't become untangled, but its emptiness and silence bother me less right now.

There is nothing in there either.

I finally arrive at our bedroom, pausing in front of the closed door. I am sure I left it open. I *always* leave the doors open up here; it can get stuffy, and I like to have the windows up for cross-ventilation. Graham wanted to put in air conditioners, but Mara says air conditioners are bad for your lungs, which I'm not sure is entirely accurate, but I couldn't risk having one visible in the background of a photo and getting called out for it online.

I stand in the hallway, watching the closed door. I wait to hear the garage door churning or to feel my phone buzzing with a text from Graham on his way home. Anything to save me from having to do this alone.

Nothing.

I reach out, clammy hand slipping on the cool doorknob before finally finding purchase and twisting, pushing the door open soundlessly.

There's something in my bedroom.

It stands by the open window, across the room from the door, directly in front of the en suite bathroom.

Human sized, human formed, but with its back to me, standing absolutely still. I might have thought it was a statue except that I can see it breathing, even from all the way over here, as if its lungs are so large they require more space to expand. There is no light in the bedroom, but the glow from the hallway pools inside, allowing me to see enough to know this is not a person at all.

I know what this is. This is my dream, come to life.

The bedroom, which normally smells like sandalwood due to the expensive oil diffuser I keep on the white wood dresser, now smells like a swamp. Damp earth, standing water, bog plants. It matches the temperature of the room—humid, slightly stale.

My mouth drops open and a croak falls out. I clap my hand to my mouth as the creature, hidden in shadows, slowly begins to turn around. It locks its gaze on me, stepping forward once, twice, before rooting still again.

My stomach twists.

The eyes staring at me are completely white. I wonder if its pupils have rolled up into the back of its head or if all it has is sclera.

The creature is the general size and shape of a person, but there's something sickening about its proportions. Its arms are a hair too short, its legs a shade too thin, its face a tiny bit too long. It has gray skin with a greenish cast, almost iridescent in places, as if covered in jeweled scales. Two nubs poke from each of its temples, breaking through the pebbly forehead like goat horns.

The creature is also naked. The heat of a blush creeps up my neck, blotching my cheeks, because technically, the creature is male. I can't seem to attach the correct pronouns to it, but I can see the penis, engorged, rounded, beneath a chiseled waistline. Literally—its body looks like it was carved from stone.

Graham said they could look like anything, even something dangerous and upsetting, but I didn't expect an angel to look like *this*.

The creature shifts, moving something on its shoulders. Is it wearing a . . . backpack?

Breath huffs from my mouth hurriedly. The creature cocks its head, steps forward once again.

Oh. No. Not a backpack.

The fuzzy light from the hall reveals a pair of wings, folded against the creature's back, too big to be completely hidden. They are leathery, bat-like, dark gray but nearly translucent. Thick veins thread through the upper parts of the surface.

The creature doesn't move again; it stands there, watching me, as if waiting for something. But seeing the wings is too much. This can't be real. I must be losing my mind. There is no angel; I've been seeing things.

The floor shifts, my vision blurs, and I reach out for the doorframe, missing and crumpling to the ground.

Everything fuzzes over, and the last thing I see are the creature's feet, clawed and the color of soot.

* * *

I wake up to Graham's voice above me and a hungry vise wrapping around my biceps.

The world is a groggy smear of colors until I recall the *thing* I saw in our bedroom. A current races from the base of my back to the crown of my head, hopping along each vertebra. My throat seizes and I wheeze as my eyesight clears, wildly looking around, thrashing in Graham's grip.

His hands are the restraints I felt on my upper arms, and he tightens further as I begin to flail and cry, "Where is it? Did you see it?"

"Camille! *Camille!* What the hell is going on? Babe, are you OK?"

I go limp at the decibel of his words. We rarely fight, and I've only heard him raise his voice once, a year ago when his friend's wife called me "dumb" and said I was only feeding a "sexist kink." Graham freaked out, ordered her out of our house. He doesn't see that friend much anymore, and his wife has been banned from interacting with us.

"I'm sorry," I whisper, sagging against my husband's broad chest. He smells like leather and country air. And something else, something floral that reminds me of springtime.

"Camille, how long were you unconscious for?" he asks, cradling my head. His dark eyes stare down at me. There are little lines in his brow I've never noticed before. When did those get there? "We should get you to a hospital."

My focus snaps back to reality. "No," I plead. "No hospital. I'm OK. I . . . didn't eat much today. Low blood sugar."

I can't deal with the questions I'll face at a hospital. What if I slip up and mention all the hallucinations and dreams I've been having the past week? They might try to put me on medication, and Mara and her troop of influencers have been very clear about the dangers of medication. And while the wariness of medications and vaccines in my online community is at odds with what I know to be true, I try to stay in line.

"No hospital," I say more firmly, when I notice Graham's eyes are crinkled and his mouth is twisted. "I'm fine. Please." I wiggle free from his arms and shift across the floor so that my back is against the wall near the door. I smooth the off-white dress, patting my legs at the same time as if making sure they're still there.

"OK, OK," he says, putting his hands up in surrender. "You sure you're all right?" His beard is disheveled, like he was anxiously rubbing it back and forth with his hand when I was unconscious. His lips are slightly larger than usual, as if they're swollen.

"Yes, babe," I answer, clearing my throat so my voice sounds less infirm. "I'm glad you're here. Thank you for taking care of me."

"Anytime, Camille," Graham says, smiling at me, the worry lines vanishing from his charming face. "Thank God you're OK."

He means it. Graham doesn't use God's name arbitrarily like other people. He is truly thanking his God, and it warms me to see how worried he was.

"Camille? Want to stand up?"

"Yes," I reply, glancing around the room once again, looking for evidence of what I saw. But there's only our tastefully decorated bedroom. Could I have imagined it?

Graham helps me get to my feet, casting an appraising eye up and down my body as if searching for something he's not seeing. "You're positive you're feeling fine?" he asks again.

"Yes," I repeat, smiling to erase the exasperation bubbling within. I don't want to think about this anymore. I'm too tired.

"Good," Graham says, matching my smile. "I'm hungry. Did you make me dinner?"

C H A P T E R

8

THE EYE APPEARS in my dream again, but now it's different. The old script has been thrown away. This time, it jumps right in. Its voice presses me down into the mattress with fervor and insistence, and I can feel its displeasure furrowing into my limbs.

You wanted a baby.

I try to close my eyes against the whirling wings, which are once again spinning around the oculus, but as before, I am frozen, forced to stare as dizziness washes over me.

I do, I think. *Please, stop.*

The wings stop moving. The eye wetly blinks and goes completely white.

You wanted a baby, it repeats. *You prayed. You offered a gift. I arrived. You asked for a baby.*

You arrived? Wait, are you the—

DO YOU WANT A BABY?

The thunder of the voice splits open my scalp and drives into my brain, grinding my molars and scraping out the insides of my chest cavity.

I wake with a violent inhale, a drowning woman resurfacing, not knowing if this will be her last breath.

Everything is quiet. The bedroom is empty. Truly empty—Graham is not by my side. A different pain surfaces, brushing against my heart with a latent sensation like stinging nettles. Where is my husband?

I slap a hand on my nightstand, searching for my phone, waking the screen up. There, sent one hour ago, at 1:24 AM—a text from Graham.

Didn't want to wake you after your little episode earlier! You get your rest. Just wanted to let you know that I'm starting the weekend early. Staying at Bobby's place tonight so we can play hooky and watch the game tomorrow. See you soon, love you.

My stomach drops alongside my phone, the device slipping from my slack fingers and landing on the mattress with a soft *thwump*.

Graham and I went to bed together. I hadn't bothered trying to sleep with him—he was doting and almost cloying as I served him a late-night dinner, insisting on helping me with the dishes. I shuddered to think of Mara's response if she could see my man doing domestic work. Graham gently tucked me in bed after, saying he was going to watch some TV and come up shortly. I fell asleep almost immediately, completely wiped from the incident earlier and my week of unsatisfactory sleep.

But now I have to admit that my loving husband has abandoned me in the middle of the night.

Not abandoned, I try to tell myself. *He was so kind earlier. He saw you were OK, so he decided to take a much-needed break from work to be with his good friend.*

That has to be it. Even though Graham keeps saying how busy work is. Even though he's never left the house this late before. Even though his wife passed out hours earlier.

Graham warned me his schedule would change when we moved out here. He'd have to commute to his office every day, which is an hour away from our new home. And being a C suite officer means he's in high demand—he dismissed my suggestion he work from home half the time. "I have to be there, babe," he said. "You agreed to this. We might not have as much time together. My job is how I can afford this lifestyle for us, remember?"

I backed down immediately. Graham provided for me and supplied our wonderful life together. I understood that in these new circumstances, work had to come first. I didn't think our life would look like this, though.

"He smelled like perfume," I murmur, finally recognizing the floral scent I got a whiff of when Graham held me in his arms after finding me on the floor. Holy Peony from Dior. I've only ever smelled it in magazines.

I kick the blankets off my legs, suddenly too warm.

The voice from my dream echoes in my head: *You prayed.*

I thought the creature was a hallucination. The product of a mind warped by stress and lack of sleep. But maybe *this* is what the dreams have been pointing to the whole week. This could be the answer.

A real angel. Not a frightening presence, but something too beautiful and grand and *special* for me to even appreciate. I think of the eye in my dreams. The grayish green of the creature's skin. I thought it looked like a dead thing, but what if I misunderstood? What if I wasn't being stalked by this creature—what if it was trying to give me a gift?

I wouldn't be the first to do it this way, after all. How else did Mary give birth to Jesus? Immaculate conception is all well and good, but perhaps it was a cover for the less palatable truth—to have a baby, sex must happen.

And Graham isn't having sex with me.

I remember the smell of Holy Peony on my husband's neck.

A thick, soupy lava pours across my chest and dribbles down my spine and breasts. Why shouldn't I have this one thing? I've hoped and prayed and begged, and nothing has worked. A good wife doesn't get angry, and she definitely doesn't blame her husband for anything, but how can I be a good wife without a baby? How can I create a perfect life for us if my husband keeps disappearing, returning home far too late smelling like flowers and sporting bruised lips?

I need this. *We* need this. And if Graham won't help me, I'll have to help the both of us myself. I'll be doing it for our love.

What stories are you telling yourself, Camille? says a voice hiding in the corner of my mind.

I crawl from bed and stomp over to the window, shoving aside the gossamer curtains and staring out into the black abyss of the backyard. There is no moon tonight, yet I can sense the swaying of the wheat field beneath me, a sea I can't touch but can smell on the wind.

The world outside my window seems so far away. I have been surrounded by flat fields of wheat and corn, the looming presence of the forest at the back of our property, and the paved road that cuts through the landscape, going nowhere I can reach. Even the sky itself has started to feel oppressive, a heavy weight threatening to collapse down on top of our utopia.

Embers pulse inside me. I don't know what to do with this unfamiliar emotion, the pieces of which have been stacked one by one over the last few months, or the last few years, until a tower of resentment has reached my heart.

"Stop it," I whisper, my words creaking like the painted floorboards under my feet. "Don't be ungrateful. You wanted this. Your life will be perfect as soon as you have a baby."

A soft scraping comes from behind me.

When I turn around, a shape is in the doorway of the bedroom, the dim glow from the nursery's night-light framing its body.

A gasp slips free, and the shape flickers, as if made of static. In the heady darkness, it's hard to make out any details from my spot by the window, but my eyes are adjusted enough to recognize the lurching posture, the outline of wings, the almost reptilian head. This is the same creature that made me faint in fear hours ago.

My heart whips and flutters like a flag in the wind. I bite down, front teeth sinking into the smooth plumpness of my bottom lip as I take a hesitant step away from the window, toward the center of the room and the en suite bathroom. Our positions from earlier have been reversed, and I mimic its staccato steps.

The creature stays in the threshold of the doorway, not moving. I can make out its eerie eyes, glowing white like twin moons, pitted and shadowed, but without it having pupils it's impossible to tell what it's looking at, if it's tracking my movement.

Aware of my vulnerable state, my bare legs exposed in my beige cotton sleep set, I make my way slowly to the center of the large bedroom without incident or movement from the creature by the door. The bathroom is five feet away. I could throw myself in there, lock the door, and . . .

What? I don't have my phone. It's on the bedside table closest to the entrance of the room. I can't call Graham. Would he even pick up if I did call him, or is he *busy*?

My blood is pumping, but there is curiosity laced in my adrenaline, and I get a whiff of Holy Peony again. My skin grows hot.

I can't shake the dreams, Graham's insistence that angels don't always look the way we expect them to. I crest a wave of impulsivity, triggered by my clenched stomach, the tight fists at my sides, and the heat building around my neck.

"Are you an angel?" I ask, the words raw and unformed in my mouth.

The creature in the doorway doesn't move, doesn't answer. Maybe it can't speak English. Maybe angels have their own language. Or they can only speak in dreams.

"An angel," I say again, my voice quivering. "You're an angel?"

As if to confirm, the creature shifts, takes one step forward. It's not particularly tall, but somehow its one step has cleared five feet of space. It's fully inside the bedroom now.

"You were sent here to help me?" I ask. "Help *us*? God wants us to have a baby?"

Again, the creature steps forward, blank, white eyes staring at me or at nothing at all. It's difficult to tell.

"You're an angel," I whisper, and this time the creature does not move, only stands near the bed, arms limp by its sides.

Stop calling it a creature if you think it's an angel.

I can't help it. It's unlike any version of an angel I've seen before, and though it's here to help us *(Do you really know that?)*, I can't shake the persistent fear that lingers in the scaffolding of my bones.

If I'm not meant to do this, let Graham text me right now, I think, sending the prayer up to the heavens.

I wait a minute for God to consider my request and wake up my husband, remind him he has a wife at home. Then I wait a minute more, thinking of how I threw the penny in the wishing well. Strange things have happened since then, but I've had realizations too. Things I would rather not think about are bubbling to the surface, and I'm not sure I appreciate it. I want my life to be the life I was promised when I married Graham; I want to be the best wife possible, and I want to be a mother. Maybe just this once, it's OK to take matters into my own hands.

My phone is faceup on the bedside table near the creature. I hold my breath, watching the screen, but it stays dark. The creature—the angel—remains motionless.

I don't know how long I stand there, waiting for Graham to hear my prayer and text me, but eventually it becomes clear that he's not thinking of me at all. Which means I am meant to do this. I am meant to get us a baby in a different way. Mara Shoemaker wouldn't approve. My father wouldn't approve. But at this moment, I don't care. *God* has approved this, and the desire to fix my relationship and bring a child into this world devours me whole. This isn't a choice—it's fate.

I move around the bed slowly, the creature (*angel!*) getting more defined as I draw closer. Its nakedness, the rough, scaled skin, the thick muscles corded across its chest and stomach. White eyes move in their sockets as I step forward. Heart hammering, I reach out and pick up one of the creature's hands, which is motionless and hanging by its side. Its fingers are black tipped with blunted claws, but its palm is surprisingly smooth and warm and *human.* I expected it to feel cold and rough like stone, but instead there's a humid heat emanating from its skin.

I step closer, and the room lightens suddenly as the moon shows its face, slipping out from behind the dark clouds that covered it. I glance behind me; the bed is cast in a pearly light, the comforter looking soft and luminous in the glow of the moon. The curtains part with a cool breeze, and the scent of pine and wet stone fills the room.

It's another sign, I think. Where there was darkness, now there is light.

I turn back to the creature. Now that I'm closer to its face, the creature's skin looks softer, more human, though the color is unsettling. With so little space between us, I can see now that its eyes, consumed by white, are bloodshot, but instead of spidery red veins, there are threads of black lacing around the inner edges of the sclerae.

I cut my gaze away from its eyes—they are too disconcerting. Instead, I lift the edge of my cotton shirt and pull it over my head. Next I step out from the matching shorts, leaving them on the floor in a puddle. I stand in front of the creature, breasts bare, skin tingling, in my lacy white underwear.

The voice from my dreams reverberates in my mind: *DO YOU WANT A BABY?*

"Yes," I whisper.

I reach out and place a hand on the creature's manhood, which shifts beneath my fingers, erect and eager.

I look at the hollow in the creature's collarbone, right under its throat. Reaching out, I touch it with my free hand, index finger caressing the divot. The creature's skin has an ombré effect of light gray to pale green, and this particular area is the lightest and softest spot on its front side.

"Give me a child," I say.

Without warning, the creature lifts me into the air, muscled arms wrapping around my waist, carrying me the few feet over to the bed. It gently lays me down on my back, face expressionless. It has no hair, just an eruption of black bone near its temples and a collection of shiny, dark-gray scales over the top of its head like a helmet.

I tug down my underwear, tossing them to the side of the bed Graham usually sleeps on, opening my thighs, shivering as the night air touches my body. I am thrumming with anticipation, nerves, anger, but I need this. I *want* this. I think about how I ached to be touched by Graham and how he rejected me or used only my mouth for his pleasure.

The creature hovers over me, long, clawed hands coming down to rest on my hips. Then it lowers itself, head near my stomach, trailing down until it reaches my pubic mound.

"What are you doing?" I ask, breathless. "Baby. I need a *baby*—"

I'm cut off by the creature's mouth against me, hot and darting like an electric current. This is not what it is like with Graham. My body responds in a way I don't understand, arching, lifting, hips pinned in place by the creature's smooth palms. A fire builds inside my chest, trailing down to meet the creature's tongue, which flickers insistently inside me. When I break, I scream out in grief and delight and rage.

Swiftly, the creature's face emerges and I gasp, reaching down for it, connecting us. It pushes against me, and we fall together. Its body smells of loam and wheat, as if the field outside has bundled itself into a human-shaped suit of scaled skin. There's something tangy in the scent of its body as well, reminiscent of moldy bread or rotten vegetables. I try to breathe through my mouth as we move as one, our bodies rocking together seamlessly in a way Graham and I never do. The creature's arms are propped up near my head now, and when I glance at its face, I'm relieved to see its unnerving eyes are closed. Its eyelids look like the texture of dead leaves, and its mouth, parted, reveals a layer of needle-sharp teeth.

The creature's wings, much bigger this close, unfurl and lower, wrapping our bodies inside a cocoon of darkness and soil-scented membrane. The skin on my arms and legs prickles, hairs lifting as if they could touch the wings surrounding them.

Arrector pili.

Our rhythm picks up urgency until I feel the fire building inside me again, my breath coming fast and loose and wild. I turn my face away from the creature as I shatter a second time, and in the same instant, a burning-hot liquid releases inside me. I shriek, but the heat is a pain that ripples with pleasure, and a satisfied whimper falls from my lips.

A baby. I will have a baby.

The creature pulls away, eyes open now. The wings fold back, becoming smaller, resting against its shoulders. The creature appears to look down at me, spent and panting on the white sheets. There is no change in his face.

No, not *his*. It's not a man, I tell myself, almost scolding. An angel. A creature sent from the heavens to save me and my marriage. He—it can't be a man. Because that would mean I cheated, and I would never cheat. That's not what a good woman does.

But there's a twisted bundle of nerves in my stomach that won't stop writhing despite the aftershocks of desire pulsing through my lower half. I take a shuddering breath, lifting myself up on my elbows as the creature steps away from the bed. I look down at my body as if expecting it to be different, but it's not. Yet I feel the creature's seed inside me, and I clamp my thighs together as if to help it take root and grow.

I am sticky with sweat and my own daring. The creature has gone back to standing perfectly still, arms by its sides, face blank and eyes wide.

The moon, present throughout our copulation, vanishes again. The heavy clouds that sheathed it earlier are back, and the first sprinkle of rain begins to fall. The air coming in through the open window tastes like electricity and fog. Naked, I pull free from the tangle of sheets on the bed and hurry over to the window, pushing down on the frame to shut out the raindrops, which are pattering harder and harder against the glass now. I peer out at the dark wheat field, the ridged line of the forest in the distance that looks like a smear of black paint. Seconds later the sky cracks open with a burst of lightning. In the flash from the white light, I catch a glimpse of a dark shape moving away from the house, melting into the high stalks of wheat.

When I turn around, the room is empty and the creature is gone.

CHAPTER

9

GRAHAM DOESN'T COME home until the next evening.

He texts me in the morning to check in, see how I'm doing, and then later in the afternoon to request steak for dinner.

I act like nothing is wrong, like nothing has changed. But it has. As I move through my chores, check my social media likes and messages, take a few photos of my bread-making setup, my mind is elsewhere. I'm not sure if last night was real or a dream.

Graham was my first. He was so kind, so loving. He explained that sex was supposed to hurt the girl. "It's very normal," he said gently as I winced underneath him.

I knew that wasn't true, but I pretended otherwise. My perceived innocence pleased him, and I enjoyed that.

Eventually it stopped hurting, but sex with Graham was fast, intense. I liked it because I liked Graham. Or rather, love. I *love* Graham. I accepted our sex life—his compliments on my appearance, and his furious appetite in the beginning after I explained I didn't have much experience. Sometimes when he wasn't around, I would quietly explore my own body, imagining Graham touching me in such a way. He never did, always asking, "Did you come?" and then smiling at me when I lied and said yes. When our sex life started to dwindle shortly before the move, part of me was relieved. The larger, stronger part of me was distraught.

I want the intimacy. And more important, I want the baby.

But even when Graham couldn't keep his hands off me, our sex was never like what happened last night. I wonder if that's because Graham never got me pregnant. Maybe you only have sex like that when you conceive.

No wonder all those influencers have ten kids, I think ruefully.

I remind myself I'm one of the lucky ones. My husband loves me. He would never hit me or scream at me.

Why, then, did I so quickly turn to the creature—the angel—for help? Why can't I stop thinking about the encounter? And why do I feel no guilt?

When Graham enters the house, I'm kneading dough, flour dusting my arms, blouse rolled up to my elbows.

I can't help it; love springs in my heart at the sight of him. His eyes are blurry, as if he's exhausted, and he needs a fresh shave, but everything else about him is so familiar. His pressed pants (that I wash, iron, fold, and return to his closet), his dark eyebrows, his square jaw. I fell for him right away—he was exactly what I wanted because he knew what *he* wanted.

We can get back to how it used to be. We're so close.

"Welcome home, love," I say, leaning toward him so he can kiss the tip of my nose. "How was your night with Bobby?" I almost stress his friend's name, but at the last second, I decide not to. Maybe Graham was telling the truth. Being negligent is better than being a cheater.

"It was fine, nothing special," Graham says, squeezing my shoulder, looking down at the dough. "How was the rest of your night? And today? No more fainting episodes, I hope?"

For a moment, I worry Graham can see the truth on my face. But then I notice he's not looking at me; his phone has dinged and he steps away, leaning against the counter to read the message, standing so that the screen is angled away from me. He doesn't see my expression, and even if he did, I didn't do anything wrong. I accepted the gift God gave me. Gave us.

Is that what you're telling yourself?

"Shut up," I mutter to the voice in my head.

"Huh?" Graham says, distracted as he types away a response on his phone.

"Uh, nothing," I reply hastily. "It was good. No more passing out. Lots of housework today. And now bread making."

Graham must hit send, because he finally looks up from his screen and eyes the dough in front of me. "New batch of sourdough?"

"Your favorite," I reply, smiling through the frown threatening to break out across my brow.

"Oh, by the way, this was taped to the front door. I saw it from the driveway," Graham says, passing me a slip of paper. "You should call her."

I take the paper with flour-speckled hands and unfold it to see loopy handwriting with pink hearts: Renee's name and phone number along with the words *Love to go for that jog soon!*

"You read this?" I ask as I refold the paper and rest it on the counter. I've been a little lonely, yes, but Renee is . . . a lot. I'm not sure I want to be friends with her even if we have some similarities.

"Sure. Wanted to see who was leaving notes on our door in the middle of nowhere," Graham says. "I don't want to freak you out, but there are some weird rumors about this area."

"Oh?"

Graham sighs, like he's already regretting mentioning it. "Cryptic warnings about the woods. That they aren't safe. Nothing to worry about, darling. Farm animals go missing all the time. It's part of country living. There's probably a bear or coyotes in the forest."

Renee mentioned something similar, but I was not made aware of any security issues in the area at any point during the home-buying process. Then again, Graham handled everything. I tagged along to viewings, offering my opinions and throwing my arms around my husband when he agreed that this house was the best choice for us despite its distance from his job. Never did I hear that the forest was unsafe, although it definitely has a certain *vibe*.

"Am I safe here, all alone, every day?" I ask, once again wondering how Graham could leave me in our bed in the middle of the night, especially if he heard the woods are dangerous.

"There's nothing to worry about, babe," Graham says, patting my cheek as if I were a beloved dog. "Predators are completely normal out here in the country. We're not in the suburbs anymore, remember?"

"I know."

"This is what you wanted."

Is there a hint of accusation in his voice? A tiny stress on the word *you*, as if this isn't what Graham wanted too, as if he didn't leap at the opportunity?

"Yes," I reply. "It's been amazing so far." I change the subject. "What would you like to do this weekend?"

Graham, almost unconsciously, glances down at the phone in his hand again, before answering me. "Why don't you call this Renee woman? Go for a jog, maybe visit her place? You've been cooped up here for a while. Fresh air will do you good."

"I go for walks every day outside," I point out, even though that has stopped in the last week.

"Still. It's good for you to be friendly with the neighbors."

"I thought maybe we could spend some time together," I say, not wanting to touch him due to the white dust all over my hands but feeling the magnet of his body pull me closer in space.

"That would be great," Graham says, smiling. "But I'm golfing with the boys tomorrow. Don't worry," he adds, seeing my expression. "I'll be home for dinner this time, I promise! It's an early tee-off, so I'll be back late afternoon."

I try not to let my disappointment show. I had pictured a lazy day together, taking selfies for social media, going for a walk along the road, hand in hand, curling up together on the couch to watch a movie. Maybe we could even make love, see if we could replicate the oceanic sensations I experienced last night.

"We'll have a romantic evening together, OK?" Graham promises, chucking my chin. "I'll stop and get a cake from that organic bakery you like. Maybe a bottle of wine?"

I'm not a big drinker—Mara says alcohol is bad for your skin and makes you unseemly, but she allows for an occasional glass or two of an expensive, classy red wine, so sometimes I will enjoy a pricey bottle with Graham, portioning it out over several days.

I nod at him, my smile stiff. "That sounds perfect."

"Then it's a date," he says, planting a kiss above my left ear. "All right, I'm going to go watch some TV. What time is dinner tonight?"

* * *

Graham goes to bed earlier than me, which is rare. He seems tired, worn out, and he keeps reminding me of his early tee time as if it's an award, something to be celebrated, perhaps forgetting that I regularly rise at that time to get his breakfast ready and prepare the house for the day. When we have a baby, I'll have to start getting up even earlier, so I consider it practice.

After I finish putting away the dishes from dinner, wiping up all the counters, and tidying the living room where Graham planted himself for hours, I'm utterly exhausted. I haven't fully recovered from the events of last night, even though the experience was short.

I tiptoe into our dark bedroom—once again, Graham hasn't left any lights on for me—and a strange, giddy sensation floods my stomach to see his lumpy, blanketed shape on the bed I writhed around on last night.

I changed and laundered the sheets. Remade the bed. Sprayed lavender sleep mist on the pillows and comforter. There is no evidence of what happened. But still, seeing Graham sleeping there causes a stir in my groin, a pull of desire inside my flesh.

I move quietly through the bedroom into the en suite bathroom, closing the door so as not to disturb Graham, setting about my nighttime routine with cleansers and lotion.

I'm brushing my teeth when the swells start in my stomach. They rock and swirl like whirlpools, sending waves of nausea through my body. I spit out the toothpaste and gag, dropping the brush against the marble counter and gripping the sides of the sink, abdomen clenching as my stomach heaves in vain. Nothing comes up, but my eyes water and my mouth turns as dry as sandpaper.

I wait for a few minutes to see if I will be sick, but eventually the rolling in my stomach dies down, and I splash icy-cold water on my face, letting the rivulets drip down my wrists and forearms.

Maybe I'm imagining it, but it feels like there's a twitching deep inside me, a leaf poking its head free from soil.

A woman always knows when she's with child, Mara said on her last pregnancy announcement post, a photo of her golden face surrounded by her other children. *Our ancestors didn't have tests or doctors to tell us what we know in our hearts. Every woman knows when she has created the miracle of life.*

I look at my reflection in our giant mirror. My skin, freshly clean, slightly pink, is coated in a sheen of lotion that makes my face shiny in the fluorescent light. The edges of my mouth curl up as excitement courses through my blood.

It's too soon to be the angel's, I think gleefully. This must be Graham's child!

Twin suns of regret and joy crowd together, trying to eclipse each other. Maybe I didn't need to lie with the creature at all. Maybe I was already carrying Graham's child and the first pregnancy test was inaccurate—that happens sometimes. I should have taken another test to be sure.

I cheated for nothing.

"I did not cheat!" I whisper out loud, hissing at my reflection in the mirror, lines forming on my forehead as my smile fades. "I did what I needed to do. What God wanted me to do."

I take a deep breath, easing the frown from my face, elevating my smile to its rightful place. This is amazing news. Remarkable news. Mara is right—I can feel it inside me.

Tomorrow I will take a pregnancy test, several of them, to make sure. I can't do it now—I want to capture the moment on socials and I need time to prepare my look. Besides, it will be so much better to test tomorrow and have good news for Graham when he comes home from his golfing day.

Maybe I can record his reaction! Think of the engagement a post like that will get on social media. I might even go viral, catch the attention of Mara Shoemaker and her iconic group of wives. For a moment, I vividly imagine myself entering Mara's sacred online inner circle, being invited to all the virtual events, the group chats, being tagged in her posts. It *could* happen.

It all starts with this child. My future. Our future.

I sigh, looking dreamily at my reflection.

Everything is going to be OK. Everything is going to be perfect.

10

DESPITE ALL THE fuss Graham makes about his early wake-up, I'm up even earlier, cooking him a quick breakfast and filling a to-go cup of coffee he can drink in the car.

The eye did not interrupt my sleep last night, and I already feel calmer and more rested.

When Graham finally stumbles down the stairs, eyes bleary and mouth creaking with yawns, he grins to see me already up. I'm wearing a short-sleeved floral maxi dress, and my blonde tresses are slightly curled, draping down my shoulder blades.

"You're the best," he says, giving me a half hug as he takes the egg sandwich and thermos.

Graham is wearing a light-blue polo shirt and perfectly pressed khakis, thanks to me. I laid them out for him before bed yesterday. A baseball cap is jammed over his dark hair, and his beard scratches my bare cheeks as he presses a kiss against my skin.

"Have fun," I say. "I can't wait for our date night later. I think it's going to be *very* special."

He yawns again, giving me a wink. "Me too, babe."

Then he lumbers away to the garage entrance in his office. The car growls, the mechanical door purrs as it opens, and the gravel crunches, signaling Graham's off into the predawn morning.

The house is suspended; a clock's ticking hands are audible from the living room. I pause in the subsequent silence, inhaling the lingering aroma of warm coffee beans and fried egg. The scent of Graham's breakfast sticks greedily to the inside of my nose, and I gag again. Stomach twisting, I rush from the kitchen, throwing open the door to the downstairs bathroom and stumbling over to the porcelain toilet just in time to lift the lid.

I squeeze my eyes shut as thick, hot liquid spills from my mouth, splashing against the bottom of the bowl. Stomach contracting, I feel my hands slip from the rim, clammy and shaking. My hair tumbles forward, and with my eyes still tightly closed, I quickly swipe my fingers through the strands, catching them and pulling them away from my face.

My throat burns as if the liquid is actually boiling and not just heated from my insides, but finally the retching slows down. I spit a few times in the bowl, gasping for air, and then open my eyes. My vision is blurred by tears, so I sit back on my heels and release my hair, wiping at my face. I glance at the bowl, hand reaching for the flush.

I almost vomit again when I see what's inside.

Blood. What looks like buckets and buckets of blood. But it's not normal blood—it's half coagulated and nearly solid. Like soup that's been sitting out for days. And it's dark. Not bright crimson but burgundy, streaked with black and brown, almost like menstrual blood. I gag again looking at it and quickly flush the toilet, leaning back to avoid the spray. For a moment I'm worried the thick blood will clog the pipes, but it vanishes, leaving a slightly sulfurous smell in its wake.

This isn't good. Pregnant or not, vomiting blood is a bad sign. Am I seriously sick? What if everything that has happened over the last week or so is because I'm ill?

Cramps twist inside me, and I double over for a moment, holding my stomach.

Wait. Something is . . .

I straighten, rubbing my belly. There is a roundness there that certainly wasn't present yesterday. Trembling, I use the sink to pull myself to my feet, staring in the mirror at my bloodshot eyes. Then I pull at the fabric of my maxi dress, fingers disappearing in the folds of flowers, hiking the skirt up and up until I can bunch the material into a clump and shove it under one arm, exposing my lower half and stomach.

Staring down, I can't see the elegant nude lace of my underwear; it's hidden by the swell of my abdomen. Skin stretches over the bump, pale and taut. With my dress tucked under my arm, I reach out with my free hand, stroking my belly, feeling the curve, the warmth of the shape that is now part of me. As my hand reaches the middle of my stomach, there's a sudden pressure, a quick movement, and something slams into my palm from inside.

I cry out and jerk my hand back, stumbling toward the shower as if I can back away from my stomach. I freeze as the movement comes again, sharp and fast. This time I catch it: a protuberance, the size and shape of a grape, punching up underneath the skin of my belly.

My breath squeezes out of my throat, unwilling and forced. Tentatively, I place a palm back on my stomach, and once again, something kicks into me with enough force that my hand is knocked off the bump.

I let the fabric drop, the maxi dress falling down to hide my belly and legs. Sweat gathers on my brow as if waiting for permission to fall. Somehow, between dawn and now, I have started showing.

I hobble forward to the mirror again, bending over, digging through the storage space under the sink, pulling out a box of pregnancy tests. I always have them on hand, but today I tear into the packaging feverishly, not bothering with my camera, not thinking about the social media video I planned. Something is wrong, and wrong things don't go online.

Smiles, not frowns.

Twenty minutes later, three positive pregnancy tests look up at me from the counter, their pink lines self-satisfied smirks.

I press both hands into my stomach, feeling the soft material of my dress rub against my tight skin. I wait, but nothing moves inside me this time, as if the confirmation was what it wanted.

Not Graham's child, then, I think.

I may be young and a bit naïve, but I'm not stupid. This isn't how pregnancy is supposed to go. You're not supposed to throw up blood and then immediately discover a baby bump that already contains a kicking child when hours earlier there was nothing. But you're also probably not supposed to have sex with wishing-well creatures that you find in your bedroom.

Angel, I insist angrily. *It was an angel. That's why this feels so weird. It's a divine pregnancy. I'm sure it will be different than a normal one.*

It's easy to tell myself that and return to the mirror, smiling at my reflection. It's easy to ignore the voice in the back of my head that has been offering warnings and contradictions for months now, even before we moved. Because this, ultimately, is what I wanted. My greatest wish was to have a baby so I could save my marriage, establish my place online, and have someone, finally, who would love me completely. Does it matter how we got here?

I am undeniably pregnant. Who cares if there's an underlying sense of foreboding hiding inside my joints and woven in among my fascia?

I picture Graham's excited face. I'll tell him at our date night. He'll be so proud and happy. We'll be a real family now; things can go back to how they were before we moved. Get better, even.

I grin at myself in the mirror, ignoring my bloodstained teeth, the dark crescents under my eyes, and the drawn quality of my skin. I'm too busy imagining the photo shoots, the content, the adorable child I will have. I have so much to do to prepare.

Humming, I turn away from my reflection, and the baby starts to kick again.

*   *   *

Graham is late.

I try hard to not be annoyed. He texted, after all, apologizing for the delay. He said a short storm passed through and delayed their game for a few hours and they were finishing up now.

We'll still have our date night! ☺

It's more than a date night now. I use the extra time to prepare our dining table, laying out the fine china Graham's mother gifted us at our wedding, lighting soy candles and dimming the lights, setting up a charcuterie board with local meats and cheeses. I cook Graham's favorite—sirloin steak—and I look away when the sight of the raw meat makes saliva gather at the corners of my mouth. I'm pregnant; I'll have some strange cravings now. My father told me my mother used to eat pickles dipped in peanut butter when she was pregnant with me.

I step back, looking at the scene I've set. It's romantic—the candlelight, the soft jazz spinning on the record player in the corner of the living room, the wafting aroma of the steak. I remember to get out our fanciest wineglasses. I won't have any drinks now, of course, but Graham should still be able to celebrate.

I text Graham, asking his ETA, but there is no answer. I bite down any resentment, breathing through the static that grows in my chest. He has no idea what I'm going to tell him. If he did, I'm sure he would cut his game short and come rushing home immediately.

The candles flicker, their wax half melted.

I check my reflection in the floor-length mirror in the living room. I have showered and changed, taking time to marvel at the new shape of my body as I washed my stomach with gentle circles. Now I'm wearing a crew-neck cotton dress, off-white, intentionally shapeless and loose. It hides my bump easily—I want to surprise Graham. My hair is styled half up, half down, and I'm wearing a tiny bit more makeup than I normally would to make my eyes pop. I'll be on camera, after all.

My phone and tripod are set up on the coffee table, pointed at the dining area that lies between the living room and the kitchen. I've positioned the shot so that I'll capture the whole table and Graham's honest reaction. I'll be able to edit out anything I don't want later. My heart hums thinking of all the comments and likes I'll get.

The initial shock of the sudden pregnancy has worn off, and I haven't thrown up any blood since this morning, so I'm writing it off as a freak thing. I feel fine. Better than fine, really. Happy. Excited. Energized.

I shift back and forth in front of the mirror, fixing my hair, pulling my dress tight to see the bump again as if to make sure it's still there. The baby has been quiet for a while after spending most of the morning kicking away. Maybe it's sleeping. I pat my stomach.

"Get your rest, sweetheart. We have a big life ahead of us."

Gravel crunches outside and my heart leaps. Graham is finally home. Abandoning my reflection, I rush over to my phone, waking it up, starting the recording. Then I hurry into frame, taking my seat at one end of the table, the opposite end set for my husband.

As Graham enters the house, wanders through the open kitchen, catching sight of me on the other side of our breakfast bar, my stomach churns. The baby isn't moving, but my insides are, shifting and rocking, and the smell of cooked meat suddenly makes me feel sick.

Don't you dare throw up right now.

"Welcome home, darling," I manage.

Graham is flushed. The baseball cap he left the house with is no longer on his head, and his hair is slightly mussed, a cowlick flipping up above his left ear. His blue polo is rumpled. He's forgotten to take his shoes off at the door like I always ask, but I can't scold him tonight. Not for that, and not for being so late after promising to spend time with me.

"Hi, honey," he says, clomping into the dining nook. "What's all this?"

"Our date night. It's a very special one."

"Baby, I have to shower. I've been golfing all day. Can this wait?"

I'm extremely conscious of the phone pointing at the table, knowing I'll have to edit this entire exchange out. It doesn't accurately represent the love and kindness in our relationship. Anyone watching might think Graham is vaguely annoyed by the spread I've served him, not bothering to comment on it at all. They might think the crinkle around his eyes is dismay instead of exhaustion. And they might wonder why he doesn't greet me with a hug and a kiss or remark about all the work I've done to make it smell and look good in here.

Usually, I would say *Whatever you like* and let Graham tromp up the stairs to take a twenty-five-minute shower, hustling around the kitchen to try to keep the food warm. But this is not every other night. This is important. His shower can wait.

"Did you bring home the wine?" I ask instead. "We have to celebrate."

His hands are empty. He always leaves his golf clubs in the garage, but he wouldn't have left the bottle of wine there, would he?

"I forgot, sorry," he says, rubbing his hand over his face as if trying to swipe away his tiredness. Doesn't he want to know what we're celebrating?

"That's OK," I try again. I need to set this up so I can cut around all this and still make the reveal amazing. "I probably shouldn't be drinking wine anyway."

Graham finally takes the bait. "Why not?"

"Darling, will you sit at the table for a moment?" I say, my voice soothing. "I have something to tell you."

Perturbed by my request, Graham slides into his chair, nostrils flaring as he takes in the scent of the steak in front of him. "What's going on, Camille? Are you OK?"

Perfect. This is where I'll start the video.

I smile at him, aware of how I'm framed both in the camera and in my husband's eyes: angelic makeup, expensive and flowing dress, the beatific expression carefully plastered on my face.

"Graham Deming," I say, like I'm about to ask him to marry me. "I am pregnant."

For a brief second, Graham's face collapses. It's so fast and violent I almost miss it, because he adjusts his expression a millisecond later, a beaming grin taking up his entire face. He places his hands on the table and lifts himself up, leaning forward. "Are you serious? Are you *sure*?"

"Yes," I say, matching the width of his smile, getting to my feet so he can come embrace me. But Graham doesn't move from his side of the table. "I took three tests. We're having a baby."

"Lord," Graham murmurs, as if he's praying, casting his eyes to the surface of the table. "My Lord."

"It's finally happening, babe," I say, internally urging him to come around the table and hold me. He needs to be affectionate here. That's what people will be looking for online. "We're starting our family." He still doesn't move, so I add, hearing the note of desperation in my voice, "I love you."

This finally gets through to him, and he looks up at me. "I love you too." He blinks a few times, as if he's clearing away misty eyes, and skirts around the edge of the table, coming toward me and wrapping me up in a bear hug.

"I'm pregnant," I say again, my words muffled against Graham's polo. He smells like laundry detergent and sweat. I get another whiff of Holy Peony against his neck.

"I'm so happy for you," he replies. He must have forgotten to say *us*.

He pulls away, and this is where I will end the video. Anything else would be too long, and besides, I've gotten the content I need. "I'm so excited! We have so much to do to prepare. A baby!"

"Oh, darling, is that why you passed out the other day?" Graham asks. "You were pregnant and didn't know it yet?"

"Ah, yes," I lie, smiling at him weakly.

"How are you feeling?"

"Good." I don't tell him about the blood or the baby trying to punch its way out of my stomach, which has already swelled an alarming amount in one day.

I wait for Graham to suggest we go to a doctor or a hospital so I can get checked out. Fainting spells are common during pregnancy, because the blood vessels dilate and there's a rise in blood supply and heart rate, but Graham doesn't know that, nor does he seem bothered by it anymore. It's as if the fear from finding me unconscious on the floor has dissolved with the passage of time. It's in the past, so it no longer matters to him.

"We'll be a real family, finally," I tell him, squeezing his hand.

"That's right," Graham says, kissing my forehead.

"I can't wait to meet our baby," I say. "You'll take time off work, right? I'm going to do a home birth. All natural. Like God intended," I add, because he'll like that. "And you'll want to spend some time with the baby right after so it imprints on both of us."

"Oh," Graham says, eyes flicking away. "Yes, I want to be there for all of that. But work is so busy this time of year." Didn't he say that a month ago when we moved in and he stopped spending so much time with me? Didn't he say that a few weeks ago as an excuse for not having sex? "There's no parental leave. Not for men. That would be silly. You understand, right, babe?"

"I understand," I say immediately, the words tumbling free as my brain spins itself in circles. This isn't right. The baby was supposed to change things. Make it better between us. Maybe he needs some time. He'll change his mind. We have nine months, after all. He can't still be this busy in nine months, right?

I don't dwell on the fact that there are no grass stains on his shoes or that when I checked the weather at the golf course after Graham's text about a storm, there were only clear skies. I don't focus on the fact that, for the briefest instant, Graham's face fell when I told him the news.

"How far along are you, anyway?" Graham asks, eyes trailing down my face to my chest and torso.

I pause, unsure how to answer this. Our sex life dwindled before we moved, but the fact that I woke up this morning with a flat stomach and then had the belly of a woman who is two months pregnant in the span of a few hours complicates things.

The baby should not be moving around the way it was earlier. A few flutters *might* be possible, but not the disturbing strength I saw in the bathroom. I shove away the memory of my skin stretching, jumping, with force. Maybe I imagined it.

Best to be vague. "I think I'm fairly far along," I say. "I thought maybe I was stressed, you know, with the move and everything. Not having my time of the month in a while. But then I noticed I was gaining weight and now I'm starting to show, so we're getting there!"

"We should get you a midwife," Graham says, but there's a question in his voice like he's not actually sure, like he's never really thought about what comes next. "A doctor?"

Under no circumstances can I go to a doctor or a hospital. I certainly can't have someone like a doula or a midwife come here either. Anyone trained will see that there is something . . . different about this baby. I can't tell them it's a holy child, "helped" into this world by an angel, so I have to do this on my own. I have to lie, and hope Graham doesn't fight me on it.

I think of Renee's note, sitting on the counter, and I seize the opportunity. "You know what I was thinking?" I say, as if I've been mulling it over for a while. "Renee, our neighbor, the one who left her number? When I met her, she told me she's a midwife. She can help out. She'll be able to come over during the day too, so we won't bother you when you're off work."

This suggestion causes Graham's brows to flatten and his forehead to smooth. "That's a great idea. Wonderful. Let's do that." He leans forward, kisses me chastely on my lips, and then pulls away. "Can I go shower now? Then we can eat together, OK?"

"Sure. We'll have to tell our family. Your mom will be so happy. My father too."

"Definitely." He throws it over his shoulder, already in the kitchen, as if he can't wait to get his clothes off and stand under scalding-hot water.

When I hear Graham's footfalls on the stairs, I edge back across the living room, pulling my camera from the tripod, stopping the recording. Graham didn't even clock it. I watch the video, pausing at the moment I told him the news, trying to zoom in and examine his face. But his expression is so fast, so fleeting, that I doubt anyone else will notice his hesitation.

If I try hard enough, I can stop noticing things like that too.

11

PEOPLE ONLINE DON'T focus on Graham's less-than-ideal reaction to the pregnancy news when I trim the clip, edit it, and post it the next day. The opposite, in fact.

I lean against the kitchen counter on Sunday morning, finished with my dawn chores, letting Graham sleep in so I can read through all the comments on my video. Back at our old house, we'd be getting ready for church right now, but we haven't found a new congregation yet in all the hustle and bustle from the move. That's fine. It gives me time to salivate over my social media.

Look at how the first thing he does when she tells him is pray! That's a true man.

He's so overwhelmed with emotion! It's so sweet when they hug!

You two are so gorgeous, your baby is gonna be a real looker!

No one catches the split-second crumple on Graham's face, and that makes it easier for me to convince myself I didn't really see it. Besides, I'm distracted by the real coup: Mara Shoemaker herself likes my video. There's no comment, and she still doesn't follow me, but it's reached her orbit, which means the video has been picked up by the algorithm in our online community, boosted enough that her attention has been sparked.

My fingers sweat against the phone screen as I tap over to Mara's profile, greedily staring at her page: the obscene number of followers, the effortlessly curated aesthetic she adheres to. I follow Mara on all her accounts—Instagram, TikTok, even her Pinterest page. Mara is older than me, a millennial, and her biggest following is on the app she's the most attached to: Instagram.

There's a new photo on her grid: a line of homemade bagels cooling on a rack, looking dappled and mouthwatering in the light pouring in through Mara's kitchen window. The caption says *Delicious folic acid-free bagels! My own special recipe! Just learned about the dangers of folic acid in your body, so trying out these new versions of an old favorite. Stay safe out there! You and your children deserve healthy, pesticide-free bodies.*

Folic acid?

I've sent Mara messages before—reactions to her lives or stories, gushing messages about how inspiring she is—but she's never responded. I don't hold it against her; she's busy with all her children and her fulfilling life. But I need to try again.

Hi Mara! I saw you liked my pregnancy announcement, thank you! Love your latest post, but I've always heard folic acid is very important for pregnant women. What do you recommend for someone who needs to consume that for their growing baby?

I'm surprised when Mara answers me not even three minutes later.

Hi! Folic acid, along with any other preservatives or additives, are dangerous to you and your baby! I recommend going as natural as possible. Only use food you make yourself to make sure none of the government's invasive additions are in there. Esp. for your children! XO.

My fingers begin typing out a response before I can stop them, about how pregnant women should be taking 400 micrograms of folic acid daily to help prevent neural tube defects, but when I read back the words I've tapped, I flush and delete them one by one. Who am I to question Mara, with all her followers and enviable life? She's healthy, her children are glowing. She knows what she's talking about.

Thank you! I tap out instead. *I'll cut out folic acid starting now!*

I vehemently ignore the tiny voice in the back of my head that questions whether or not this is a good idea. That insists, in fact, it's a terrible idea, knowing what I know about the human body.

"This is what my community does," I whisper to myself. "It's part of our lifestyle. It will be fine. Mara is fine."

For the first time, I clearly hear the lie in my voice.

Inside me, my child clenches like a fist, sending spasms of pain across my back.

"Honey? You OK?" Graham walks into the kitchen in his sleep shorts, chest bare and covered in wiry dark hairs. His eyes are bleary and he shuffles toward me, pecking my cheek. "You look like you're in pain."

"I'm fine," I say, straightening up, offering a smile as I put down my phone, still thinking about folic acid. "How did you sleep?"

"Eh. Fine. I could really use some coffee," Graham mumbles, looking around the kitchen for the pot.

Shit, I think. I forgot. I forgot to make Graham's breakfast.

"Oh. Oh, Graham, I'm so sorry," I say, darting to the side, grabbing at the marbled container I keep the coffee beans in. "I thought you were going to sleep in longer. I don't have anything ready."

Graham huffs but shrugs as if it's no big deal. I grab the mortar and pestle I use every morning to hand-grind his beans as he leans against the counter, yawning. "It's fine, babe. I'm going to go back to bed for a bit, then, OK? You can bring it up to me when it's ready."

"I will. I'm so sorry, again. It must be brain fog." He looks confused, so I clarify. "From the pregnancy. This happens to some women."

"Well, hopefully not too often," he says, trying for a joke that trips and falls flat on its face. He pats my shoulder as I turn to the counter, crushing the beans with a twisting motion as my lower back continues to ache.

"Do you want food as well?"

"Coffee for now."

He drags his feet as he moves out of the kitchen, plodding back up the stairs as I rush to get his drink ready. My stomach presses against the counter, and I wonder if it has gotten larger since yesterday. It feels bigger, like I need more space to maneuver than I did before. I didn't really notice when I pulled on my royal-blue maxi dress earlier; I was too excited about posting the video and spending the day with Graham celebrating the news. But now the fabric across my belly feels uncomfortably tight.

I need to buy some maternity clothes ASAP. I should see what links Mara has in her bio. She'll know all the best stuff.

Ten minutes later, I join Graham in the bedroom, his coffee resting on a wooden serving tray along with an alabaster cloth napkin, a silver coffee spoon, and a sprig of lavender in a tiny glass vase. I make sure to snap a picture of the setup and post it to my story with the caption *Serving my king in bed today* before heading upstairs.

"Thanks," Graham says as he grabs the cup of coffee from the tray, not noticing all the other little touches I went to the trouble of creating. "I need this."

"Sorry, again," I say, chewing my lower lip, catching myself and forcing a smile instead. "There's a lot on my mind. And I was distracted. People are congratulating us."

"Huh?" Graham asks, looking up from his slurping. He's reclining in bed, his back propped up by the same pillow I screamed next to when I was with the creature.

Angel, I correct myself.

My cheeks warm at the memory, and I swallow. "Oh," I say, trying not to stutter as I push away images of leathery wings and humid scaled skin, the sensation of it inside me, moving effortlessly. "I posted about our pregnancy on social media. Everyone's being very supportive."

"You already posted about the baby?" Graham says, raising a brow. He hasn't noticed my blush, or maybe he thinks it's because I'm embarrassed getting caught posting our news online.

But Graham knows the deal. He knows I sometimes get free things for the house from my accounts, and he knows I have to keep up with my followers. Graham isn't on social media. He's fine with appearing on my page, but he doesn't know the nuances of how these things are done, how huge pregnancy announcements are in my community.

"We haven't even told our family and friends yet," he reminds me.

Not my friends. Your friends.

I banish the thought with a flick of annoyance as the treacherous, amorous memories finally start to fade away. Graham's friends are my friends too. It's normal I don't have any female friends my age when I barely went to college and don't work in an office or something horrible like that. Besides, look at all the well wishes I'm getting from my friends online!

"Sorry," I say sheepishly, offering him a conciliatory smile. "I was excited. Here, let's tell our family today. Right now!"

"Aren't you supposed to wait to tell people until a certain time has passed?" Graham asks. "That's what Brian's wife did."

I'm surprised he knows this; Graham hasn't been the most tuned in to the female body in the past.

"It's OK," I reassure him. I gesture to my stomach peeking through the blue maxi dress. "I'm starting to show. We're past that."

"Can I see it?"

For a second, I am conflicted. Right now, the baby is mine. Us two together, sharing one body. If I show Graham, what if the illusion breaks? What if he looks at me like I'm crazy, says there's no bump at all even though I can see it through the fabric of the dress? What if he confirms my greatest fear—that none of this is real and I'm losing my mind?

I shake the concerns away. Graham is my husband and this will be our child. He deserves to see. Maybe it'll make it more real for him too. Maybe he'll finally express the joy and eagerness I expected from him.

For once, I don't worry about modesty. I clamber next to Graham on the bed, sitting on my knees and pulling up the dress, exposing my round belly, looking at it with a heart pumping full of love for this being that hasn't even breathed air yet. This child will change everything. It might be an unusual pregnancy, but I don't care.

If only I could tell Graham the truth. He would probably appreciate it, being so religious. But that's not an option—I can't risk what might happen if he *didn't* appreciate it. Or believe it.

"You see?" I say, placing a hand on my belly and flicking my gaze up to my husband.

"I see," he repeats softly. "A baby."

"*Our* baby," I insist.

"You're going to be an amazing mother," Graham says, and there's a tenderness in his voice that surprises me.

"I am?"

He reaches over and gently takes the hem of my dress from my free hand, releasing it, letting fabric fall back over my stomach, covering the bump. "Absolutely. You are so caring and organized and tidy. You're going to be incredible."

My heart pounds with every word, the compliments filling me like sweet honey dissolving into hot tea. This is it. The moment I was looking for. Graham and me coming back together, finding that connection we had at the beginning when we were in sync and excited for our future and family. And most importantly, his reaction makes it all real. I'm not going crazy.

"And you'll be a great father," I say, inching closer to Graham, turning my face down to his. I rock forward, the bed soft and supportive underneath my knees.

There is a cobweb behind the smile Graham shows, a sticky net that mars the shape of his lips. "I hope so," he replies, giving me a dry kiss on the cheek, pulling away quickly.

The stale air sits between us for a minute as Graham's eyes travel down my body to the bump under my dress. The room feels expectant and breathless, and for a moment, I wonder if we will make love. If Graham will touch me the way the creature did.

But then Graham's phone chimes, and his expression dims, and the moment passes. He rolls off the pillow supporting him and reaches for his phone on the bedside table. I shift off the bed, already feeling the different weight of my body, the way I have to move more intentionally. Graham reads a message, his face somber, and then turns back to me. "Well. Now what?"

I want to regain the momentum we had. Keep the celebration going. I chirp, "I'm going to call my father. He'll be so excited for us."

Graham nods, again offers a smile that makes me think of spiders.

My father picks up on the fifth ring, and there are waves crashing behind him; he's on the beach, as usual. He was able to retire early due to his illustrious law career and the payout from my mother's life insurance. Retired life in Florida suits him. "You certainly took your time!" he jokes when I tell him. "You've been married for five years!"

"Three," I correct him, smiling at Graham, who's watching me now, his face blank, as if his mind is elsewhere. "Together for four."

"Yes, yes," my father says, and I can picture him waving his hand as if it's inconsequential. "Well, congratulations! I can't wait to meet the little bugger. I hope it's a boy. I can teach him some football moves. Get yourself a star athlete, yeah?"

I insist on Graham calling his parents next. They live out west, which is probably for the best, because I've always gotten the sense that his mother doesn't like me much. She's never outwardly rude or belittling, but on family holidays or at our wedding, I would catch her staring sometimes, eyes narrowed, lips pursed, as if she were examining cuts of meat and found mine lacking.

But when Graham calls her, his mother's tinny voice bursts through the speakerphone, and if she's feigning her enthusiasm, she's doing a good job. "Oh, my first grandchild!" she shrieks. "Goodness, I wish we lived closer. Maybe you two can consider coming west? Not now, obviously, you just moved, but down the line. You'll need help. Babies can be a handful. Oh, this is such wonderful news. My first grandbaby," she repeats before calling out for Graham's father, her voice muffled. "Richard, get in here! Graham has news!"

Graham warms to his parents' excitement, and he tells his mother they should come visit once the baby is born.

"Camille must get checked out immediately," Graham's mother says. "Make sure the child is doing all right."

"Don't worry," Graham says, and for the first time since learning about the pregnancy, he sounds confident and calm. "We have a midwife."

Oh. Right.

The lie I made up about Renee. I have no intention of calling her in front of my husband, but after hanging up with his parents, Graham bugs me about it until I finally do. I tell her over the phone that I'm pregnant, and would she like to come over to chat tomorrow? To Graham, hearing only my side of the conversation, it sounds like I could be talking to a midwife instead of a stay-at-home mom. Renee's scream of delight pierces my ears and is audible even to Graham.

Renee and I make lunch plans, and I drop the phone on the bedspread, sighing loudly in contentment. For the first time since yesterday, the baby moves. It's a jerky twist that sends a roll of cramps throughout my lower half, and I hide a wince, sitting back down on the edge of the mattress, a few feet away from Graham.

"You know," Graham says thoughtfully after all our calls are finished. "It's Sunday. We should start going to mass again. With the baby coming, I think it's important we find a new church."

"All right," I agree. "There must be something nearby."

"I'll look around," Graham offers, and I'm pleased he's taking such an active role. "Find a good place we can start attending. We'll need a community too. My friends and family are great, but they're too far away to really count on if we need them."

I don't point out that Graham doesn't seem to have a problem with how far away everyone is now, being that he spends 90 percent of his time working or back in our old neighborhood with them. "That sounds great," I say instead. "God finally answered our prayers, after all."

Graham has no idea how true that statement is.

"Mm-hmm," he replies, scrolling through his phone. "I'll go out for a drive in a bit, see what I can find."

My heart sinks. "Oh, today? I thought maybe we could spend some time together. Plan. Talk about baby names?"

"Darling, you're better at all that stuff than I am," Graham says, finally peeling himself off the bed, as if the idea of going church hunting has energized him. "I completely trust you to make the right decision." He pats my knee, scruff above his top lip twitching as he smiles. "I'm going to shower."

Graham takes his phone into the bathroom with him, and after the lock clicks and the shower turns on, I creep over and press my ear against the crack in the doorframe. Over the ambient rush of water, I can hear the murmur of Graham's voice, too low to make out any words. After a few minutes, his voice stops, and several seconds later, the splash of water against tiles becomes louder as he gets into the shower.

I lean against the door of the bathroom, both hands on my queasy stomach, forehead damp with sweat, waiting for the baby to move.

It stays completely still.

II

Second Trimester

CHAPTER

12

G RAHAM HAS FOUND us a church.

Or so he said last night when he finally came home after spending hours driving around the countryside, apparently searching for something suitable. When I asked why he couldn't look online, he insisted he needed to see the place in person to make sure it would be the "right fit" for us.

The next morning, I rise with the dawn as usual, yawning and rubbing my eyes, drained from a night of restless fidgeting. I kept trying to find a position that was comfortable for both me and the baby, but every time I thought I had settled in, the child inside me would punch and I would have to start again. At least the dreams with the winged eye have stopped.

It's not normal to have an active baby in my belly so early in the pregnancy. This must be some side effect of my . . . communion with the creature.

Angel.

Perhaps a blessed pregnancy moves faster than a regular one. Or maybe this really is Graham's baby! Maybe the negative pregnancy test was a dud and I've been pregnant this whole time.

Don't lie to yourself like you lied to him. You've had your period regularly. This isn't Graham's child.

I do not appreciate the frequent appearance of this voice in my head as of late. I squeeze, throttling it until the thought cuts off. I drag myself out of bed and down the stairs, hands curling around my little bump, feeling the heat radiating from my belly. My ankles are strangely sore, my mouth is tender, and there's a painful itch in my lower back, as if there are bristles of hay tangled around my sacrum.

"This is our baby," I whisper as I step into the kitchen, which is dark in the predawn glow. "Everything will be perfect once the baby gets here."

As the sun rises, I fix Graham porridge and coffee, start the laundry, and unload the dishwasher. I set out the glazed folic acid–free cranberry scones I made from scratch yesterday when Graham left me alone to look for churches. By the time my husband makes his way downstairs and seats himself at the breakfast bar, exhaustion is already creeping into my bones.

How is this fetus so heavy already?

"I'll be home on time tonight," Graham says after eating his breakfast, glancing down at the bump visible beneath my brown dress. "Do you need anything?"

I beam at him, forgetting my weariness. He's so sweet to ask. "I'll check my list and text you if I do. Thank you, babe."

"I'd love some steak for dinner," he says. "We have any?"

I nod. "From the farm. I can cook it up tonight."

When he leaves, the house feels colder and larger, his presence so rare and precious that even our home withdraws when he's gone.

The morning inches forward slowly, and fatigue is a constant companion, leaning its head against my shoulder as I flip the laundry, tidy up the entryway, dust Graham's office, and scroll through my social media comments. I posted a photo of my scones, tagging Mara, effusively thanking her for her advice on living a folic acid–free life and for her recipes, and it's doing well. Mara herself has liked my post again, and this time she leaves a comment! Two red-heart emojis. It sends a thrill of validation through my bones. Mara's acknowledgment opens the floodgates; other women are replying in the comments, eager to bake their own batch, drooling over the perfect staging and scrumptious cranberries peeking out from the baked goods.

Truthfully, the scones had a bit of a strange taste, flat and musty. But the internet doesn't need to know that.

Eventually, I end up back in the kitchen.

I stand at the sink, washing the dishes, my bump rubbing against the counter as warm suds drip down my forearms. The long sleeves of my umber-colored dress are rolled up past my elbows, the fabric starting to dig uncomfortably into my upper arms as I rhythmically sponge the bowls from breakfast.

Looking up, I gaze through the window in front of the sink, watching the swaying waves of wheat in the muted sunlight. Thick clouds cover the sky today, and the temperature has been dropping. Summer is slowly staggering to an end. I wonder what our first winter will be like in this new house. Will we get a lot of snow? Will Graham be on top of any shoveling?

A ping of gratitude for the baby shoots through me. I'll have something to distract me through the dreary cold season.

The baby moves, a twisting sensation with notes of pain, as if the child's limbs are attached to my nerves, and a bowl slips from my soapy hands and clatters at the bottom of the sink. I rip my eyes away from the window, hurriedly retrieving the dish, exhaling when I see it's not broken. I rinse it off, shaking droplets of water free as I place the bowl carefully in the bamboo drying rack.

When I look back up at the window, the creature is standing there, staring inside the house.

A shriek dies in the back of my throat, mouth too dry to allow it to escape. The water runs, splashing merrily down the drain as droplets roll over my wrists and fingers.

The creature's wide, white eyes look even more unsettling in broad daylight—its sclerae are the color of rancid yogurt, and though there are no pupils, I can sense it looking directly at me, separated only by a pane of glass and a few feet of drywall and insulation. Its grayish-green skin, so rough and scaled, makes it look like a dead thing walking. I can't see its hands, tipped in black claws, but I imagine them on my bare body, palms surprisingly smooth, humid body heat covering me like a swampy breeze.

My cheeks flush and my neck grows hot. I haven't seen the creature since Thursday night. Or rather, early Friday morning. I assumed our "contract" was over. The hallucinations have stopped. I haven't seen the eye in my dreams. My child grows in my stomach, yet here is our family's savior, watching us through the window with an empty expression.

"Go away," I whisper, knowing it can't possibly hear me through the glass and the rush of water in the sink. "Please go away. Thank you for the help, but it's over now. The job is done."

The creature doesn't move, only stares. Its eyes rove in its sockets, as if it's scanning my face and throat, reading my lips through the glass.

The baby moves again, a deeper, more violent jerk this time, and I gag with pain, stepping back from the sink to clutch my belly with wet hands as if I can enfold it in tenderness and stop the discomfort.

An earsplitting screech cuts through the cramping in my stomach, and I glance back up. The creature is running one long, dark claw down the outside of the window, tracing a vertical straight line on the glass. The sharpened tip of its nail leaves a trail, a razor-thin mark that drags for several inches before the creature stops, lifting the finger and pressing its palm against the glass, covering the line it made.

For the first time, I get a good look at the underside of the hand that pressed into my hips, slid upon my body. The creature's palm is startlingly human if you ignore the dark nails protruding several inches from the tips of its fingers. The skin on the palm of its hand isn't gray or tinted green. There are no scales there either. Seeing the lightly tanned skin, the same kind of crisscrossing lines that decorate my own palms, eases the tension in my chest.

I move back toward the window, leaning forward, careful not to squish my stomach against the counter, and reach out, placing my own hand against the cold glass. Our fingers mirror each other—the creature's slightly larger than mine. The glass fogs up, as if the damp warmth of the creature's body is migrating through the windowpane.

The baby stills, and the pain abates. The three of us—me, the creature, the baby—hold our breath, motionless, waiting. I tear my eyes from our hands, pressed against opposite sides of the window, and watch the creature's face once again. It does not blink, like a snake, but it has eyelids. It closed its eyes when we were together.

Our gazes meet: mine brown, the creature's white. I open my mouth, not sure what's going to come out but being pulled along by a tether in my chest, a fishhook that I wasn't aware existed until now.

The jarring buzzer of the doorbell interrupts.

I jump, pulling away, glancing over my shoulder toward the hallway. When I turn back, the window is empty and the creature is gone. The line it left with its claw is still visible on the glass.

13

I HEAD TO THE front door, pushing away the encounter with the creature.

It meant nothing.

Renee stands on the doorstep, eager and grinning. I forgot. I invited her over yesterday for lunch. It completely slipped my mind. I'm not prepared for her, especially not after what just happened.

Renee is wearing a pair of worn jeans and a pink shirt with the words *Fun Mom* stitched on the front next to a graphic of a martini glass, sloshing out clear liquid and olives. Renee's dark hair is bundled up on the top of her head and her lips and eyes are bare, free from makeup.

"I'm so excited for you!" Renee shrieks as she shoots into the house like a human cannonball. "Oh my God, look at you! You're showing already! You knew the other day, didn't you? You little sneak! No, don't worry, I get it. Sometimes you want to wait until you're certain. But my goodness, you hid it well! I had no idea. How far along are you?"

This was a mistake.

Renee doesn't stop talking as I lead her through the hallway and kitchen, pulling out a stool for her at the breakfast counter. "Can I get you a cup of tea? Coffee?" I offer instead of answering any of her rapid-fire questions.

She blinks. "Oh. Yes, tea, please! Or actually, we should celebrate! Got any champagne?" She exaggerates a wink, her wide mouth grinning. Her tongue is stained red.

I stare at her from across the counter, trying to smile through a clenched jaw. "Um, I'm pregnant, remember? And it's not even noon."

Renee laughs. "I'm kidding, I'm kidding. Tea is fine! Do you have anything caffeine-free? I try to avoid it after eleven AM if I can. What am I saying, of course you have caffeine-free options; that's all you can drink now!"

Why is her energy so chaotic? "I have chamomile . . ."

"Perfect!" Her voice is so loud and raw, it's like releasing an unbroken horse into my home, letting it charge around, getting far too close to my preciously curated decor.

I try to change the topic as I put the kettle on. "How are your kids? They were feeling sick, right?"

"You're so kind for asking!" Renee clucks. "Yes, but they're on the mend. We're all feeling much better now. Millie's new thing is finding bugs in the backyard and bringing them into the house. She leaves them in the bathtub, and we're trying to potty train Henry now and he gets upset if he goes to the bathroom and sees worms. I can't say that I blame him!"

I tune out Renee's chatter as the water boils, opening a cabinet and pulling out the mason jar of loose-leaf chamomile I bought at a local market last year and two mugs.

"My goodness, why am I talking about myself?" Renee stops her stream of consciousness and grins at me again. "What about you? Tell me everything!"

I will do nothing of the sort. I steep the tea, eyeing the water level in both mugs to make sure nothing spills on my pristine counter. "Do you take honey? Milk?"

"Nope! Good the way it is!"

I place a mug in front of Renee, keeping the breakfast bar between us. I'm not interested in sitting with her, no matter how sore my feet and back are. The living room and sliding glass door are behind her, and for a moment I wonder what would happen if the creature slunk into the house while she was here.

Sitting on her stool, Renee wraps both hands around the mug, sighing at the warmth. "Mornings are starting to get chilly. I thought we had longer. Summer is really slipping away fast, huh? So. Tell me!"

I daydream about sitting down. My neck aches and my stomach feels denser today than it did yesterday, but I don't want to move around the counter and be closer to the abrasiveness of Renee's voice. I grab my own mug of tea and lean against the counter instead, letting the steam waft against my chin.

"Well, we're having a baby," I say cautiously. "I'm very happy."

"Me too!" Renee explodes. "When are you due?"

This is the tricky part. I can't admit that I don't have a doctor, and I can't very well say I don't know when my child is going to be born. If my suspicions are accurate, then four days ago I conceived. Today I look almost three months pregnant. If growth continues at this rate, it's very possible that the baby comes before the full nine months. There are no guidelines for a pregnancy like this.

"I'm due this winter," I decide to say, keeping it vague, hoping it's a correct estimate.

"How exciting! You must be far along, then! Do you know the gender yet?"

"Um, no. I want it to be a surprise." It's true, but not for the reasons Renee thinks.

"Well, you must be pretty pregnant, but I couldn't tell at all last week! You're lucky. I was so obviously preggers the whole time for both my babies. I miss those days, though." She sighs, almost wistful, and pauses for a moment, as if her batteries have run out. Renee snorts and shakes herself, plugging back in. "I mean, every woman is different, but it's almost like you started showing overnight," she jokes, and I hide a flinch.

She's prying, and I don't like it. I barely know what's going on with my body, and now I have to try to explain it to this woman who is essentially a stranger. This lie to Graham has backfired badly.

"I can't believe how beautiful you look." Renee sighs. "This dress on you is stunning. I can't wait to see all your maternity clothes. I bet you'll be the best-dressed pregnant woman in the whole state."

Then again, maybe Renee isn't so bad. I relent, trying to relax. She's happy for me, showing the level of emotion I secretly wanted from Graham. I should allow myself to revel in it.

"I'm getting everything prepared now," I tell Renee, taking a sip of the tea. It's too hot, and the taste is off. "But if you have any tips for a first-time mom . . ."

Renee's face lights up, and she leans forward on her stool. "Do I! Well, first of all, don't buy anything. I have so many baby books, baby clothes, toys, you name it. You can have anything you want—Zach and I are done, ha! And it's not like they're being used now."

I look down at Renee's pink martini shirt and sincerely doubt that anything this woman has fits the style I'm imagining for my baby, but I nod and smile at her blithely. I let her describe the parenting books she has, her advice to hold the baby as much as possible. I let her warn me to not cosleep with the child and assure me that bottle is just as good as breastfeeding.

I don't tell her that I'll have no choice but to breastfeed my baby—my community expects it. Demands it, really. But now that I'm thinking about it, I'm realizing something potentially alarming: My breasts feel normal.

The rest of my body appears to be adapting to the pregnancy, growing or changing, but my chest is the same size it has always been. There are no aches or tenderness. No changes in appearance to the nipples. Six to eight weeks into pregnancy, your breasts are supposed to grow. My stomach looks to be beyond the six- to eight-week mark, yet I'm still an A cup.

Is there something wrong with my milk?

Shreds of anxiety flutter in my lungs as Renee continues to talk, oblivious to my predicament.

This is why you should be going to a doctor, the voice in the back of my head points out.

But I can't. It's not worth the risk.

"Do you have family nearby? Someone to help you as the time gets closer?" Renee asks, cutting through my silent panic.

"Oh, um, yes," I lie. "Graham's parents might come to stay for a bit after the baby is born. And I have a midwife." I don't add that Renee herself is the stand-in for the fictional midwife I've created.

"I have a friend who used to be a midwife," Renee says. "Not for me! I need all the drugs and modern medicine I can get! Oh, I can't wait to meet Graham." She's somehow finished half her tea even though it was piping hot. Apparently the taste isn't bothering her like it's bothering me. "His response was so sweet."

I pause, lips on the mug, slowly lowering it back down. "What?"

"Oh, I didn't tell you!" Renee says, excited. "I saw your pregnancy announcement video online! It popped up in my feed. I found it last night after you called."

"Uh, wow," I say. The geotag must have pushed my video to people in the area. Like Renee.

"I followed you," she continues. "Your photos are beautiful."

"Thank you," I say absently. There have been so many new followers since I posted the video that I must have missed Renee.

I can't decide how I feel about her having access to my content. All my other online friends are strictly virtual—I've never met any of them in real life. They aren't around to catch any exaggerations or white lies when I post. But Renee lives down the road. She's been inside my house. If I have a pimple one day and I edit it out in a photo, will Renee call me out? I'm unfamiliar with the dynamic of this kind of female friendship, and I'm not sure I want it.

"And I didn't know you used to be a scientist! How cool!"

Renee's words screech into my brain, freezing my blood. The already-moldy taste of the tea grows bitter in my mouth. I gape at her. "W-what did you say?"

"Oh, nothing," Renee replies, startled by my reaction. "Just that I didn't know you had a science background. I saw a comment on your latest post before I came over here. Are you—"

I stop listening, throwing myself at my phone, unlocking it feverishly and scanning my notifications, finding the thread of comments on my anti–folic acid post I missed while I was having a stare-down with the creature.

"No," I moan softly. "No, no, no."

The comment is near the top, bolstered by an upsetting number of likes: *I find this very surprising, Camille. You know as well as I do that folic acid is important for pregnant people. Your focus in CAST was literally on biology and the human body. What the hell happened to you?*

I tap on the username. It's a private account, and the profile picture is too small to identify, but I vaguely recognize their name: Melody Lateef. She's not following me.

Pulse throbbing in my neck, I swipe back to my post. Nested underneath Melody's comment are several more from members of my community:

Folic acid is bad for babies!

What is CAST?

You don't know what u r talking about.

To my horror, Melody has replied to the last one: *I absolutely do. I knew Camille years ago. We both attended a prestigious science program. Camille dropped out for some reason. I never heard from her again, and then I came across this travesty on my Explore page. She could have been one of the top biologists in the country. Now she's lying about folic acid on the internet. Sad.*

"Camille?" Renee's voice comes from far away. "Camille, are you OK?"

My fingers are shaking so hard it's difficult to delete the thread of comments, but I finally manage it. I tap back over to Melody's page and block her.

"Camille! The baby! You need to sit."

I look up at Renee. The room is swaying. Maybe she's right. I tiptoe around the counter and slide into a stool next to Renee, who leans in, expression alarmed. Her hand closes around my bicep firmly, as if to keep me upright.

"What's going on?" she asks.

"I'm not a scientist," I insist, becoming aware of the frothing liquid inside my chest, the bloom of embarrassment spreading over my cheeks. How many people saw Melody's comments? Oh God, did *Mara* see?

"It's all right," Renee says soothingly. "I thought that comment was a bit rude. But not a big deal. Just breathe. What were they talking about anyway? CAST?"

I answer automatically. "Coleman Aptitude in Science Track. It's a specialized nationwide program for freshmen and sophomores in college."

I can't force the full truth out of my mouth. How I had to pick a topic and create a thesis, do research and experiments, write an abstract and defend my work. How the program proved to me that I wasn't meant to be a scientist.

The memories bubble up, pressing against the top of my skull. My joy at getting into the program, my father's dismay, his insistence that I didn't need more schooling, that it was more important for me to stay home and help him with the house and chores. But I loved biology and the human body, and thanks to my grades and all the science fairs I won in high school, I got an academic scholarship to a local university so my father couldn't come up with an excuse to stop me from going. I attended CAST the summer between my freshman and sophomore years. I never made it to my second year of college.

"I haven't heard of that program," Renee admits. "What did you study?"

"Prion diseases," I murmur. Catching her confusion, I clarify. "Fatal neurodegenerative disorders caused by misfolding of the prion protein in the brain. My focus was on kuru. A disorder that used to be common among the Fore people of Papua New Guinea."

Renee blinks. "What's kuru?"

"It spread from the funerary custom of eating the brains of deceased family members to help free the spirits of the dead. But the brain is where infectious prions are most concentrated," I explain, unearthing research I haven't thought about in years from the recesses of my mind. "My work was about using what we know about disorders like kuru to reduce prion proteins in the brain and potentially find a cure, or at least halt the progression of, neurodegenerative illnesses like Alzheimer's and Parkinson's."

Renee, for once, falls silent, her face slack with shock. I bite the inside of my cheek, wishing I never posted a photo of those stupid scones.

I don't tell her the rest. How I loved the program, up until the peer review section, where I had to defend my thesis in front of other students in CAST. They poked holes in my work. They called it "lofty" and "overly ambitious." They waited for me to respond, to argue against their concerns, but my throat grew too sore to speak. I opened my mouth and imagined frothy vomit spilling out instead of words. Shivering, I fled the room.

Outside, kneeling on the concrete curb, I called my father, crying.

"I told you," he said. "This isn't your path, Camille."

"Then what is?" I sobbed.

"The path your mother couldn't finish," he said sadly. "That's your destiny. Not this science stuff."

He was right. It's easy to gather compliments and helpings of love when you devote your life to taking care of others. Science wasn't kind—it criticized me and disappointed my father—but when I dropped out of CAST and college, I was rewarded: I met Graham a year later. I never told him about my science background. He loved me without it.

My father was right. *This* is my path.

"It's OK," Renee says, breaking me from the past. "No judgments. It seems like you're very happy now without the science stuff." She slightly stresses the word *seems*. Renee's eyes are tracking around the house, noting the spotless kitchen, the freshly cleaned floors. "I could tell from your page that you're more . . . traditional anyway."

Her presumption grates against my skin. Renee doesn't know me. I *like* taking care of things. I'm *good* at being a homemaker. And what does she do all day that's really so different from what I do? She's a stay-at-home mom, after all.

The hot liquid in my chest spills over, transforming into heaving anger. How dare Melody leave that comment after all these years? How dare Renee judge me for living a more traditional life? I left behind a career that didn't work for me, just like Mara did. Just like my mother did. And in return, I got love. My father was so proud when I quit school and came home, picking up the pieces of my shattered dream. He helped me get the job at the growing center, saying I should use my biology skills to make beautiful things flower. I never told him that botany and biology were different fields.

I was worried at first that my father would be disappointed when I started dating Graham, feel like I was replacing him, but after meeting him, my father was thrilled.

"Your path," he reminded me after his first dinner with my future husband. "This is your path."

No one tears apart my work now. On the contrary, my friends online praise it; Graham appreciates it. I loved science, yes, but it was a love that hurt. This is where I'm meant to be.

Tension drains from my shoulders. I steady my inhales, patting my perfumed hair.

Everything is fine, I remind myself.

I deleted the comment, I blocked Melody. I'll restrict comments on the post to avoid any more incidents. There's no way Mara saw it. She's too busy, and she gets thousands of notifications every day. Nothing to worry about.

"I know I invited you over for lunch," I say to Renee. "But I'm not feeling so well. Rain-check?"

There's a hint of sadness in Renee's smile. "Of course. You looked like you were going to faint a few minutes ago. You rest. And"—she pauses, licking her lips with a stained-red tongue—"I'm sorry. If you felt . . . Well, I think you're doing an amazing job. OK?"

I soften to her again. She's nosy, but I think she means well, unlike Melody. "Maybe after I give birth, we can go for runs," I offer. "Help me lose the baby weight."

Renee glances down at my body appraisingly. "Hon, you're already so thin. Don't get wrapped up in that weird pregnancy 'bounce back' narrative everyone loves so much. Your body is making and feeding a human!"

That's easy for her to say. She's not trying to become a huge influencer like Mara Shoemaker. I'm young and attractive. It's expected that I have my baby and then return to my ideal form. That's what Mara does, and she's got *eight* children.

"Sure," I say, trying to smile. "I'll walk you out. Maybe we can try this again sometime soon?" My stomach is doing flips. The baby isn't moving, but there are pangs coming from my womb as if a gong is ringing against my innards.

"Absolutely," Renee says as she helps me from my stool. When we reach the frosted-glass door, her eyes flicker over the tidy hallway, the pristine entryway. "Like I said, I have tons of baby stuff. You need to vent or need a second opinion on something, you ask me. And enjoy this while you can. Your house will never be clean again after the baby arrives!"

I smile sourly and bid her farewell as she walks over to her car. She's parked off the road, on our lawn. She couldn't have pulled up on the driveway? Her tires are flattening the grass.

I watch her drive away, a tug of longing in my chest. She can move around so easily with her car, not tied to the house like I am. Graham and I talked about a second car. The move to the country made me think it might be necessary, but Graham failed to understand that there might be reasons I'd want to leave the house besides getting cooking and cleaning supplies. I can't blame him, though. It's not like I have any friends or family nearby to visit.

The second-car conversation might need to happen again once the baby arrives, though. We haven't yet discussed schooling or extracurricular activities, but I'll want to give our child the adventures I didn't experience when I was a kid—everything I missed out on after my mother died.

The path your mother couldn't finish.

I've been at the door staring at the paved road for a while, Renee's car long gone. Clouds stretch overhead, rolling like the underside of waves. The air hangs static and smells of faint pine and overgrown grass. The countryside surrounds me, smears of golden brown and green. Sometimes in this house, when I'm alone, I feel like the only person left on the planet.

When I finally turn away from the door, my stomach groans. I am starving; the nausea and adrenaline brought on by Melody's comments have worn off. I usually eat small portions—Graham likes me to have a lithe figure and trim waist—but I've never been this hungry before, even with portion control.

The craving comes upon violently, urgently. I rush down the hallway and into the kitchen, looking around frantically. I can't tell what it is I want, but the compulsion to eat *something* digs its fingers into my stomach and won't leave. I remember the strange taste of the tea. Maybe I need something heartier.

I open the bread box on the counter, tearing off a hunk of fresh sourdough and stuffing it into my mouth, gnashing my molars against the tangy bread. It's like using an eyedropper to fill an ocean. Nothing happens. Before I know it, I've eaten the entire loaf of bread, which tastes strangely acidic, and the ache of hunger still throbs inside my stomach. The baby is shifting around now, as if trying to avoid the food I'm sending down to it.

Panting, I reach into the fridge and pull out the glass container I keep our butter in. Dissolving a single pat on my tongue every so often is not enough anymore. I am hungry, so hungry, and nothing I eat seems to satisfy the pit in my belly, so maybe the fat and salt of my favorite food will satiate me. I grab the stick of butter, lovingly formed by my hands a few weeks ago, and bite into the end, chewing the creamy, slippery pieces that try to shoot from my mouth, making a break for it. Butter smears across my lips, sticks to my gums and throat as I gag, trying to swallow.

My mouth is working harder than it needs to—my teeth come down with astonishing gravity, and my tongue is in the way. I wince as a blister of pain followed by blood fills my mouth. Unthinking, I spit, letting blood splash the stick of butter I'm holding. I gaze down, tongue throbbing, looking at the red stains on the butter, watching beads of blood soak into the slippery surface.

The baby lurches up, a shark trying to breach the surface of the ocean. I pretend it's all due to the child I'm carrying when I lift the remaining bloodstained butter to my face and gnaw on it.

The flavor is unlike anything I've tasted before—metallic and sweet, silky and tangy. I drop to my knees and inhale the rest of the stick, smudging blood and butter all over my face, hands, and dress.

When I'm done, I drop the glass container on the floor, the bottom cracking. I pant, the baby kicking joyfully inside my stomach.

We have raw meat in the fridge, waiting in its plastic wrap. The steak Graham requested. I was going to cook it for his dinner tonight. But I'm still hungry, and the baby is growing and twisting within me.

"OK, sweetheart," I say, patting my bump, lurching to my feet. "Let's feed you."

I open the fridge again, stomach growling at the sight of the bloody meat.

CHAPTER

14

THE FOLLOWING SUNDAY, Graham insists on going to the church he found.

I try not to be surprised that the church exists—Graham was gone for so long last week that I wasn't sure he was actually doing what he said he was doing.

We rise from bed together, and I cook Graham bacon and eggs. When he's not looking, I shovel several pieces of raw bacon in my mouth, choking down their slippery bodies, patting my belly when the baby hops in pleasure. I leave the eggs alone— the baby doesn't like them. It doesn't like anything except meat. Raw, if possible.

The past week consisted of me fielding texts from Renee asking if I would like this item or that item from her attic, experimenting with the types of food I can keep down, and tracking the growth of my belly, which is expanding much faster than it should.

Going to church will be a welcome reprieve—I'm starting to feel stir-crazy. The house is perfect; I always complete all my daily chores, but I'm much slower than usual, and my energy has dipped. I struggle to wake in the morning, and my body aches. The texture of my hair is strange, straw-like, and there's an unfamiliar brittle quality to my skin. But it's early in the pregnancy—maybe I'll even out. Be more like Mara and the other influencers online who glow with youth and health when they're with child.

"Ready?" Graham asks after breakfast, holding out an arm to me.

He's been better this week—no late nights, no vanishing from our bed in the early hours of the morning. He's on his phone a lot, but I don't mind as long as he's home. He's making an active effort to be involved, which I appreciate.

The other night, I modeled a few maternity dresses for him. He smiled and clapped and told me I looked beautiful even though when I looked in the mirror after, my skin was pale and there was a hollowness to my cheeks that hadn't been there before.

But it doesn't matter. Graham is coming back to me, as I hoped.

"I'm ready," I reply, taking Graham's arm, his warm muscles flexing under his shirt. He looks especially handsome in his blue button-down, scruffy beard finally trimmed, eyes relaxed.

I check my reflection in the hall mirror as he guides me through his office to the garage door. For the occasion, I've chosen a rust-colored midi dress, belted and long sleeved, showing off my bump but in a subtle way. My hair is in a tasteful bun, and I'm wearing dark-brown suede ankle boots and a camel-colored cardigan in case the church is as chilly as the morning air is right now. Summer is definitely on its way out the door.

I thrum in excitement as we settle in the car. It feels like forever since I've been anywhere besides the new house. Graham tells me to get comfortable, that it's a thirty-minute drive.

I'm not in the car often, but I think it might smell different. A little sweet. I look around for an air freshener but can't see anything. The scent is faint but lingering, as if it can't quite release its hold on the leather interior of Graham's Audi.

Holy Peony.

The fields whip past in a blur of gold as the sun crests over the trees of the encroaching forest. Graham takes the winding roads at a higher pace than I would like, considering the baby and my rotating nausea and hunger, but he is playing folk music at a volume that indicates he's not interested in talking.

When we pull up to the church, the lot is full of cars, and I clear my throat to mask a squeak of anxiety. I haven't been around this many people since we moved.

I heave myself out of the car, wishing Graham would come around and open the door for me like a gentleman, but he's already out and walking toward the church.

The building is small and white, with a little steeple and a letter board out front that says *Jesus is watching!*

The church is on the side of the road, between two farms, but there's a few acres of grass and a small garden. Several oak trees provide shade beyond the parking lot. People are trickling indoors, but I catch up to my husband and pull him to the side before we enter, nodding at my phone.

"Picture," I say, and Graham sighs, used to this.

I turn the camera, beckoning Graham closer to me, and extend my arm so I can take a selfie of the two of us. I carefully frame the church steeple in the background, checking the lighting on my face. I look more haggard than usual. I'll have to retouch this one. Graham's itchy bearded cheek, rubbing against mine, makes my smile strained.

"Look happier," I whisper through my clenched teeth. "We're at church! We're having a baby!"

Graham obediently widens his mouth, staring into the camera, not realizing I was talking to myself.

I take twenty shots rapidly, all at once, tilting my head in micro-movements for each one so I have angle options. Satisfied, I grab for Graham's hand, and we walk to the front doors of the church.

Inside are about twenty pews, varnished wood with floral cutouts. There's a yellow carpet that reminds me of mold, and several small stained-glass windows create a well of pity in my chest—they must not be able to afford anything grander. The altar at the front of the church is as small as the rest of the space, crammed into an arched nook next to a diminutive pulpit. A priest moves around the tabernacle, his back to me, his white robe shifting around his ankles. I expect the church to smell like old books and melted candles, but instead there's a mildewy scent, rank and oppressive. It settles on my skin and leaves a layer of grime on my hands and face.

The amount of people in the small church makes it feel claustrophobic.

A ring of sweat gathers around my collar, and when I swallow, my esophagus weakly protests, pain following my saliva as if I have a sore throat. Inside my womb, the baby shifts.

Something is wrong.

My vision tunnels and dark-gray clouds edge around my peripheral—an approaching storm I can't blink away. Clutching Graham's hand tightly does no good; my clammy fingers slip through his grasp and I stumble, tripping over the ugly carpet and reaching out for the nearest pew. I catch myself on the wood, which is smooth and dry under my wet hands.

"Are you OK?" Graham's voice comes from behind me, an urgent whisper.

I can't find the words to answer him.

When I look up, vision narrow and shaky, every single person in the church has turned around in their seats to look at me.

None of them have faces.

It's as if someone has smeared their features with paint, creating a kaleidoscopic swirl of pinks and browns until there is nothing left but brushstrokes and echoes of expressions. The priest turns around too; his face is broad and empty, his arms dangle by his side.

The church is silent. Its inhabitants watch me with no eyes. The blank spaces on their faces where their cheeks might be are raised, as if the mouths I cannot see are smiling.

The people in the pew I cling to slowly begin to slide down the bench, inching closer to me. Groaning, I release the pew and back away quickly, bumping into Graham.

"Oh God, tell me you see it too," I beg, turning around to fall into my husband's arms.

"Camille, *what* is going on?" he says, catching me and lifting me up, setting me back on my feet.

The baby is kicking like mad now; the imprint of its feet patter against my stomach, a drumming, frantic pattern that beats with a speed that matches my pulse.

"Graham, don't you see—"

I cut myself off as I catch sight of my husband's face. His eyes are pitch-black, his pupils expanded to encompass his irises and sclerae: the photo negative of the creature's. Like the churchgoers, Graham is smiling, but it's a wide, forced grin. A sludgy dark slime oozes out from Graham's lips, slowly spilling down his chin. His nose begins to drip too—a slug of black goop crawls down his philtrum and pools over his top lip like runny mucus.

"Fuck, oh, fuck," I whisper, my breath hitching up into my throat as I squeeze my eyes shut, hoping when I open them everything will be normal again.

"Camille, what's wrong? Everyone is staring at you," Graham hisses.

I open my eyes. Black is streaming out of Graham's pupils now, inky tears that leave stained tracks on his cheeks and bare trails in his beard, as if they're searing off the hair.

The baby goes berserk inside me. Thrashing, twisting, punching. I have never experienced this level of movement before—I don't think it's even biologically possible. Yet it's happening, and I can barely stay on my feet. Pain envelops me, blinding me even further as my forehead burns and my hands go numb.

"I need some air," I manage to stammer. "I don't feel good. I'll be back."

Pew benches scrape as I tear myself away from my husband and stagger to the front doors only a few yards away. My vision breaks down further, becoming a mere pinprick of light that I desperately follow as the rustle of clothes and light footfalls dog my steps.

I fling myself toward the door, expecting to feel fingertips on my neck, pulling at my hair, scratching my back, at any second.

I burst through the doors of the church, air wheezing into my lungs as I careen away from the entrance. The doors clunk behind me, and I spin around, ankle boots crunching on the gravel. Panting, sweating, holding my stomach protectively, I watch the church doors as strands of hair escape my bun and stick to my wet skin.

No one emerges. Not even Graham.

A guttural moan pushes free from my mouth as I slowly back away from the white building, trying to gulp down the fresh air. The baby's frantic movement slows, but my guts are churning, hot and soupy. A gorge of queasiness rises, and I hurry around the side of the church, heading to the giant oak tree at the other end of the parking lot.

I make it behind the trunk of the tree in time to drop to my knees, dark-red dress puddling around me, the weight of the baby making me lurch forward. When I vomit, I close my eyes and pray it's not getting all over my new outfit.

My chest burns—hot, raw, but it's different than when I threw up blood. This time, it's as if what's inside me doesn't want to come out and my throat is too small to allow for easy passage. Whatever it is gets lodged, and I choke, panicking, eyes flying open as I realize I can't breathe. I slam a fist against my sternum, pounding on my breastbone as if I can force it out, but nothing happens.

I gag on hands and knees, saliva running from my open mouth, heart racing, tears pouring down my cheeks.

Please, please, I pray. *Please don't let me die here. Don't let my baby die.*

An intense pressure comes from my womb, but not low—it's high, as if the child's head is pressing into my rib cage. Then a sudden, painful jab, and my throat expands, the substance trapped there rushing up and out, heaving over my lips and splattering against the brown grass.

It's mud. Damp, dark soil, packed together and clumped with clods of dirt and severed roots that wiggle like pale worms. It keeps coming, a literal mudslide, pouring from my churning stomach until I'm empty and crying.

The slippery wet mud stains my dress and oozes next to the oak tree. I sit on my heels, clutching my bump and wiping away the sweat and tears on my face with the back of my free hand.

My womb is quiet again, the baby calm. My throat is parched and feels like the inside of a garbage disposal. I want nothing more than to lie down in a dry patch of grass and sleep until I forget about everything that has happened today.

Squeezing my eyes shut, I take three deep breaths, pinching the bridge of my nose and trying to regain some semblance of composure. When I open my eyes, the speckled sunlight filtering through the leaves of the oak tree catches on a shiny glint amid the wet soil. I peer at the steaming sludge that has come out of me.

Half-buried, head up, poking out from under a hard clump of knotted dirt, is a single copper penny.

CHAPTER

15

MY BRAIN UNHITCHES from the cart of my body as I stare at the coin.

I can no longer feel the air on my skin or see the sun in my eyes. I am lost above everything, floating away; my spirit catching on the branches of the oak tree, the only thing keeping me from launching into the endless sky.

"Camille?" Graham's voice carries through the parking lot.

I startle, snapping out of my trance, peeking around the wide trunk of the oak tree. My husband is weaving between cars, craning his neck, looking for me.

A rush of relief washes over my heart. I can see the whites of his eyes, even from here. There are no black stains on his face. He appears normal, unchanged. Everything I saw in the church must have been another hallucination. Maybe the baby's aggressive activity inside my womb made me feel ill.

It's fine; this is all fine, I tell myself. *Not normal, but fine. You're OK, the baby is OK.*

I can't pinpoint the exact moment I stopped believing the lies I tell myself, but it doesn't matter. I accept them anyway. I have to. There's no other option.

I glance back at the pile of mud, which is slowly starting to congeal in the morning sunlight. It feels wrong to leave the penny here, even though the sight of it is disturbing in a way I don't feel like naming. I check again for Graham; he's getting closer. I can't let him see this.

Sliding my hand into the muck, I snatch up the penny, shake off clumps of mud, and stuff it down my dress, tucking it into my bra. The penny is damp and cold, despite having come from my warm insides, and a wet drop rolls down my breastbone and lands on the stretched skin of my stomach. Using the tree to lean on, I heave myself to my feet and step around the trunk, tottering back into the parking lot as Graham spots me.

"Camille!" He rushes over and stops a few feet away. "Whoa. What's going on? You look really sick. Is that *mud* on your dress? Are you feeling OK? Should we call Renee?"

"Why would I want her?" I snap before I can stop myself. Graham's face pales in shock, and I shake my head in apology. I keep forgetting that Graham thinks our neighbor is my midwife. "Sorry, babe. I-I feel really nauseous. I think I need to go lay down. I'm sorry about church."

He watches me carefully. "That's OK."

"It was . . ." I shouldn't ask. But I need to know. "You didn't see anything . . . weird in there, right?"

"*Weird*?" Graham repeats, his brows scrunching together. "Weird like what?"

"Oh, nothing," I quickly cover. Graham, I am realizing, is not a good liar. The crinkle of his confusion is genuine. He must not have seen what I saw. It *was* all in my head. "I think I need some rest."

"Oh, OK," Graham says, edging a step closer to me, looking wary, as if I'm a wild dog that could bite at any moment. "Let's get you home. You can call Renee there. Have her check you out."

"Maybe it was the car," I offer. "I do feel a bit carsick."

"I could see that," Graham concedes. He's not touching me. Why won't he take my hand? Give me a hug? Something? "Those roads are pretty windy. And you're probably more sensitive to that kind of thing now in your condition."

I nod, grateful he's accepting this but craving his touch. "Definitely. I don't think we need to be alarmed. I need rest. Please."

"Absolutely, darling. Come on, let's get you back to the car."

Our footsteps crunch across the parking lot, gravel skittering out of our path. I expect Graham to take my arm, offer a hand, check in with me in any way again, but he doesn't. He lets me get into the car by myself, promises to drive slower, and puts his music back on.

As he drives, I place both hands on my stomach and stained dress, feeling the penny press against my breast, still cold.

*   *   *

When we get back home, Graham insists I see Renee, but I manage to convince him it can wait until tomorrow morning when he's at work.

He tells me not to worry about lunch; he'll go meet his friends in town so I can rest in bed.

"That way you'll be right as rain and ready to cook dinner later," he says, handing me a glass of water as I peel my ruined dress off and slip under the covers in my bra and panties.

Graham averts his eyes.

I want to take a shower, but I'm physically exhausted. My throat is sore and scraped and my stomach aches fiercely from the baby's intense movement at the church. I need to nap first, rest. Then I can get clean and do the rest of the household work for Graham.

"Are you sure we shouldn't have Renee come look after you now while I'm out?" Graham asks.

The last thing I want is Renee sniffing around, but I can't tell Graham the truth. "I'm feeling better already. I'll be back to normal after a nap," I swear, and he gives in.

I wish he wouldn't. I wish he would make more of a fuss over me, even though it's not what I want—I don't want him poking around and realizing how unusual this pregnancy is. I don't want him to notice that things aren't lining up, that I'm not experiencing anything remotely similar to his married friends who already have children.

But even so, I want to feel like my husband cares about me. He does; I know he does. He came looking for me after I ran out of the church; he drove us home no questions asked even though he was excited about joining a congregation again. Graham isn't as demonstrative as he used to be, but maybe that's normal. We are evolving as a couple. As a family. And I have no doubt that he'll be a good father—able to provide a supportive and stable environment for me to raise our children in. He's already doing it. Last Monday, Graham handed me the credit card, the black one with no limit, and told me to get whatever we need.

"Should we hire help? A nanny?" he asked at the same time.

"No," I protested. "That goes against everything we stand for. I can do this by myself. I *have* to do this by myself." Besides, a nanny wouldn't be as oblivious as Graham, and I can't imagine the outcry if my followers—or, God forbid, Mara—found out I wasn't rearing my firstborn child by myself.

Instead, I excitedly used Graham's credit card to order everything we would need. I already had quite a bit: changing table, crib, stroller, mobile hanging from the ceiling. But with the credit card I was able to fill the nursery with burp cloths and baby monitors and clothes. So many baby clothes. I ignored Renee's constant offers to donate her used clothes and toys and purchased organic baby booties, hand-stitched onesies, beige and white blankets. I bought a new lamp—the base looks like a curled vine, the stand a stalk that reaches up to the wicker lampshade. It gives the nursery a sweet, natural feel. I ordered something called a "Social Media Baby Set" from Etsy with accessories and matching taupe-colored numbers so I can take pictures of the baby every month, counting down to the first birthday.

Yesterday I set up the baby monitor, which will record both audio and video, transmitting recordings right to my phone.

"We're all ready for you," I told the baby, rubbing my stomach. "I can't wait to meet you."

I couldn't have done any of that without my husband's funds. I have to be grateful for the help he provides. I'm one of the lucky ones.

Graham leaves, promising to be back for dinner. I try not to think about how, once again, he's leaving his wife home alone after a frightening incident.

It's not his fault, I insist. I told him I was fine. I downplayed the whole thing. He should be allowed to go get some food with friends. It's not like I can feed him in this state.

In the back of my mind, there is that annoying voice that demands I seek professional help, but I shoo it away like always. This is a special pregnancy. Nothing about it can be changed or helped or explained by science, no matter how much I respect it.

Are you sure? You're eating raw meat. You're vomiting mud and seeing things. These symptoms you're having could be indications of larger, more serious issues.

I am not a violent person, but if I could beat that voice and stuff it into a sealed box, I would do it in a heartbeat. Why can't I trust the process? Trust the wish I made at the well and the angel that was sent to me after?

The penny burns icy cold against my chest. With Graham out of the house, I dig the coin from my bra and shift the blanket off my body so I can place the penny on my baby bump.

I can't be sure it's the same penny that I dropped in the wishing well. I didn't look closely at the coin before I threw it down the hole with a prayer and a hope. How would the penny get inside me anyway?

I know how, the irritating voice says, and I want to strangle it.

I scoop the penny off my stomach and awkwardly roll to my side so I can shove it in the bedside drawer under my new book about unusual pregnancies. I think about reading a chapter, but nothing in there applies to me. What I'm going through can't be found in a book. Besides, I'm not a scientist, not anymore.

Instead, I reach farther back into my drawer and pull out a sheaf of papers. I flip through them, printed photos of Mara's account. Her beautiful grid, her comments, images of her home and children. It settles my heart, tracing her glowing face with a finger, rereading my favorite captions. I like having these physical representations of her on hand. It feels more real than perusing her page from a phone screen. If I study her hard enough, I can be like her, I know it.

I stare at the image of Mara's folic acid–free bagels. Thankfully, no one else has come out of the woodwork after the debacle the other week, but I'm too terrified to post anything else that could be misconstrued as being science related. I've been sticking to aesthetic content and pregnancy updates only. Science is not supposed to be a part of my life anymore.

Sighing, I return my Mara papers to the drawer and settle in for a nap, the weight of my stomach pulling me into slumber almost instantly.

When the eye, the winged one I haven't seen for weeks, appears on the ceiling above me, I try to squirm away. Frozen to the mattress, my bare belly exposed to the blinking oculus overhead, I am forced to stare as the wings start spinning again.

The voice comes, heavy and directionless, and I am not surprised, but I attempt to cringe away from it anyway.

Do not go back, it says.

I attempt to part my lips, trying to find the words and push them free, but I can't get a good grasp on them, can't find the moisture in my mouth to loosen them.

Do not go back there.

The eye blinks above me, and the clash of its eyelashes sounds like the steel of swords ringing against each other.

It is not safe.

I trusted the angel before. It was frightening, but I listened to it, and it gave me a baby. I can't ignore it now. Not when it's giving me a direct, clear order. There is nothing to interpret here. Nothing to make sense of.

The blank-faced people in the church. The mud I vomited. The unease of the baby in my womb. None of that can happen again.

I can't talk, but I cast my thoughts up toward the eye: *I understand.*

The angel seems satisfied with this response, because the wings around the eye stop their dizzy spinning and the blinking ceases. The room goes quiet, and we stare at each other for a moment, the giant irisless eye and my small brown ones.

The penny that used to hover in the angel's eye is gone.

The world goes dark, and I wake up.

*   *   *

The next day, I feel normal. I do my chores and make Graham's breakfast. I walk him to the garage and agree to text him after Renee comes over to "check me out."

After, I return to the kitchen and chew on a raw pork tenderloin as the baby twitches happily inside me, savoring the meaty juices that run down my chin and the earthy scent of uncooked flesh. The faster I eat, the better I feel, and soon I've consumed the whole thing, the slippery chunks of meat gnawed into manageable bites and greedily swallowed.

By the time Renee shows up, I have tea and fresh scones waiting for her, glad I didn't tell her anything about what happened at the church when I invited her over. She thinks we're becoming friends, and I would never dream of being rude enough to admit to her that she's only a buffer between me and my husband.

"So happy you texted after last time. I know you were upset by that rude commenter, but I'm glad you're feeling better now," she says as I let her in the house, suspiciously eyeing the plastic garbage bag she hauls on one shoulder. I lead her to the breakfast bar, where the tea and scones patiently wait. Renee slings the garbage bag to the floor next to the stool and places her hands on her hips, spinning to take me in. "My goodness, you look . . . I mean, it's only been a week since I last saw you! Well, what— how are you feeling?"

I'm a bit miffed by her tone. I worked hard to look presentable today. I'm wearing a peach-colored linen dress that I thought did a good job of hiding how large my bump has gotten in the past few days, and I carefully created a double-braided hairstyle that hides the strange discolored patches that have started to pop up near my golden roots. When I looked in the mirror earlier as I applied blush and bronzer, dotting concealer under my eyes to minimize the dark bags, I thought it would be difficult for anyone to see the waxy texture of my skin or the limpness of my hair.

I am still waiting for that natural pregnancy glow, the one Mara has every time she's with child. "I'm great," I say firmly. "What's in the bag?"

Distracted, Renee looks down at the bulging garbage bag at her feet. She smiles, clapping her hands together excitedly. "I hadn't heard back from you about what you might need, and you don't know what you're having yet, so I decided to bring a bunch of stuff from both my kids. You'll have options!"

My heart sinks. Why can't Renee take a hint? I ignored her texts about what supplies I needed, so she made the decision for me?

"That's kind of you, but we really don't—"

"Let me show you!" Renee interrupts, bending down to untie the garbage bag impatiently. Her movement wafts her familiar, stale, fruity scent toward my face, and I cough to cover a gag.

Renee worms one hand into the tight opening and stretches the mouth of the bag, revealing glimpses of bright baby clothing piled inside.

I place a hand at the small of my back, my body aching with displeasure and exhaustion. Inviting her over again was a mistake. I should have lied to Graham and used this time to clean instead. I'm so much slower these days, especially with all the breaks to order and eat raw meat while I prepare Graham's normal meals.

"This was Henry's first onesie. Isn't it cute? I love the little giraffes. And here's Millie's sweater set. This is great for the winter; you should definitely take it." Renee digs through the garbage bag—*a garbage bag, of all things!*—and points out different outfits. She pops up for air, straightening and spotting the scones. "Oh, yum!" She rises and shoves the end of one into her mouth, noisily chewing, flaking bits of pastry all over my shining floors.

The baby shifts in my womb, and I imagine placing a hand at the back of this woman's neck and smashing her forehead down on the counter.

I shake my head, startled by the vision. I glance down into the open bag instead. The clothing she has presented to me is not what I would have chosen. In fact, I didn't. I think of the beautiful, neutral-toned outfits neatly folded and tucked away in the baby's dresser upstairs. I don't know the baby's gender, but it doesn't matter—I won't be dressing the child in ugly, bright-blue or pink colors anyway. Instead, we'll be in matching palettes: muted, simple tones that go well with our charmingly minimalist house.

There's no way I'm dressing our baby in any of the items Renee has brought over. I spot a neon-green hat with black trim, a royal-purple onesie with a cartoonish bear head on the front, and a pair of baby booties designed to look like puppy paws.

I can imagine my followers' disdain to see my baby dressed like a Walmart catalogue.

I suppress a shudder. "Thanks so much; you really didn't have to do that."

"It's no problem," Renee says, munching on the scone and spraying crumbs over her chest that drop down to the floor. Her lips are slightly chapped and red, but it doesn't look like she's wearing lipstick.

"How's your family doing?" I ask.

"Kids are back in school!" Renee says, clapping her hands together. In the same instance, her chin dips and her eyes lower. "I wish I could have been there to see them off."

"Oh, were you busy?"

She looks up, as if remembering I'm there. Clearing her throat, she tries on a thin smile that's too small for her wide mouth. Renee says, "Ah, yeah. Doctor's appointment. Maybe next year." She attempts to cross her fingers, but her index finger stacks on top of the middle finger instead, and she has to use her other hand to manually move her fingers into the correct gesture.

I don't want Renee to ask more questions about my pregnancy, so I steer the conversation back to her life. "What type of diapers did you use? Same kind for both children?"

Renee launches into an energetic rant about the specifics of her favorite diaper brand, and I tune her out. I already know I'll be using the same handmade cloth diapers Mara promotes on her page.

After I spend another agonizing hour making small talk, dodging questions by asking Renee for newborn tips, she finally leaves.

I knot up the garbage bag she's left behind and drag it over to the garage, tossing it into a corner behind Graham's toolbox.

At the exertion, the baby kicks rapidly, and I pat my stomach. "I know. I'll get us something to eat."

I turn off the light, dousing the empty garage in darkness, and return to the kitchen to feed.

16

PREGNANCY DOES NOT suit me, and it's infuriating.

The photos I take have to be heavily filtered. I get creative with poses and garments that hide my thin limbs, my washed-out skin. I do not look like Mara or any of the other influencers I follow who glow with radiant pride when they're carrying a baby. I look feeble and sickly. It limits the amount and quality of the pregnancy content I was so excited for. But maybe that's for the best, because there are things about my pregnancy I can't explain and don't want to draw attention to.

My stomach is growing at an alarming rate. A month and a half in, my belly is fully rounded, the baby a heavy burden on my back. Yet at the same time, I lose weight elsewhere. My arms and legs become sticklike and fragile; my hair starts to fall out in the shower in long golden ropes. Using the changing weather as an excuse, I wear knit hats to hide the strange, discolored patches in my natural coloring.

My gums have started to bleed, sometimes when I'm eating, sometimes on their own. I'll taste the hot salty liquid dribbling down the back of my throat and know my upper molars are leaking again.

And no matter what I eat, no matter the quantity of raw meat I consume, crouching in the corner of the kitchen at midnight after pretending to eat the cooked food I serve Graham, I cannot release the hunger that grips my gut. I secretly order extra steaks from the nearby farm, getting them delivered when Graham is at work.

It's the baby. Consuming my energy, eating my resources, craving strange foods that should make me sick but give me a bizarre burst of adrenaline instead. I've wondered if eating the raw meat has given me a worm or illness, but I can't stop. The baby wriggles happily in the womb when I eat meat, and I vomit up anything else.

But it's all worth it, because I love my baby. Even though these "quirks" mean I won't be able to do a cute pregnancy photoshoot, unable to trust a professional photographer to examine my withering body through a lens, or a photo-a-day video compilation because of the inconsistent and puzzling growth in my belly.

Instead, I set up my tripod in the backyard and use the self-timer on my phone to take photos in my new, pricey maternity dresses during golden hour. The rays streak my skin and make me look healthy, my body too far away from the camera to reveal any details.

It's the only time I've been near the wheat fields since I got pregnant, and I haven't seen the creature again since it appeared in the kitchen window. The line its claw left is still there; Graham hasn't noticed. He's rarely at the sink.

I'm not necessarily avoiding the field or the well, although Graham's and Renee's warnings about staying away from the forest ring in my ears whenever I look out the windows. It's more that I don't want to confuse the creature. I told it all those weeks ago that it was over and our interaction was done. I don't want it to come back.

I select the best photos from my private shoot in our expansive backyard and post them online alongside lush captions bursting with gratitude.

These photos, carefully edited and filtered, with the waves of wheat visible in the background, fallen leaves on the ground under my bare feet, get me noticed by Mara once again.

My heart leaps in excitement when I see the notification, and the baby responds in kind, kicking at my kidneys with ferocious strength. I have to sit down, wheezing, but the pain doesn't matter because Mara has liked my photo *and* commented!

I have the same dress! You look amazing. Must be from cutting out that folic acid ;)

"Three whole sentences!" I whisper in awe, rubbing my aching belly, leaning back on the couch in amazement. "And she remembers who I am."

Mara must get thousands of messages a week, but she remembered our exchange and, more importantly, recognized me! I tap to her Instagram profile, checking her "following" list, but she's still not following me back. That's OK. We'll get there. She knows me now. I'm on her radar.

I reply to her comment: *Thank you, love! It takes more work to make folic acid-free food but it's so worth it! I've never felt better.* ☺

It's a lie. But I'm not going to tell the world that I'm having the weirdest pregnancy ever. I'm not going to announce that I had to accept the help of a creature (*Angel,* I correct myself for the umpteenth time) to conceive. And I'm not going to admit that food without folic acid is a pain in the ass to make.

Nothing about this process is what I expected. The fragility of my body, the sourness of my insides, the skeletal look of my face. This pregnancy is heavy with unpleasant surprises that I try to ignore. I should be grateful. I *am* grateful. I've finally gotten what I wanted.

But the truth is that my pregnancy is full of lies.

In the evening, Graham and I are sitting on the couch—him watching boxing, me knitting a pair of baby socks using a soft, oatmeal-colored yarn—when he turns down the volume during a commercial.

"How far along are you?" he asks, looking pointedly at my bulging belly, which I've tried to hide in loose-fitting garments. "You seem much more pregnant now than you were a few weeks ago."

Black is not my color—it doesn't fit the vibe I'm going for—but dark colors are more slimming, so I've been wearing ebony shifts and charcoal cotton maxi dresses in maternity sizes bigger than I need. Graham, surprisingly, has noticed.

"Turns out I was further along than we thought," I fib. "I'm close to birth, Renee says. Maybe a month away."

"Seriously? But the rest of you looks . . . normal. Or like maybe you've lost weight? Aren't you supposed to get bigger—" He cuts himself off, cheeks tinged red. Graham gestures downward, glancing at my chest. "You know . . ."

My breasts are not any bigger. Of course Graham would notice *that*. I've always privately thought he was unimpressed with my naturally small chest. He would never say anything—Graham is too classy and modest for that. But I've had my suspicions.

"They *are* bigger," I lie again, trying not to sound like I'm arguing with him. Good wives don't bicker with their husbands, but I'm tired and my back hurts and the baby was rolling around in my stomach like it was tumbling down a hill earlier today. "I went up one cup size." I turn to face him, a hint of challenge in my voice. "Do you want to see?"

I watch his expression, lit up from the TV, looking for signs of arousal, still hoping that maybe the baby will connect us in a way we haven't had in a while. But Graham's face shutters instead, and he turns away from me, eyes glazed and no longer roving over my body.

I barely notice my disappointment.

Graham shrugs. "It's weird, that's all. Your stomach is growing but the rest of you is shrinking."

Graham might not be the most scientific man in the universe, but he knows that babies take nine months to be born. I've been visibly pregnant for a month and a half. He's going to question this. I have to try to explain it away, and I'm hoping his fondness for physical beauty will override any intellectual concerns he might have.

"Some women lose weight in pregnancy," I try, shrugging and smiling at him. "I guess I'm one of the lucky ones. I was pregnant for a long time without realizing. My . . . period is pretty irregular as it is." I hesitate to talk about menstruation— Graham doesn't like it; he thinks it should be private and kept quiet—but the benefit of that is that he often doesn't know or notice when I'm on my period.

Graham glances back at me. "Wow," he says, trying for a smile. "Only you would lose weight while carrying a baby."

Just like that, he lets it go, turning back to the TV. Disappointment mingles with relief. He believes, somehow, that I've been pregnant for eight months already, even though he lives with me. Even though he surely would have noticed. How can he accept this so easily?

Because he doesn't care?

Shut up, I snap at the voice skulking around the edges of my consciousness. He's not that educated about the female body. All his schools were religious. He didn't have sex ed.

Maybe this is a good thing. I don't want Graham prying—I don't want to have to explain the truth and hope he believes me. But I don't want him this disengaged either. He's not asking enough questions. He's not concerned about this pregnancy the way I am. He doesn't notice my bleeding gums, my exhaustion, the patches of darkness in my usually bright hair. Or maybe he thinks it's normal.

He isn't worried, and it makes me feel utterly alone.

But when Renee comes over the next day when Graham is at work, she *is* concerned.

"You don't look so good, Camille. Have you seen a doctor?" she asks, sitting next to me on the couch, a pumpkin spice–scented candle burning on the coffee table. "You've gotten sonograms and stuff, right?"

"Yes," I lie. "Everything is fine. I'm having a . . . tough pregnancy. I'll get through it."

"Yes, you will," she says, patting my hand. "You're a tough cookie. Look at all you've done already! You're going to be a great mom."

I smile at her. This is why Renee has become somewhat of a constant fixture in my life. She's annoying at times, but she's also supportive and generous with compliments. And she hasn't said anything judgy about my lifestyle since the folic acid incident. So I allow her to come over to "help" me. In reality, she mostly eats my food and tells long, rambling stories about her children, exuding the tart smell of squished grapes drying in the sun. Sometimes she'll be wearing strange things—today she showed up in one of *her* maternity dresses, twirling around the kitchen when I showed her inside.

"Do you like?" she asks now, tugging at the crimson stretch dress patterned with garish yellow leaves. "You would make it look so glamorous. I thought you could have it if you want."

I do not want. Not at all.

But I'll put up with her bizarre behavior and intrusive personality for now, because it's nice to interact with someone who isn't Graham. The baby isn't here yet, and Graham doesn't invite me to hang out with his friends anymore, saying I need to rest.

Although he still expects the house to be clean and his meals to be cooked. He is out of reach, a mirage in the desert I am not getting any closer to.

Renee isn't ideal, but she's someone to talk with.

"What else did you bring?" I ask her, nodding to the tote bag at her feet near the couch.

"Oh! Baby name books!" Renee squeals, bending over and dumping out the contents of the tote bag so that they sprawl out between us on the sofa like a physical barrier. I'm grateful for that; they'll keep her from touching me too much, from rubbing her hands on my belly with such longing that the hair on the back of my neck stands up.

"Wow, thanks," I say, picking a book up and thumbing through it, landing on the *N*'s, scanning the page. No matter what the gender, I will not be naming my child Nemo.

"This one is great," Renee says, nudging a book called *Name That Baby!* toward me on the couch. "They have a nice mix of traditional and modern."

I close the book on Nemo and pick up *Name That Baby!* instead, flicking through it, not really looking. I want to do this with Graham, not Renee.

"Maybe next time I can come over to your place," I say, not because I actually want to but because I'm itching to get out of the house for a while, even if it's to go down the road. "I could walk there. It would be nice to do a long stroll."

"Oh, gosh, you don't want to come to my house," Renee laughs, looking around the tidy white living room. "Why would you ever want to leave such a beautiful place? And come over and sit in melted crayons and walk around mountains of stuffed animals and trip over shoes? Trust me, stay in your pregnancy bubble as long as you can, because once that angel is out of you, you'll never have a moment's peace again!" She says it lightly, but there's a hard kernel nestled in her words that makes me wonder if she's jealous.

"What did you do before your kids?" I ask, genuinely curious. "Like before you became a stay-at-home mom?"

Renee smiles, flipping randomly through the baby name book I discarded, pausing on one page, squinting, and then shaking her head. "You can't name your baby Scooter. Even if it's a boy. No way." She looks over at me. "I was a manager at a restaurant. It was high pressure and fast paced, but I was great at it. When I got pregnant, though, Zach and I decided it made more sense for me to stay home with the kids. Save some money on childcare, and I'd get a break from the restaurant life. It ages you, you know?"

I don't know, but I nod carelessly. I glance at the golden wall clock that hangs over the TV, its abstract, circular body supporting two metal arms that slowly tick around its face. It's almost time for me to start prepping dinner. And my stomach is gurgling, the baby adjusting inside me as I picture the raw steak waiting for us in the fridge.

"What about you?" Renee asks.

I draw my attention back to the woman on my couch. "What *about* me?"

"After the whole CAST thing, did you ever go back to school?" She pauses, closing the book in her hands. "Study anything else? You're clearly very bright, and you're so good at social media. Did you take a marketing class or something?"

I pull back, stone-faced. I don't want to talk about CAST again. It was bad enough the first time; I only told her the truth because I was in a state of shock and distress. But I have to give her something. "I don't have a college degree. I've always been good at photography, though. And interior design. Seeing beautiful things in my head and replicating them in the real world. This is what I was meant to do, and I'm not ashamed of my choices."

It's the answer I've used in the past when people ask about my hobbies and assume that because I stay home all day, I am boring or stupid. It's the safe answer.

I never talk about CAST or how invested I was in science when I was younger. I never speak about my interest in biology and the human body. It's too "masculine." That's what my father said when I was growing up, anyway.

"Science and math are for boys," he would grunt when I excitedly showed him my grades. "Good job, honey, but let's focus more on what matters, OK? How's your cooking elective coming along?"

Renee nods at me emphatically. "Oh, sure. There's no shame in leaving college if it's not for you. But I wonder . . ." She trails off.

"What?" I ask, challenging her.

"Well, it's . . . It sounds like you were really talented. I looked up that program after we talked. CAST? Apparently only eight students get in every year. It's very competitive," she replies, not meeting my eyes, flipping through the baby name book again. "I get it if you decided it wasn't for you. But why not try something else? You're so young. I'm wondering how much of the world you've gotten to explore."

My palms get hot and I try to force a smile, feeling the creases of a frown wrinkling my forehead. "This is what I want to explore. My home. My family. My life here."

"But what do you *want*?" Renee pushes, glancing at me again. Her eyes are almost as big as her mouth, and when she blinks, it's like her gaze is sliding around the room before roaming back to my face—back and forth, back and forth. "What do you *really* want?"

"This." I gesture to my stomach. "This is what I want. Always has been."

"Really? This is what you wanted to be as a little girl?"

"Well, yes," I say testily, placing a hand protectively over my bump. "I had to take care of my dad when I was little because my mom died. I'm good at taking care of people. I was destined to be this way."

I won't tell her about the start of CAST, how I saw a different future unfurling—one where I could use biology to help people. I left that dream behind when it became clear that science, like so many other industries, was all about rejection and judgment.

"There's a difference between being good at something and wanting something. Is this what you *want*?" Renee presses. When she sees the expression on my face, she adds, "You know, parents are supposed to take care of their children. Not the other way around."

"My father was very busy," I say, bristling. "He needed me."

"Is there anything you've done that you've liked just because it was for you? Not for social media or your husband or your baby?"

Her presumption pricks my skin and I clench my jaw, but I can't help thinking about the strength training I tried, how powerful it made me feel, how I missed it when Graham said I shouldn't do it anymore. I think of the walks I took in the wheat field behind the house, the ones I went on alone before my pregnancy without Graham's knowledge. I think of the biology classes in high school—dissecting frogs and pigs didn't bother me. I loved learning about how living creatures functioned, especially humans. But when I told my father, he said I was too pretty to be a scientist. He didn't support my choice to attend CAST, but the praise and love he heaped on me when I quit showed me I made the right decision.

"I'm getting tired," I say instead of telling Renee any of that, pretending to yawn, and then actually yawning seconds later. "I think maybe you should go."

"Oh, all right," Renee says, shoulders slumping. "If you need anything, text me. I'll leave the books here. You can ignore the highlighted names. Those were from me, years ago. Feel free to mark them up in your own way."

I escort her out, and when I'm sure she's gone, I wander back into the kitchen, resting my head against the cool stainless steel of the fridge, letting my breath fog up the metal surface.

Oh, ew. I need to brush my teeth, I think, wrinkling my nose.

My breath smells like rotting meat and freshly tilled soil. I hope Renee didn't notice. But even if she did, who cares? Who is she to judge me? Pry into my "wants" and insinuate this life isn't what's best for me? It's not her business. My life may be tumultuous right now, but everything will be better when I give birth. The baby will make everything normal.

Will it? Even though nothing about its conception or this pregnancy has been normal?

I hate that voice.

My stomach groans in response, as if it's conspiring with my conscience, and I sigh, pulling my head back from the door and opening the fridge. I tear into a packet of sausage links, gnashing the meat against my molars. The baby flaps happily in my womb as drool dribbles down my jawline. I wolf down the raw meat, but it's not enough. I dive back into the fridge and remove the steak hidden under a bag of spinach.

I thought, at first, that the red liquid oozing from the steaks was blood, but then I did some research. It's actually myoglobin, water mixed with an iron-rich, oxygen-binding protein found in the muscle tissue of vertebrates. It's delicious.

I plunge my tongue into the spongy meat, licking up the myoglobin.

Maybe things aren't perfect. Maybe this process is difficult and strange. Maybe this isn't what I pictured. But I don't care—when I connect with the baby like this, feeding us in the most natural, primal way I can think of, it feels *right*. I was meant to do this.

I swirl my tongue around the steak, my lower half vibrating at the thought of the creature making the same lapping movements inside my body a month and a half ago. The baby jumps in my stomach, demanding, and I bite into the meat, moaning as the rich, earthy flavor bursts across my taste buds. The metallic smell settles in my nose, and I almost purr as I consume the raw meat, sucking the juices off the ends of my finger and licking the Styrofoam tray and plastic wrap that housed it. When I'm done, the baby settles, and I drop the garbage on the floor. I'll pick it up later.

I sink to the ground, holding my stomach, sated. The hunger will come back—it always does. But for now, the baby and I are fed and at peace. I look down at the bump, large next to my skinny arms and prominent wristbones. My hands are constantly cold now; my feet too. All my blood is in the middle of my body, helping create a human.

I sigh, wiping my mouth with the back of my hand.

Renee's words ring in my mind. What do I want? It used to be Graham. Then a baby. Now I have both, and if I'm being honest, I'm not sure what else I expect from life.

What do I want?

What does anyone want? To be happy, healthy, fulfilled. I want to be like Mara Shoemaker, displaying my beautiful life online so that others may be inspired, to show what a good wife and mother I am to the people that matter the most. I've always interlaced my happiness with others, with the person I'm taking care of. That's what it means to be a woman.

But something about that rings hollow now. It's like the reflection of the moon on tranquil water: beautiful and alluring, but an illusion. If I can tear myself away from the mirror image and look up, what will I think of the real moon?

Maybe there are things I can do that don't cater to others. Things the men in my life have gently rearranged or removed so my attention would drift back to them.

Graham has not come back to me the way I wanted. In fact, he's drifting even further away. His affection is limited, and there are times where I think I can see gaps in his kindness. Has that always been there and I'm just noticing now? Or could it be that this man simply isn't who I thought he was and only now, with the impending arrival of someone I already unconditionally love, am I realizing it?

I extend my legs out ahead of me on the kitchen floor, the tiles cold on my bottom and thighs. I lean against the door of the fridge and look up at the ceiling.

I haven't seen the creature in a while. There have been no strange dreams or visions since the incident at the church. Yet there's an absence there. I miss it.

Groaning, I roll over to one side and use the fridge handle to drag myself back up to my feet. I squat to pick up the steak packaging I left on the floor and take it over to the garbage can under the sink.

The baby kicks, once. I pat my stomach absently, acknowledging my child.

I can't stand here all day. I have chores to do. Meals to cook. Graham expects me to keep house, even if I'm growing a baby.

This is my life, and I must love it.

III

Third Trimester

CHAPTER

17

I T HAPPENS A week later, an hour after Graham leaves for work.
I'm in the dining area, sandwiched between the open
kitchen and living room, spraying lavender cleanser on the table
and wiping it with a microfiber cloth, when a sharp popping
sensation reverberates inside my body. A scraping movement
deep within makes me shudder. Warmth blooms near my
vagina, then unfurls into heat as liquid slides down my inner
thighs.

I lift my skirts to watch a white, viscous substance crawl
down my legs, dribbling toward the spotless floor.

I should put down a towel, I think numbly as I track the liquid's path with my gaze.

But I don't move; I don't want it to come out faster. The
white continues to flow out of my body; there are streaks of
crimson mixed in, blending with the white, creating a kaleidoscopic pattern of banded pink on my shins and feet.

When your water breaks, it's supposed to be clear, perhaps a
pale yellow, odorless, thin, watery. But this is thick, like glue,
and smells of a freshly dug hole. Blood cuts through sections of
the deluge like poorly mixed acrylic paint.

It's OK, I tell myself as the tacky substance begins to pool around my feet. *My water breaking doesn't necessarily mean the baby is—*

Agony twists inside my body, everything going black for a second as I'm overcome by a convulsion so great and violent that it brings me to the floor, bruising my kneecaps. One leg slips out to the side, skidding on the slick puddle, but I catch myself by tipping forward, both hands landing on the dry floor a few feet in front of me.

I breathe through my nose as another racking twist rips through my uterus, my eyes dampening from the strength of it.

"You're early," I pant as the baby shifts. It feels like a frightened cat is trapped inside my womb, tearing at my uterine lining with needled claws and fanged teeth, crawling around, positioning itself so that it's ready to escape the home it spent far too little time in. Is the baby OK? Why is it moving around so much?

Nothing about this has been normal. Why would I think the birth would be any different?

A scream erupts from my mouth as a new contraction detonates, shaking my flesh, eating away at my atoms. I could split apart entirely—the story from the Bible about the two women who each claimed a baby was their own pops into my head. The king offered to cut the baby in half so they could each get a piece. One woman immediately released her claim, and she was declared to be the true mother, a woman who couldn't bear to see her child slashed apart.

I should be the mother, the true, noble woman who can't stand seeing her baby killed, but instead I am the child, ripped apart down the middle. No one is here to release the claim on my body. No one is here to save me.

On all fours, panting, in too much pain to even scream, I can't help thinking about how awful my hair must look, sticking to my sweaty face and neck. How the *fuck* do those bitches take glowing pregnancy photos seconds after birth? Or during? Mara had a photographer at the birth of her fifth child.

I am suddenly consumed with hate for every woman in my community who insists natural childbirth is the way to go, who acts like you're not a woman unless you're a mother, who demonizes anyone who has a pregnancy that doesn't imitate their own.

Another wave of pain passes through me, and I choke back a dry sob at the thought of giving birth here, on our living room floor, alone, like a cow.

A *shush* comes from across the room, and I look up as the sliding glass door opens.

The creature steps inside, and the lights in the house darken, like clouds consuming the sun. It leaves the sliding glass door open, and the brisk fall breeze whips through the house and cools my dripping face. I inhale greedily, taking in the smell of the wheat, the promise of rain, the distant pines in the forest.

"Stay with me," I groan as another contraction, faster now, ripples my skin. The baby is clawing itself free from my womb, peeling away layers of my insides, scoring the walls of my body as it goes.

The creature moves farther into the room, face impenetrable, white eyes wide and empty. Maybe it's here to kill me—I would welcome it at this point. But the creature does nothing, only stands several feet away, watching. I don't care. I'm grateful I'm no longer alone.

*   *   *

Labor lasts four hours.

This is not normal. Yet the unnaturally short process is something I pay for in pain. I cry out when I have enough spit to unstick my tongue from the roof of my mouth; I am unable to move from my position on all fours, knees numb against the wood. Sometimes it feels like my bones want to die, and my muscles wrap around them tighter and whisper, deeply, intensely, *Not yet darling, not yet.*

The creature moves closer to my side, and two hours in, it crouches down and peers at me with glassy eyes, as if it's observing an anthill with mild interest.

Near the end, my arms weaken, trembling, and I start to fall face forward, unable to hold my front half up any longer.

The creature moves for the first time in an hour, arms slowly extending so that it catches me, the underside of its scaly forearms pressing against my sternum and collarbone as my head droops toward the floor. My hair hangs in lank, sweat-soaked snarls, draping over my shoulder. I can't lift my head. I lay limply in the creature's arms as it props me off the stained floorboards.

The smell of wet soil is overwhelming.

"It's coming," I croak, not knowing if my companion understands me, an angry pressure building at the core of my body.

A hot wet rush gushes from my vagina; a blistering rip radiates through my lower half, and I automatically push, squeezing my child from its previous home with throbbing tenderness. The baby is starting to slide free, and I panic, not wanting it to hit the hard floor. I squirm in the creature's arms, drawing out the last bit of strength I have, placing my sore hands back down on the floor to support myself.

"Catch the baby," I grunt, hoping it understands, hoping it can at least intuit what I'm asking.

I breathe a sigh of relief as the creature releases my chest and smoothly disappears from view, moving around me, toward my rear. It has seen me naked before. It has made me break against it like a wave on a rock. It helped create this child, but nothing has felt as intimate as this.

Graham should be here, I think, but then push the thought away. This birth has been alarming and unusual. He can't see this. He can't know the truth. I did this for *us.*

I wish there were someone here to tell me to push, but there isn't. I must tell myself.

"Push!" I scream, and I feel the baby breach, cool air playing on my face from the open sliding door. "One more! You can do it!"

A waterfall of pain releases inside me as the baby breaks from my body, falling away, leaving a wake of tiny tremors in its place. Quickly, I crane my head back, making sure—and yes, the creature has caught the child and is gently moving it away from my body. The umbilical cord is strange—dark green and pulsing. Maybe I'm not seeing it right.

My job done and my energy entirely spent, I collapse to the ground in a sticky pool of liquid that used to be inside me. I roll onto one side, watching as the creature cradles the baby, who is quiet and still.

"Is the baby . . . is it . . ."

The creature looks at me, eyes large and white and empty. Its wings unfurl suddenly, and there are tears in the leathery membrane, black veins spidering through the skin. It sweeps its wings around us—me, the creature, the baby—and we're plunged into a quiet dome of gray light. It smells like the forest—tree bark and freshly dug soil and animal scat. For a moment, my pain vanishes and a blanket of calm falls over me, easing my lungs.

Then the creature pulls back its wings and the baby is screaming, writhing in its arms. The pain returns, causing my vision to falter for a moment. I am swallowed up by the monsoon raging inside. For the first time, I wonder if I will survive this birth. Women have died this way for generations. I could easily join them, especially because nothing about this pregnancy or birth has been accurate or expected.

I blink rapidly, clearing my eyesight in time to watch the creature gnaw off the umbilical cord, which falls wetly to the ground with a dull *slap*. Nausea rises, but I push it down. I need to deliver the placenta. I can't tell the difference between the burning, pulsing aches and the residual contractions meant to push out the placenta, so when it comes, a few minutes later, it is almost a surprise. It's like a jellyfish slipping out from a cave. Still on my side, the placenta slides down my leg and into the puddle of white goo and blood.

I gaze up at the creature, at the bawling baby in its arms. I have a daughter.

"Oh," I breathe. "Oh, please, give her to me."

The creature doesn't obey me. Instead, it transfers the baby into one arm, scooching forward on its heels to help me into a seated position with its free hand. It shifts me so that my back leans against the sturdy dining room table, my legs stretching out in front of me like dead logs.

The creature finally hands me the child, and I press her against my hot chest, my beating heart. She freezes immediately, falls silent. When I look down at my baby, her nostrils are flaring like a dog's, sniffing the air, sniffing my skin. She opens her eyes, regarding my face.

My stomach clenches. Her eyes are pure white. She has no pupils, no irises. Just snowy sclerae that look as if they've been bleached.

I lift my gaze to find the creature with the matching eyes, but the living room is empty. The sliding glass door remains open, but my baby's biological father is gone.

CHAPTER

18

THE FIRST PHOTO I post of my daughter gets me sixty thousand likes and a deluge of comments.

I am overjoyed, but the photo had to be carefully posed and edited—in it, I sit in the rocking chair in our beautiful nursery, holding the baby in a bundle of beige blankets. You can see her face, tiny features, eyes closed. I am wearing a knit hat, a braid resting against my shoulder so it's less obvious how much hair I've lost. My impressive wedding ring is visible on my left hand, supporting my daughter—I made sure it was in the shot.

I had to color-correct the whole thing, since both my child and I look slightly gray and worn. I made the photo warm and bright, and with my giant smile and the sleeping baby's tiny face, the illusion works. People go wild.

I get five hundred new followers right away, one of which is Mara.

I dance around the nursery, singing to the baby. My daughter is on her back in the crib, and I have been folding clothes, organizing her outfits for the week. Graham left for work a few hours ago, and I can't think of a better way to start the day than spending time with my baby and finding out Mara Shoemaker has followed me back after all these years.

"We did it, darling! She only follows a hundred accounts," I croon, cradling my phone to my chest as my daughter's big white eyes gaze up at the mobile over her head. "She has a one-in, one-out policy. She literally unfollowed someone else to follow me! All because of you, Sweetheart!"

Sweetheart.

Graham said he'd take care of all the paperwork, and we picked a name for our daughter. But as soon as we did, the name left my head. Instead, I started calling her Sweetheart. Graham, amused, did the same. I can't tell if it's to placate me or if he genuinely likes it, but it doesn't matter.

She is Sweetheart, her original name forgotten.

Graham was shocked to come home a few days ago and see me on the couch with our baby. He couldn't believe it, even after I explained that Renee had helped me deliver Sweetheart and clean up after, even though in reality I had to do it all myself.

But his surprise petered out after a few hours of me repeating my lies. Again, I wished he would press more. Ask why I hadn't called him to be there, interrogate me about the timeline of this pregnancy.

I won't let Graham's obliviousness ruin this for me, though. And at least he seems pleased, fawning over Sweetheart, who is miraculously always sleeping when he's around. Graham hasn't seen her white eyes yet.

He doesn't notice her other abnormalities either. Such as her grayish-green skin, not as saturated as the creature's but conspicuous enough that she looks sickly and claylike in certain lights. The scent of soil that cuts through the baby powder. Her weight; Sweetheart is *heavy*. I weighed her on our bathroom scale—she's thirteen pounds, and perhaps that accounts for the unimaginable pain I was in during childbirth. The weird thing is that she doesn't look large—it's like she's a Russian nesting doll with hidden bodies inside her.

Before he left this morning, Graham said, "I'm going to work very hard, babe. I'm going to make as much money as possible so I can provide a beautiful life for you two."

"Yes," I said. "I wish you could be here to spend more time with her, though."

"I'll work hard now so that I can be there for her later," Graham explained.

I wondered if Graham was more enamored with the idea of being a father than actually doing any of the tasks required to be one. "I understand," I conceded.

"Oh," Graham said before he headed out the door. "By the way, I'm going to be late tonight."

I shake my head, pushing away the memory. I can't think about that now. Not when I finally have my baby *and* the tacit approval of Mara Shoemaker!

I have to commemorate this occasion. Pulling up my photos, I find the album marked *Mara* and select one of my favorite selfies of her—Mara in front of a dreamy beige wall in her house. I save her best shots so I can use them as inspiration, but this time I open one of my many editing apps and upload Mara's photo. I scroll through my own selfies until I find one that looks proportional, adding it to the app. Some background-removing magic, a little AI assist, and suddenly my face and Mara's face are next to each other in front of her beige wall. The lighting is slightly off, but it looks good. Real. Like we're posing together in her home, best friends.

Smiling, I save the photo. I won't post it anywhere, but I'll print it out and frame it. Keep it in my craft room. It's the perfect way to mark the dawn of our new relationship.

Hovering above the crib, keeping an eye on Sweetheart, I return to Instagram, typing out thanks to people in my comments section.

A series of texts flurry through at the top of my screen: the group chat we're in with Graham's parents.

More photos please! I can't wait to meet her, Graham's mother says.

Grimacing, I scroll through my photos to find something appropriate to send. I have shot and edited a dozen carefully curated photos of Sweetheart for my father and Graham's parents. I send one now: my daughter curled up, face nuzzled in one hand.

An angel! Do you have any of her awake?

My throat constricts.

Next time she's up I'll try to get one, I tap back. *She's a big sleeper!*

I'm underselling it. Sweetheart's sleep schedule is more like a sloth's than a human baby's. Newborns are supposed to sleep twelve to sixteen hours a day, but Sweetheart sleeps closer to twenty. It's not normal, but when she's awake, she seems fine, so I decide everything is proceeding as it should.

Lucky, lucky, comes Graham's mother's reply. *I wish Graham slept when he was a baby!*

Come on, Mama, I just wanted to spend all my time with you, my husband responds a minute later. He's added the winky-face emoji.

I put the phone away, feeling a bit queasy, turning back to my daughter.

Sweetheart is considering my face, nostrils flaring. She opens and closes her mouth rapidly, but no sound comes out. She doesn't cry; she never does. She sleeps, then wakes in the middle of the day when Graham is at work, staring at me.

A dribble of drool pools out from her lower lip as she sniffs the air.

She's hungry. But we have an issue: I don't have milk. My breasts never filled out, and there's nothing to feed my baby with. I didn't want to try a bottle—Mara hates bottle-feeding—but I had no choice. I secretly overnighted organic baby formula to the house, only for Sweetheart to refuse the bottle. I'm not sure what else to do. It's been several days since Sweetheart's birth, and she has yet to eat anything. I'm starting to panic.

Sweetheart's full-moon eyes fixate on my face. At least, I think she's fixating on my face. It's hard to tell when there are no pupils. Maybe her pupils and irises are the exact same shade of white as her sclerae, or maybe she doesn't have any at all.

"Should we try some formula again?" I ask her, as if expecting her to sit up and answer me. And why shouldn't she? I've run out of astonishment. Since the move, my life has been full of miracles.

A wet warmth releases inside me, and I cringe.

Hold that thought.

"One second, darling, I need to go to the restroom," I tell Sweetheart, darting next door into our bedroom and the attached bathroom.

With my phone in my hand, I switch over to the baby monitor app so I can keep an eye on Sweetheart.

In the bathroom, I remove the thick sanitary napkin from my underwear, staring at the wet soil smeared on it. It's not quite mud, more like dark, damp earth. Like something dug up from the inside of a well. The soil has been coming out of me since childbirth. I expected lochia, vaginal bleeding that isn't dissimilar to a period. I even prepared myself for the occasionally frightening lochia clots. I told myself this could happen for weeks.

I did not expect wet dirt smelling of iron and misty mornings.

At least it's slowing down. The first twelve hours after giving birth were the worst—the earth slithered out of me like a mudslide. I irrevocably stained four pairs of underwear and went through eight sanitary napkins. At one point, I simply folded a washcloth and shoved it in my underwear. I was lucky Graham was at work for the worst of it—I don't normally wear pants, but I crawled into soft joggers and clamped my thighs around the washcloth. Curled up on the rug in the nursery, I watched my baby, wincing as the clumpy soil drained from my vagina.

Sweetheart sniffed hungrily in her crib, chalky-white eyes nearly glowing through the wooden rungs keeping her in. After that first screaming fit following her birth, she was mostly quiet, as if she was committed to observing everything around her before making comment on it.

After changing my pad, I wash my hands and walk back to the nursery, cheerfully grinning and clapping my hands together when I see Sweetheart in her crib.

"Hi, baby!" I sing to her. "Here, let's get you out of there, and we'll have another shot at the bottle. But don't tell anyone! It's our little secret."

I spread out one of Sweetheart's blankets on the floor of the nursery. It's densely soft, the color of tea with milk, waffle knit with organic yarn. I made it myself, and I wonder if there's a photo opportunity here as I adjust the edges, returning to the crib to lift my daughter out. I gently place Sweetheart on her back on the fluffy blanket and step aside, pulling out my phone.

Sweetheart's eyes are open, unblinking and vacant. The whiteness that once unnerved me in the creature I now find lovely. Looking into her eyes is like looking at fog captured in a jar, or spider silk that's been melted down and mixed with milk. Her eyes remind me of the most beautiful parts of nature: mist on a lake in the fall; the clouds that cap the highest peaks. Sweetheart's eyes reflect things I have never seen, probably *will* never see, and I love her all the more for it.

But others will not see the beauty in her inhuman eyes, only shifting snowy sclerae framed by black veins. I won't be able to take a photo of her face. Not when she's awake like this. Instead, I angle the camera so it captures her bare feet resting against the blanket, her toes like pearls.

"Look," I croon, leaning over Sweetheart, her face only a few inches away from my own bare feet. I bend farther to show her the photo. "We'll have to edit it. Your skin looks a bit green in this lighting. But it's cute, right?"

Sweetheart swiftly rolls over on her blanket in a way no newborn should ever be able to move, and before I understand what's happening, she has bitten off two of the toes on my right foot.

She takes the pinkie toe and the one next to it, mouth chomping down, the bones snapping in her mouth as blood dribbles down her face.

Agony starts quiet and becomes louder as the shock wears off.

"Oh," I moan. "Oh my God."

As if she can understand me, Sweetheart glances up, jerkily craning her head. No baby should be able to move their neck like that. No *human* should be able to move their neck like that.

Sweetheart watches me while she crunches on the toes, blinking, and then returns her attention to my burning foot, the blood pumping from the toe stumps she left behind. I am frozen, trembling in pain, trying to wrap my head around what just happened.

But my daughter isn't done. She considers the red gushing from my wound and staining her adorable blanket. Sweetheart swallows my toes, leans forward again, and fastens her lips around the end of my foot. Her mouth is like a warm suck-erfish; I'm the bottle, and she's drinking from me. I expect to feel her needlelike teeth again, but she feeds happily, silently, for several minutes until she pulls back, sucking on her hands.

"Oh," I whisper, looking down at my foot, my jaw ajar.

The chewed-up flesh has closed over. A thin layer of reddish skin covers the spot where my two toes used to be. A newly healed scar.

I am faint and swaying. I wonder how much blood I lost while Sweetheart fed. The pain is dulled but throbbing, inconsistent and eye watering. It could have been worse; Sweet-heart's saliva has sealed the wound, preventing me from bleed-ing out.

Sweetheart rolls to her back, kicking her legs happily, gurgling, blood bubbles popping on her lips as she smiles up at me.

That's when I get a good look at the teeth I missed.

I could have sworn she didn't have those yesterday. But now, her mouth open and her face alight with satisfaction, I can see a thin line of razor-sharp teeth. *Teeth* might be the wrong word. They look more like snake fangs; the small but deadly mouth of a reptile.

I stumble off the blanket, clutching my chest, looking at the blood splatters on the waffle knit. I'm not sure those stains will come out. Damn. I really loved that blanket. Now I'll have to throw it away before Graham sees. My gaze returns again to the gap in my toes, heart pounding, not quite accept-ing that two parts of my body are fully gone. I keep expecting them to erupt from the ends of the stumps as if this is all some twisted joke.

Sweetheart lets out a screech, a burbling, baby yelp that denotes joy. This is the most vocal and active she's been since her birth.

She should not have teeth yet, especially not the ones she has. She should not be able to move like that. She should not have blood smeared around her lips from the toes she eagerly ripped from my body.

But she finally ate. And she seems happy. Elated, even. If this is what Sweetheart needs to live, I can't possibly deny her. My pulse slows, and I drop to my knees on the floor beside my daughter, placing a hand on her stomach. The soft cotton of her onesie, which is oatmeal colored with beige buttons, is warm under my palm. Sweetheart shrieks again, a delighted crowing, bicycling her legs.

I think of the raw meat I craved during pregnancy—the raw meat I continue to eat despite giving birth. I tried to return to cooked foods and vegetables in the days after Sweetheart's arrival, but I threw them up instantly. It seems I have the taste now, and I can't go back. The deception continues—cooking Graham the same meals he's come to expect while I feed myself thick slabs of red meat when he's not around.

"Meat, darling? Is that want you want? We can do that," I say.

I set up the baby monitor so that I can see Sweetheart on the floor and hurriedly limp down the stairs, hopping over the baby gates I've already installed. Phone in hand, keeping an eye on my daughter, who gurgles happily in black and white on the blanket, I throw open the door of the fridge. My stomach churns in hunger as I tear open a packet of organically raised hamburger meat, breaking off a hunk and slamming the door closed. I vault back up the stairs and return to the nursery, panting.

I crouch by Sweetheart again, my missing toes pulsing with my racing heart, a muted blot of pain in my foot. I am not scared of my daughter, but I hold my breath when I lean down to lift her head so she won't choke on the food I'm offering. Sweetheart doesn't attempt to bite me again, only stares up at me with her milky gaze.

"Here you go, baby," I say, breaking off a crumble of meat from the piece I grabbed and hovering it above Sweetheart's mouth.

Sweetheart's lips snap shut. She squints at me as if completely offended.

"Come on, love," I murmur. "This is what you want, right?"

I nudge the meat toward her closed lips, and she twists her head, face crumpling as tears form in her white eyes.

"It's OK," I insist, popping the meat into my own mouth instead, chewing it with exaggeration. "See? Good!"

Maybe she can tell I'm lying. The meat doesn't taste the same as it did before. It hasn't gone bad; I've checked. But the piece I chew isn't satiating the way it was a few weeks ago. It's bland and dry, like cereal without milk or salad without dressing.

Sweetheart turns her face away resolutely when I try again, tempting her with another piece, this time one that drips with myoglobin. She starts to sniffle, and I can't imagine what the influencers I follow would say if they could see me trying to force-feed my newborn raw meat.

I would be canceled so fast.

Maybe she's not hungry? Maybe my toes were enough for her?

I don't want Sweetheart to start bawling, so I leave the rest of the meat on the ruined baby blanket and hold her, singing a tuneless song and rocking back and forth on my knees, trying to ignore the bizarre sensation of absence on my right foot.

My comforting movements aren't settling Sweetheart, though. She's grumbling and fussing, her little fists coming up to rub at her eyes, her mouth bloodstained.

I sigh, putting her back on the blanket. "OK. Wait one minute."

I run back downstairs, returning with the sharpest knife we have. It's quite small—I use it for deboning. Sweetheart perks up when she sees me come back into the nursery with the knife, although she can't possibly know what it's for. She doesn't even have object permanence yet. But there's an intelligence present in my daughter's face that makes me wonder. She is a special baby. All the books in the world couldn't prepare me for her.

I remove my dress, pulling it over my head, the knife disappearing in the darkness of the fabric for a moment. Dropping the dress to the floor, I kick it to the side, bearing down on the pattering of my heart and the sour dryness in my mouth.

Sweetheart lies on the bloody blanket, staring up at me, expectant.

"I love you this much," I whisper to her.

I pinch a fold of skin on my stomach, which is loose and stretched from the impression of my daughter inside me, and pull it away from my body with one hand, slicing down with the other. My aim is surprisingly steady and true—the knife passes through the outstretched skin with a keen swiftness, separating a small chunk of flesh from my stomach.

Sweetheart kicks her feet, her chubby cheeks shaking from the movement, her lips parting once again to reveal her lizard teeth. She gurgles at me as I drop heavily to my knees, the wound on my stomach freely bleeding, the piece of flesh shaking in my grip. There's a fierce burning around the cut, and every drop of blood that races from it forms a hot tire track on my bare skin.

Tipping Sweetheart's head up again, I gently offer her a piece of me. She snaps it up eagerly, making quick work of it. She used to be inside me, so maybe it's right that there are bits of me now inside her.

"Come on," I say softly, lifting her to my stomach. "Eat up."

She latches on to the wound and suckles, making happy grunting noises against my body. Her feet cease their kicking, and her tiny fists curl like seashells as she nestles against my stomach, red smearing her lips.

I sigh, a jagged, broken expelling of air that sinks to the very bottom of my body. The pain is ebbing—Sweetheart's attachment is slowing down the bleeding, and the burning is dying down to a flicker of embers.

She must be hungry after days of not eating, so I allow her to have her fill, even when I get light-headed and black fuzzy spots appear in my vision. Finally, Sweetheart pulls away from my stomach with a squelching sound. Carefully placing her back on the ruined blanket, I examine my body.

In the same way my toes are now covered in reddish-pink skin that quietly smarts and hides any evidence of a gruesome injury, the cut is healed. There's a divot in my flesh, evidence of the missing piece, but the open wound I created is gone.

Hands on my knees, naked save for my undergarments, I shiver. My daughter needs my flesh and blood to survive. In a way, it makes sense. She was created from me and she was so early—perhaps she needs more of me to continue growing.

Not daring to stand up yet knowing how dizzy I am, I watch Sweetheart, who has already fallen asleep. Her breathing is steady and deep, and the rise and fall of her chest soothes me, grounds me back into my body. Twinges of pain ricochet in my right foot and abdomen, but they are faint, already memories. It doesn't appear that I will have to die to feed my daughter—how she eats will allow me to stay alive.

There's gore smeared on her face, so I crawl over to the baby-changing station and grab the wet wipes before dragging myself back to Sweetheart. I dab at her mouth, gently rubbing off the blood, turning the wet wipe pink.

My heart is so full of love for her. Isn't motherhood all about sacrifice anyway? If this is what she needs, I have to do whatever it takes to feed her. I am happy to give up parts of myself to make sure my daughter has a healthy life.

"You are the best thing that's ever happened to me," I say to my sleeping child, setting aside the wet wipe, hoping she's dreaming.

I take a photo of her, eyes closed, blood clean from her cheeks, red-soaked blanket cropped out, and post it to my story with the words *My little angel.*

19

THE NEXT DAY, Renee shows up in our driveway fifteen minutes after Graham pulls away for work. I haven't seen her since our awkward conversation about what I really "want," but she did text me several times afterward to apologize and tell me what a good job I'm doing.

Even so, I think about leaving her on the porch, but she's banging on the door, ringing the awful buzzer, squealing through the frosted glass, "Oh my God, you had the baby?! Already?"

I have to start putting some boundaries in place here—what if she had arrived twenty minutes earlier and she and Graham had run into each other? He might have realized that she isn't my midwife.

"Please text me before coming over, OK?" I say when I finally open the door for Renee, who sails into the house with the energy of a bull in a ceramic studio.

I don't think Renee has absorbed my words at all. She's racing through the hallway, exploding into the kitchen, her head on a swivel.

"Where is she? Oh, why didn't you call me? I saw online! I saw your beautiful social media posts about her. Camille, I'm so happy! Please, let me see her! Where is she?" Renee's vibe is so frantic and enthused I'm a bit taken aback. It seems . . . dispro- portionate, given she hasn't known me that long.

"Um, she's sleeping, actually. Upstairs."

"Oh, please, can we go see her?" Renee asks, literally jump- ing up and down in my kitchen. "I won't wake her, I promise. I want to look. The photos online weren't enough."

I've never had this happen before—a follower who can fol- low me in real life. Graham's friends thought my accounts were too "girly" and they never bothered. But Renee's admiration for me and my life is infectious. Sweetheart is sleeping and the nurs- ery is dark. It can't hurt to let Renee take a peek. I haven't been able to show off my beautiful child in person yet, and Renee is always bursting with compliments.

"Fine," I relent. "But only for a minute."

As we ascend the staircase, a faint throbbing echoes in my foot. My missing toes are hidden by thick wool socks, and I hope Renee won't notice the loose fabric at the far end of my right foot. Graham sure didn't.

"Sweetheart. That's such a charming name," Renee whispers as she follows me down the upstairs hallway. "Not what I would have chosen, but very cute. How are you feeling? Is she a premie? I can't believe you just gave birth. What was your due date again?"

I turn around as we reach the open door of the nursery, smil- ing away the threat of the frown on my face, placing a finger to my lips. "Quiet, please. I'm sure you know how hard it can be to get newborns down."

"Absolutely," Renee says, lowering her voice even further. "Not a peep."

With the curtains drawn and the night-light off, the nursery is dark enough that Sweetheart's greenish skin isn't noticeable. Her face is turned toward the wall, and she snuffles in her sleep, white eyes thankfully shut.

Renee places both hands on the crib and leans over, dark hair falling past her ears. Her face is shining as she silently coos at my daughter. I fight the urge to rip the woman away from the crib and shove her out of the nursery, slamming the door behind her. It feels strange to share my daughter with someone new; I can't help the protective instincts rising within.

After five minutes of staring at my sleeping baby like a creep, Renee is finally satisfied and nods to me, the two of us heading back downstairs where we can talk while I keep an eye on Sweetheart via the baby monitor.

I don't offer Renee food or drink this time. I don't want her to stay long; I'm not lonely anymore. I have my daughter.

"You know, if you ever need a break or a babysitter, I am available!" Renee says, her voice slightly breathless as if the thought has overwhelmed her with emotion. "A nice, quiet house could be good for you. I could take her over to my place for a few hours. Or a half day, even! You must not be sleeping much."

She doesn't know jack shit.

There's no way I would ever let Sweetheart be alone with this woman. I barely know her, and besides, Sweetheart has to be protected. I'm lucky she's asleep right now. I can't imagine Renee's reaction if she saw my daughter with her eyes open.

"Thanks, but we have childcare," I lie.

"Well, come on!" Renee says, stepping closer to me in the kitchen. Her teeth are slightly purple, as if she's been sucking on grape-flavored hard candy. "Tell me everything!"

Is she slurring, or is she overly excited?

"I'd love to," I say, inching back, examining her elastic band mouth and the puffy blue coat she hasn't bothered to take off. "But we actually have a doctor's appointment we need to get to. Maybe some other time."

Renee sighs, eyes squinting. "Damn! I suppose that's important, though. Go often, make sure everything is normal and uneventful!"

Those are two words I would never use to describe Sweetheart's first week on earth. "That's right," I reply instead. "Her health comes first."

"I have to say, I'm relieved to hear you say that," Renee admits, dragging her feet as I usher her toward the front door yet again.

I pause before the hall mirror, catching sight of my wan skin, my thin hair. "What do you mean?"

Renee shifts, licks her stained lips. "From your accounts it seems like you might not . . . believe in that. You know, with you doing the whole tradwife thing and all. But then I thought to myself *No, she's got a science background; she knows how important it is!*"

My fists curl, and I smile hard. "I'd do anything to keep my baby safe."

Renee nods, returning my smile, though hers seems smaller than usual. "Just keep her away from the forest."

I pause before the threshold. This is the second time Renee's brought up the woods to me. "Is there something I need to know? Graham said farm animals sometimes go missing, but . . ."

Renee wrings her hands. "I don't want to worry you."

"Renee. Please."

She sighs, glances around furtively. "Farm animals are . . . taken. Large animals, too, not just chickens and ducks. Cows. Horses. They almost never find any remains, which is strange. It's become a local legend at this point. They say that every few years or so, like clockwork, a hunter goes into the woods to kill whatever bear or big cat lives there." She grimaces. "Not all of them come back out."

My mouth dries. "People have *died* in there?"

Renee shakes her head. "Oh, I doubt it. Local superstition, you know. But there's definitely something eating farm animals, so best to stay away regardless."

"I see," I murmur, wondering if Graham knows any of this. "Well, thanks for telling me." Striding forward, I open the door pointedly, waving Renee through. "I'll see you around."

She obeys the social cue, weaving slightly as she steps outside. Turning around, she throws over her shoulder, "Seriously, though. You ever need help, let me know. I'd love to babysit!"

As she wanders over to the driveway, I imagine running up behind her and smashing her face into the ground, driving pebbles of gravel into her skin, shattering her cheekbones.

I smile and wave as she drives off.

*　*　*

On Friday, I do a live video to officially introduce my baby to the world. To her future fans. Only a couple hundred people attend my live; Mara gets thousands, but this is more than I had the last time I did one of these, pre-Sweetheart.

We're set up on the couch in the living room, the phone propped on the coffee table a few feet away. My daughter is nuzzled against my chest, unnerving eyes closed. I've positioned a warm yellow light off-camera so that its shine offsets some of Sweetheart's strange coloring, and I've wrapped her in a dark-gray blanket to explain away her skin's hue.

Oh, it's the lighting and the blanket, I imagine saying to anyone who notices.

There's another blanket draped across my legs. The countryside has fully embraced fall now, so my body is hidden away under a long, white wool dress, but I'm not taking any chances—the scarred, shiny skin on my thighs and stomach must stay out of sight. No one will understand that I feed Sweetheart not from my breasts but from my blood.

I've been wearing thick socks around the house, and today my feet are also shoved into warm, shearling slippers that completely hide the fact that I've lost two toes.

"Let's see here," I say, squinting at the camera, reading the floating comments from my followers. "Oh gosh, hi, Andrea! I loved your last post with your kids in their school room." I read her question out loud slowly for the people tuning in: "Andrea asks, 'What are your plans for schooling? You look gorgeous, by the way.' Oh, Andrea, you're so sweet!" I laugh, noticing Sweetheart's blanket slipping in the video and fixing it. I toss my braid over my shoulder. I do *not* look gorgeous—I am getting very good at concealing my patchy hair, which hasn't grown back, my spindly limbs, and my drawn, pale skin. It's amazing what a brushful of bronzer, hats, and autumnal layers can cover up when you get creative.

I hide a wince as I shift around on the couch cushion. Sweetheart is heavy—it's like I'm holding a bag of bricks in my lap instead of a baby, and I have to move gingerly. I am still sore and swollen from childbirth. There are gaps in my stomach and thighs that weren't there before. The skin has healed, but the feeding spots are tender.

I'm also stalling. I don't know how to answer Andrea's question because it's not something I've ever thought about or talked about with Graham. Which is . . . odd. Then again, I thought we had longer. I had no idea I would get pregnant and give birth in the span of two months.

I always assumed we would send our kids to school, but the new house is so far from civilization. And Sweetheart is . . . different from other children.

"We're talking through a few options," I say, not wanting to leave too much dead air in the live video. "But I have to admit I'm leaning toward homeschooling. That seems to be the best option, given our location and values. And you've made it look so amazing,

Andrea! Shout-out to Andrea for being such a vocal homeschooling advocate for our community! Oh, here's another question: 'Who is your biggest inspiration?'" I laugh and adjust my seat once again. "That's easy! Mara Shoemaker is a pillar in our community, and if I can be half the woman she is, I'll be doing my job right."

An explosion of hearts lights up my screen as people watching send their silent approval of my statement. Mara isn't on my live—she's too popular and busy for that—but her fans are everywhere, and one of them might report back to her. Who you know is everything online; Mara follows me, and now I need her engagement. If Mara tags you in a story or a post, you can gain thousands of followers overnight.

Another question pops up on the screen, and I unthinkingly read it out loud before realizing what it says: "'Are you a real tradwife or are you faking it?'"

A curdling heat swills in my gut. My right eyelid twitches, and I smile to hide the grit of my teeth. Another comment comes immediately after, and this time I'm not stupid enough to parrot it back like I'm using a teleprompter: *I saw you used to be a scientist. What gives?*

I dig my nails into my palm, the piercing pain sharpening my thoughts.

For God's sake. I wasn't even a proper scientist; I had an interest in school, and I dropped out within a year! But clearly someone saw Melody's comments on my post all those weeks ago and took them the wrong way.

"I am committed to being the best wife and mother I can be," I say primly to the camera. "Mara left Hollywood to fulfill her duty, and I left behind my past to do the same."

A cluster of hearts sprinkle the screen—less than before, but enough that my breath untangles from my rib cage and my shoulder blades roll down my back. My palm is dampening; I glance down at the beads of blood carved in my skin from my nails.

In my lap, Sweetheart's nose twitches. I look at the camera and then back at my daughter. Her face is scrunching up, and she's starting to make grousing noises.

She's waking up.

"I, uh, well, it seems like my little lady here needs her diaper changed!" I tell the camera, trying to keep the panic from my voice. I have to end this live before Sweetheart opens her eyes or I get any other awful, judgmental questions. "This was a short one, but I'll be back next time to chat with you all!"

Sweetheart yawns and cracks her eyes open.

My free hand shoots forward and I grab the phone, raising it high so that only my face fills the frame. "Bye, everyone, see you later!"

I end the live video, heart pounding. I sigh, dropping the phone next to me on the couch, groaning as I shift Sweetheart so I can get her body weight off my knees.

She gurgles up at me, fussing. I lied—she doesn't have a dirty diaper. Sweetheart's eliminations are infrequent and unusual. Her urine is white, the same color as her eyes, and her bowel movements have the consistency and color of wet soil. In fact, they *smell* like soil: damp, packed earth that slides out of her like spilled cement. When Sweetheart goes to the bathroom, she freezes and smiles, baring her reptile teeth. I had prepared myself for blowouts and foul-smelling eliminations, but the worst part about Sweetheart's defecations is how heavy they are. I have to double-bag them and dump them in the dying wheat field behind the house.

No, when she gets fidgety and vocal like this, she's hungry.

"All righty," I say, hefting her to my chest and carrying her into the kitchen where her high chair is set up. She keeps trying to twist around and lick the spots of blood on my palm.

Sweetheart is surpassing baby milestones like they're unimportant items on a hastily created checklist—she can already sit up on her own, recognize herself in the mirror, and babble non-sensical vocalizations. Interestingly, she only does these things when it's just me and her. When Graham is home, she sleeps. When Renee pops in to drop off yet another bag of unwanted baby items, which she's done twice since seeing us earlier in the week, she sleeps. Sweetheart spends the majority of her time in dreamland, but it's curious how she times it so perfectly.

She grumbles in her high chair, kicking her plump legs and waving her fists. Sweetheart's snow-blanketed eyes grow wide and eager as she squalls at me.

"Yes, yes, I know," I say, searching for the deboning knife.

There. I left it drying in the bamboo dish rack.

We have a process now. I cut open a garbage bag, then place it on the floor underneath Sweetheart's chair to catch any drops or spills. Removing my layers, I yank up my dress and throw the skirt over my shoulder, deciding on a spot for today. Stomach is easiest. It's the most accessible for her, and the skin is still stretchy.

With precision, I cut the flesh, ignoring the initial blast of pain that radiates around the site, placing the wet knife on the high chair tray and sidling up next to my daughter so she can latch on.

I hold my dress up, breathing deeply as she feeds. She never takes too much. In the three days since she ate my toes, she's never fed so much that I've fainted, and for that I'm grateful.

When she's done, the skin already starting to heal, I drop my dress back down, wipe off her blood-smeared face, and wrap anything stained or bloody in the garbage bag at my feet, throwing it all away. I'll take it out to the cans later, before Graham comes home.

After feeding Sweetheart, I leave her in the high chair in the kitchen so she can watch while I eat my daily meal of raw steak. It's been hard, lately, to stomach anything else. The steak's lackluster flavor grows more prominent every day, like chewing gum that's been in your mouth for far too long. The hunger gnaws inside me even after I gorge myself. It's not enough. It's like there's not enough *life* in it.

Sweetheart yawns; she's ready to go back to sleep again. She only wakes to feed, and occasionally to stare at me in silence, as if trying to understand the face she sees every minute of her waking life.

I carry her upstairs to her crib, and she's fast asleep by the time I settle her in. My body aches as I return downstairs. I've fallen way behind on my chores since giving birth. It's not that Sweetheart really takes up much time; it's that I'm not capable of the speed and thoroughness I had before her. Everything takes forever, every movement is costly, and the motivation I used to have for keeping a clean home has dwindled.

I start to tidy up, but when I enter the living room to grab my glass of water—the only thing I can drink these days that doesn't make me queasy—movement catches my eye.

There's a shadow at the sliding glass door. A dark shape I barely get a glimpse of, flickering by the open space of the backyard and the fields beyond it.

By the time I hurry over, though, there's nothing there. Only a view of the yard, the brown grass, the slowly withering stalks of wheat, which are becoming muted and crunchy. I stare out the door for a moment, watching the waving wheat, looking for motion. After a few seconds, I spot something lying on the ground on the other side of the glass, resting on the concrete step that leads to the yard.

"Is that a . . ."

A dead hare. Brown body crumpled a foot from the house. I rub my eyes, making sure it's real. Its neck has been broken.

Saliva gathers in my mouth as I stand there, an eagerness burrowing in my belly. I imagine the scent of the cooling body through the glass; I imagine what it might feel like to bite into its gamy flesh.

No, I think, pulling away. *No.*

When I look up, the creature is standing among the stalks watching me, sunlight texturizing its leathery wings.

Without thinking about it, I slide open the glass door and step out, eyes locked on the creature. The air smells of dry leaves and dust, and sunlight cascades on the wheat field, making it shimmer.

The creature and I look at one another for a minute, and then it melds itself back into the field, gray skin blending with the tall stalks until all I can see is the pale glow of its eyes.

Swallowing, I turn my attention back to the hare, nudging it with my foot as if checking to make sure it's really dead.

The wheat field whispers around me. The house is an island in a sea of dying gold. Holding my breath, I shift the hare with my foot, moving it off the concrete step and to the side of the house so it's no longer visible from the doorway.

Returning to the house, I resolutely ignore the growling of my stomach, the wetness of my mouth.

20

G RAHAM ACTUALLY COMES home in time for dinner tonight, greedily lapping up the butternut squash soup I made from scratch, dunking the folic acid–free sourdough bread into the yellow broth and tearing at it ferociously before moving on to the grilled chicken.

I hurried to get everything prepared for Graham's arrival; I was distracted after finding the hare in the backyard.

"You sure are hungry tonight," I say, my voice light.

More and more often since Sweetheart's birth, I've felt like I have nothing to talk to Graham about. It should be the opposite. We should be constantly texting and talking about our daughter. But he's so physically distant, and he is completely content to have me handle everything baby related.

What did we used to talk about? I rack my brain, trying to think. His work, I suppose. His friends. His interests. His life. Occasionally I would offer up information about my day or how my chores went, but I could always tell Graham was half listening, being polite and nodding in all the right places without really absorbing anything I was saying.

But now my husband is home, it's a Friday night, and I should be making more of an effort to get us back to where we used to be. That was the whole point of this, after all.

"How was your day?" I ask. The dead hare outside our house floats into my mind, and I push it away. "Tell me everything."

"Oh, you know, normal," Graham says. "Unexciting. I forgot to eat the lunch you packed, so I'm starving. This is great, by the way," he adds, stabbing at the chicken.

"Thanks." I force a smile, pushing the food around my own plate, glancing at my phone to make sure Sweetheart is soundly sleeping in her crib. "I'm glad you like it. And I'm glad you're here for dinner. We've missed you."

"Yeah," Graham says, swallowing a hunk of half-chewed chicken. "I was going to talk to you about that. I'm going to try to be more present, OK? I know how hard you're working. I want to provide a good life for us. And Sweetheart. But I want to be around more too."

My heart lifts, and my lips spread wider into a more authentic smile. "It's so good to hear you say that, babe. I want that too."

It might have taken a while, but Graham is finally coming back to me. Thank God.

Graham stays off his phone the whole dinner. No texting, no scrolling, no disappearing in the conversation to "check" on something.

Maybe they had a fight, the voice I hate whispers in my ear. *Maybe he's pissed off, so he's coming back to what he knows. What's easy.*

I heave the traitorous thought away. There's no truth to that, and I won't dwell on it, no matter what my subconscious might mutter. I have to stay positive: Men like Graham who have wives like me don't need to cheat.

After dinner, I clean up and Graham helps, drying the plates and leaving them in our bamboo rack.

"What happened here?" he asks, tracing a finger on the window above the sink, finally noticing the claw mark the creature left behind weeks ago. "Looks like it's on the outside. Did a pebble hit the house or something?"

My throat tightens, and I shrug. "No idea. I think we're done, darling. Want to come with me to check on Sweetheart?"

Distracted, Graham follows me up the stairs, and I feel his eyes on my backside as he trails behind me. The vintage dark-orange dress I'm wearing hugs my waist and falls all the way down to the floor, covering up my body, which refuses to return to normal.

In the nursery, Graham and I tiptoe to the crib, the room glowing in the soft yellow of the night-light. We watch our daughter sleep, one fist curled near her head, the other down by her side. In the dim lighting, in her eggshell onesie, eyes tightly closed, Sweetheart looks like any other baby.

"We sure got lucky," Graham says, smiling down at Sweetheart, arms wrapped around my shoulders. We watch her face twitch in slumber together. "She's such an easy baby."

He *would* think that. He's not home when she's awake and hungry. He doesn't see her eyes, and he doesn't look close enough to notice her gray-tinged skin or the fact that she already has teeth.

"Yes," I agree anyway. "She is perfect." And though she is difficult and harder to understand than an ordinary baby, I'm not lying. Sweetheart is everything to me.

My husband kisses the side of my neck and strokes my shoulder. "She sure is."

Graham's being strangely affectionate this evening, and it's so unexpected, so rare now, that I'm not sure what to do with it.

I begin to picture a peaceful evening cuddled on the couch, watching a nature documentary or something that isn't sports, when Graham's hand slides to my hip.

"Come on," he says huskily, pulling me from the nursery and into our bedroom.

A tendril from my heart reaches out and fastens on to Sweetheart's crib—a reluctance to leave my daughter and the safety of the nursery. But Graham's grip is strong, and the attachment breaks.

In the bedroom, Graham kisses me, but it's mechanical, stale, like he's performing a scene from a script he's overpracticed. His breath starts to come heavy against my mouth, and I close my eyes and try to enjoy the sensation of his hands running down my sides, scrunching the fabric of my dress and pulling it up.

Yet I can't help comparing. The creature's touch was soft and hungry at the same time. Its hands, scaled and clawed but smooth underneath, were much more adept than Graham's. Pressed underneath the creature, I grew wet and eager. Pressed against Graham, smelling his cologne and the hint of flowers, my vagina tenses, remembering the violence that ripped through it only a week ago.

Women should wait up to six weeks before having sex after childbirth. The strange, soil-like lochia is still dribbling out of me. My legs ache and plead for rest. And I don't want Graham to see my body—the new scars, the missing toes, the frail limbs. Even though Graham and I haven't had intercourse in what feels like forever, even though it's my duty as a wife to always say yes to his needs, I can't do it.

"Graham," I whisper, pulling away. Graham ignores me and transfers his mouth to my throat, lapping against the delicate skin there. "It's too early. I just gave birth. I'm sorry."

My husband detaches himself from my neck with a suction cup sound. Drawing back, he blinks at me in confusion. "What?"

I've never denied him before. Never. "Sorry," I repeat. "We're supposed to wait six weeks."

I just had a fucking baby, I want to add, but I could never talk to him like that. Yet the thought itself is new; I don't usually allow things like that to breach my waking mind.

"Oh," Graham says, and I look away from the bulge in his pants as he runs a hand through his scruffy beard. "Right. Well, maybe you can . . ." He glances down, raises an eyebrow, smirking at me.

I used to think that was sexy. The way he wouldn't *ask* for what he wanted, instead relying on me to intuit his needs. The sad thing is that there's no question about what he desires right now. He wants his wife, the one who recently gave birth, to drop to her knees on the uncomfortably hard bedroom floor and fellate him yards away from their sleeping daughter.

But if I have to take Graham's throbbing, average-sized dick in my mouth right now and pretend I like it when he pumps against the back of my throat, I will throw up.

A month ago I would have done it, no questions asked. Two months ago I would have begged for the opportunity. Now the thought fills me with disgust, and it makes me pause.

For the past few years, my life has been about Graham. I've been terrified of losing him, terrified of letting him down. Yet now I am disinterested in something I could easily do to make him happy. I think of Sweetheart's precious face; I think of the framed photo I created of Mara and me. There are other people who cherish me now. It's not only Graham. And my daughter depends on me more than Graham ever could—I'm literally giving her my body.

Perhaps that's why I'm hesitating. Perhaps that's why there's a noticeable lack of guilt in my heart. I've already decided: I am going to do what I've never done before. I am going to turn my husband down. Because his love isn't the only love in my life anymore.

"Sorry, babe," I say again, heart pounding, bracing for his disappointment. "I'm really tired. I'm not feeling up to it tonight. Maybe another day?"

Graham stares at me with his mouth open, expression slack. He blinks several times as if trying to wake himself up. He looks like a fish caught in a net, too silly and thoughtless to understand what has happened to it.

"You . . . you're serious?"

A bristle goes through my shoulders, making me stand straighter. I fight the instinct to apologize again and nod, thinking of Mara and my daughter. I don't need to rely on Graham for unadulterated devotion anymore. "Yeah."

"Oh."

Flickers of emotion pass across my husband's face—alarm, shock, suspicion, and finally, resentment. It's as clear as the sun in a blue sky. His thick dark brows do all the work for me, spelling out exactly what he's feeling.

"Maybe next time," I say, trying to keep it light. "When I've recovered from childbirth."

Graham doesn't smile. "Right. Your health comes first."

"Thanks for understanding," I say, though he clearly doesn't. "I'm going to get ready for bed. Love you."

He doesn't say it back. He lets me go into the bathroom without another word.

*   *   *

When Graham has fallen asleep, I check on Sweetheart. She's moved slightly, but she continues to slumber peacefully. I suppose

I'm lucky that she always sleeps through the night. I'm never waking up at three in the morning to feed her like other mothers. No, all I have to do is cut off my flesh and let her drink my blood.

I slip from the nursery and ease down the stairs, moving carefully and quietly, creeping through the dark first floor. I know the house better now; I know where to dodge the coffee table and where I've put Sweetheart's bouncy chair. I know exactly how to get to the sliding glass door without turning on a single light.

Gently, I unlock the door and step outside into the cold night. The air nips against my skin, eagerly chewing through my thin cotton pajamas and feasting on my flesh. The thick socks I wear protect the pads of my feet from the rough chill of the concrete step, and my missing toes wiggle as if they are still there.

I turn the corner and kneel down next to the dead hare. I run a hand through its coarse fur, trying to swallow the hot saliva gathering in my mouth and failing. A string of drool escapes from my bottom lip, reaching for the hare desperately.

The wind rustles the dying stalks of wheat in the field, a chorus of half-life whispers that urge me on. I pick up the hare, its body cold in my hands but smelling of trees and fields and *energy*.

The moon peeks its face out from behind a comforter of clouds to watch as I rip the dead animal apart with my bare hands, unable to wait or pause to get a knife from the kitchen. I devour the hare raw, blood spotting my face, fur sticking in my teeth. Its meat is heady and orgasmic. Though it's been dead for a while, it tastes fresh in a way the steaks in our fridge don't. The meat's texture is buttery and salty and conjures up images of wildfires and thunderstorms. Maybe it's in my mind, but it even feels warm, not barely thawed and cold like the meat I was eating before.

I inhale the meal, and the groans in my stomach finally quiet.

When I am done, I slink over to the wheat field and throw the bones and gristle into the stalks.

I cannot see it, but I sense the creature is watching.

CHAPTER

21

I HAVE ALWAYS PRIDED myself on my ability to multitask, balancing all the things I need to do to keep a house running smoothly and flawlessly. I have always scoffed at the online trolls who say what I do isn't a real job or who say women like me must be stupid or boring. The amount of work I do in one day would astound them. But now, to my chagrin, I am floundering, juggling too many things at once to be successful at any of them.

Sweetheart is my priority, obviously. But I'm also cooking, cleaning, doing the laundry, raking the dead leaves outside the house, itemizing the mail for Graham to look at later, creating content and engaging with my rapidly growing social media accounts, and secretly consuming a stream of dead animals that have been left in the backyard.

It's a lot.

I text Graham, taking a break from the constant ping of social media notifications to check in with him after I finish my morning's chores: *We still on for date night?*

I'm standing in the laundry room under the stairs, brow beaded with sweat despite the chilly weather and the new house's inability to retain heat. Sweetheart sleeps in her playpen in the living room; her little snorts echo from the other side of the wall.

I'm surprised when Graham's response comes quickly: *Definitely. I'll pick up some wine.*

I'll have to pretend to drink it. The only beverage I can stomach now is tepid water. Too cold and my teeth hurt, too hot and my stomach twists. But it doesn't matter; at least Graham and I are trying.

It's been a month since Sweetheart's birth, and Graham has started to talk about taking her west to see his family for the holidays. I convinced him Thanksgiving is too soon to be traveling with a newborn and suggested they visit in the spring instead.

"Or Christmas, if they want," I said, knowing his mother hates flying and would much prefer we come to them. If we invite them for Christmas this year, at such late notice, they won't come, and I'll be off the hook. I'll have one more year to figure out what to do about Sweetheart's . . . differences.

"That's a good idea," he said, but there was a touch of chilliness in his voice.

Graham has withdrawn even more since I rejected his advances a few weeks ago. I am healed now—it hasn't been the suggested six weeks yet, but ever since I started feeding Sweetheart what she really likes, I've noticed a change in my body. I'm stronger, healthier. The wounds I create in my flesh to feed Sweetheart heal quickly, but so do other wounds. The aches and tearing pain in my vagina have disappeared.

But I don't try to make it up to Graham, and even though I have loyalty and love for my husband, he notices how I've disentangled myself from him. His late nights have become later, and he has started sleeping over at "Bobby's" house at will.

I am losing him. I am finally ready to accept that—but the sting is mitigated by Sweetheart. She is exactly what I wanted, exactly what I hoped for. Someone I love unconditionally who will love me back. Someone I can take care of forever, knowing we will always be in each other's lives.

Even so, I am not willing to give up on Graham. Weekends have been hit or miss, but sometimes he stays in, letting me cook for him, holding a sleeping Sweetheart, watching TV.

"Is it normal that she sleeps this much?" he asked once. "I don't remember the last time I saw her awake."

That's because you haven't. Because you're never home.

"Newborns sleep a lot," I replied with an even tone. "Renee says she's perfect."

"She's kind of heavy," Graham remarked, hefting Sweetheart in his arms. "She looks big. Is this the size a newborn is supposed to be? And why is her skin that weird color? Are you sure she's not sick?"

My cheeks got hot, especially at the comments on her weight. I'd been hoping he wouldn't notice that our daughter has grown extraordinarily quickly since her birth, surpassing milestones she should have taken six months to get to. Her size is closer to a four-month-old than a one-month-old. I try to keep her wrapped in blankets as much as possible around Graham and Renee, who insists on visiting at least once a week.

I thought I had been hiding it well, but perhaps not.

"Graham, darling, this is what I'm here for, right?" I said, gently taking Sweetheart from him, my forearm muscles straining under her weight, and handing him a beer instead. "You trusted me to take care of everything for four years. Trust me now with our baby. I know what I'm doing. Everything is fine. Everything is normal."

It's a mark of how estranged we've become that Graham easily accepted me at my word. He was finally noticing the differences in his daughter, but he wasn't invested enough to truly care. Not when I was content and insisted it was unproblematic.

He's learned to not ask questions beyond *How was your day?*

But I'm not sure how much longer I can keep up this charade.

I sigh, leaning against the whirring dryer, letting the vibrations hum up and down the vertebrae of my spine. It's a Saturday, but Graham claimed he had to go in to the office to do some work he couldn't finish yesterday, and I didn't fight him, instead suggesting we do a date night when he returned. To my surprise, he agreed, but now I wonder what on earth we'll talk about. The sense of ease between us has been lost since Sweetheart's birth. Or maybe it was when we moved. It's hard to tell. Time has gotten gauzy and indistinct.

I tap over to Instagram, smiling at the red notifications that keep me company as the likes and comments from my recent posts—images of Sweetheart sleeping, a video of my "Perfect Mommy Life," a snapshot of the only corner of the kitchen I found time to clean—continue to flutter in. Checking my list of followers, my heart steadies when I see Mara's familiar profile picture at the top. Every day, sometimes multiple times a day, I check to make sure she's still following me. We're interacting more and more, commenting on each other's posts and sending messages about folic acid–free recipes. It's really happening—our friendship is blossoming, and it's all thanks to Sweetheart.

I scroll through my feed, stopping on a photo Andrea posted forty-six minutes ago. She's one of the more religious influencers I follow—the one who homeschools her six kids. The post that catches my eye is a simple image of a cornfield, the hint of a porch visible in the lower corner of the shot.

Andrea's flowery font overlaid on the photo has so many curli-cues and swirls that it takes me a few seconds to parcel out the words: *For if God did not spare angels when they sinned, but sent them to hell, putting them in chains of darkness to be held for judgment . . .*

The caption underneath discusses, in oblique, delicate ways, a recent betrayal the influencer experienced at the hands of someone she considered a friend. The comments are juicy, with people speculating on the gossip. I can't concentrate on that; her personal drama doesn't interest me. But the Bible verse Andrea has quoted, which the caption tells me is 2 Peter 2:4, has jogged something loose in my memory.

A fallen angel.

Graham talked about it once, very early on in our relation-ship, using it as an example of some of the darker parts of the Bible. But I can't recall specifics, and he breezed over the topic quickly, as if he didn't want to expose me to it.

Something about angels who left heaven and became demons.

I hold the phone tightly, and I try to release the tension in my chest with a big exhale. Locking my phone, I slip it into the pocket of the custard-colored cardigan I'm wearing. Out of sight, out of mind. I shouldn't be scrolling through social media anyway.

I have so much to do, and soon Sweetheart will need to eat.

*   *   *

Graham comes home late afternoon, smelling like apple cider and barbecue.

I wonder where he was. If he was really sitting in the office, finishing up reports and closing out tech tickets like he's not a C suite manager with employees who can do that for him. Maybe he was out and about, enjoying fall, eating and drinking without his wife and daughter.

"Hi, honey," I say, kissing his cheek obediently. "I'm making dinner now. It'll be ready in an hour or two. How does trout sound?"

"Great." Graham's voice is unenthused and his smile is stiff. "Although I wish you made lamb. I brought Merlot. Not the best pairing for trout."

Well, maybe if you communicated that to me, I could have made exactly what you wanted. I'm supposed to fucking read your mind and know you're buying red wine?

I blink, startled at the viciousness of my conscience, easing a hasty smile on my face to hide the wrinkling of my brow. "I'm sorry," I say, keeping my voice light. "Next time, let me know, and I can pair the meal with the wine."

Graham pauses, perhaps hearing something in my tone I was unable to erase, scrutinizing my face as he slides the bottle of wine onto the counter. "Yeah," he says finally, deciding what he heard must have been in his own head. "Sounds good."

He looks as handsome as ever in a brown flannel and dark jeans, and he pats my shoulder like I'm a good dog before navigating around the breakfast nook and settling on the couch in the living room.

"Hi, baby," Graham coos at Sweetheart, who is sleeping, as usual, on a blanket in her playpen.

I like to have her visible when I'm cooking and cleaning in the kitchen, and from this angle, I can see her over the breakfast bar, several yards away from the coffee table.

Graham flicks on the TV, clicking over to ESPN, wordlessly accepting the beer I crack open and carry to him in the living room. His eyes dart from the TV screen to Sweetheart, who is unbothered by the noise. Graham does this—he considers it spending time with his daughter, even though she's not awake, but it makes me nervous.

Sweetheart has recently fallen into a routine where she wakes and eats midday and then sleeps again until the middle of the night, when she'll wake to feed again. But if she breaks pattern and wakes up now, there will be no way to hide her eyes. Just because it hasn't happened yet doesn't mean it won't. She's a baby. A remarkable one, sure, but still unpredictable.

Cooking dinner is a tedious whirlwind of checking on my husband and sleeping baby, roasting fresh potatoes, baking the trout, and making an autumnal salad with squash, zucchini, and pomegranate—a recipe Mara sent me. I make sure to snap pictures of the finished results so I can post it, thanking and tagging her. Everyone needs to see how close we're getting.

My heart skips the entire time, waiting for a gasp from the other room, but Sweetheart's schedule sticks once again—she does not wake.

"Graham, dinner is ready," I inform him after setting the dining room table, laying out all the food. "Go ahead and get started while I put down Sweetheart."

"Great, thanks, babe." Graham, on his third beer, leans over the playpen to stroke Sweetheart's downy head and then slouches over to the table, nostrils flaring. "Smells great. I'll get the wine open. And maybe you can change while you're up there?"

Already lifting up Sweetheart, pressing her solid bulk against my chest, I glance down at my outfit, perplexed. Then I realize— I've been so busy today, torn in so many different directions, that I forgot to style myself the way I normally do.

I'm wearing soft taupe cotton joggers and a matching long-sleeved top with a half placket of wooden buttons. I am usually barefoot in our home, but I have used the approach of colder weather as an excuse to wear slippers, thick socks, and even shoes inside. Graham hasn't noticed I'm missing two toes, but apparently he notices right away if I dare to wear anything made for comfort instead of style.

Grimacing, I glance at Graham, considering his face. I am comfortable and warm. The shiny pink skin on my stomach and thighs is hidden away. The body that has changed drastically since my pregnancy is concealed—I am no longer limber and sun-kissed. My skin is sallow, my hair is getting darker, and all the time I spend carrying Sweetheart's heavy body around the house is giving me muscles where there used to be fragility.

But that is not who Graham married.

When I return downstairs, phone in hand to keep an eye on Sweetheart via the baby monitor, I'm wearing a cashmere ribbed midi dress in oatmeal that I've paired with a burnt-orange cardigan. I can't very well show my bare feet, so I've opted for suede moccasins instead. A matching oatmeal-colored bandanna covers my thinning, oily hair, and my makeup is neat and pristine.

"Much better," Graham says, smiling as I join him at the table. He's already started to eat, the smudges on his wineglass telling me he's had more than a few sips as well. "Everything is excellent."

He's putting in an effort tonight. It's the most complimentary he's been since I refused to perform oral on him a few weeks ago. Maybe that means he's forgiving me and warming up to the idea of being a loving family again.

Is that what you want?

If I could throttle that voice, I swear I would. Instead, I smile at Graham and start to pick at my plate of food. My true hunger is growing, gnawing at my insides and itching my intestines. All I want is fresh meat. Still warm. The blood so tart and steaming that you could almost imagine it pumping through the body. Viscera drooling through my hands and puddling at my feet. Licking a bone clean, sucking off the cartilage.

Hot saliva floods my mouth, and out of desperation, I try a bite of the trout and nearly gag. How the hell did I eat this cooked crap before? The oven leeches all the flavor from it, all the wildness.

"So, hey," Graham says, with an intensely casual air that immediately makes me alert. "Now that we're here, talking, we should discuss Sweetheart's baptism."

Well, that would be why Graham is on his best behavior tonight.

"OK," I say carefully. "What are you thinking?"

"She's already a month old. You didn't want to do immunizations, and I agree with you, but we really do need to get her baptized as soon as possible. It's important."

The truth is that I would immunize my daughter if she weren't who she is. Mara and the others would tell me not to, would say that vaccines can hurt my baby, but this is the one thing from my past I can't simply set aside and forget. Part of my thesis for my CAST project was proposing a version of a vaccine to prevent or halt human prion diseases, which might one day be expanded to a vaccination for neurodegenerative disorders. Of course, the peer review ripped into my work, saying active vaccination isn't a good option for human prion diseases, given the very rare incidence rates, but my thesis argued that the long genetic incubation period of prion diseases could be used to our advantage for—

Stop.

I draw away from the whirring part of my brain, clenching my jaw. CAST doesn't matter; none of this does. The important thing is that at the end of the day, I love Sweetheart too much to risk anything happening to her. Which is why I gave Graham a bullshit excuse about not believing in vaccinations. The reality is that I can't bring Sweetheart to a doctor. And I can't bring her to a church either. Graham has been good about not nagging me to go back, but that leniency has come to an end.

My mind spins; I need to buy some time. "Let's wait a little longer. You know your parents will want to be there. Why rush it? Let's do it in the spring when she's six months. Maybe do it out west. We can stay with your parents. Do it at their church."

Graham's eyes light up at this. "Oh. That's . . . not a bad idea."

My shoulders relax, dropping away from my ears, and my breath comes easy again. Graham is at his most malleable when it comes to his parents. They are strict, devout Catholics who showered him—their only child—in affection and compliments growing up. It was hard for him to move to the Midwest for his job, to be so far away from them, so he jumps at every chance he gets to see his parents.

"Then it's settled," I say, grateful he took the bait.

"We should go back to church in the meantime, though," Graham continues, spearing a forkful of trout and shoveling it into his mouth. He makes a satisfied noise at the taste, and before he swallows, he sips from his wine. A twist appears on his lips as his throat works. "Would have been better with a white wine. Why are you smiling like that?"

I adjust—my grin must be too manic, but I can't help it. I was picturing him choking.

What the hell is wrong with me?

A frown tries its hardest to settle on my brow, and I work to counteract it. Exhaling to soften my features, I try again. "Sorry about the wine-pairing mix-up. Next time we'll coordinate better on date night food and drink."

"Uh-huh." Graham is undeterred. "So, church. We should go back. Especially now that the baby is born."

Under no circumstances can I go back to that church. Or, I suspect, any church, and I certainly can't expose Sweetheart to a potential reaction like the one I experienced almost two months ago.

"I kind of like the idea of starting her once she's been baptized, you know?" I say instead, trying to keep my voice level. "A new beginning. That's supposed to be her introduction to the church anyway, right? We don't want her to pick up any bad habits before that. Let's wait."

Graham's brows are raised, but he reluctantly nods, as if my suggestion that a baby could learn bad churchgoing habits were completely reasonable. "Yeah. I guess that works. I'm a little surprised you don't want to go sooner."

You are? Do you even know what I want? Do you not remember what happened the last time I went to that church? Or do you not care?

I grit my teeth as if grinding down the poisoned thoughts and continue to force my smile. "I want everything to be perfect. Besides, I was thinking we could read to her in the meantime. Passages from the Bible, you know?"

Graham nods, tipping his head to the side and slurping again from his wineglass. "Yeah, I like that idea. Nice family activity."

One he'll participate in for one week and then forget about, leaving it all to me.

It's for the best anyway. I have to limit the time Graham spends with Sweetheart. She's growing fast, and eventually she's going to stop sleeping so much and start opening her eyes more.

I want to steer the conversation away from religion, but I also can't stop thinking about the Instagram post I saw earlier, and this is as good a segue as I'm going to get.

"What do you know about fallen angels?" I ask Graham.

He pauses with his fork near his lips. "What?"

"Fallen angels," I repeat.

"What . . . what made you think of that?"

"Oh," I say vaguely, "someone I follow on Instagram posted about them. She's very religious, and I couldn't remember what their deal is."

"'What their deal is?'" Graham repeats, raising an eyebrow. He's right, it doesn't sound like me, but I don't care. Graham pops some trout into his mouth and chews slowly, watching me. "This isn't really dinner conversation."

"Tell me anyway." I wait, watching him, and his face changes when he realizes I'm not going to drop it like I usually do. "I remember you talking about them back when we were dating. What did you say then?"

He looks at me with reluctance, almost like he's nervous. And maybe a little irritated that I don't recall the exact words that came out of his holy mouth four years ago. "Well, they're exactly what they sound like. Angels who were expelled from heaven. They're a little controversial."

"Why?"

Graham is getting into it now, sliding into the instructional voice he uses when he's explaining something to me that he thinks he knows a lot about. "There are different thoughts on them, but generally speaking, they're angels who sinned and left heaven. Some think they mated with human women, producing Nephilim, which were later destroyed by God's flood. Their souls were left to wander the world as demons." Graham realizes the words that have left his mouth too late, carried away by all his years of religious instruction, forgetting he was talking to a soft, simple woman. "I shouldn't have told you the thing about the . . . the mating. Sorry."

I fold my lips into my mouth, trying not to show my clenching jaw. He thinks me so sheltered and delicate. All he knows of me is what I've shown him. He has no idea what I am capable of. What I'm doing to raise our daughter.

"These Nephilim," I say, ignoring his last statement. "What's up with them?"

He gives me another weird look but answers, "It was thought that they were giants. Beings of great strength and stature. The . . . spawn of the fallen angels."

I tense at the word *spawn*. It sounds impersonal and crude. I think of Sweetheart curled in her crib, fist in her sharp gaping mouth, softly snuffling as she shifts in sleep. I tap my phone, pulling up the live recording of my daughter in the nursery. She's visible in the infrared light, resting on her back. My chin drops at seeing her so calm and peaceful.

"Do normal angels ever mate with human women?" I ask, tearing my eyes away from the video feed.

Graham chokes on his wine. "What's with these questions, Camille? Are you feeling OK?"

"Do they?"

"Lord forgive her," he mutters. "No, Camille, they don't." Graham's voice is snappish now. "That's the whole point. Angels taking on a human form is perverse, a sin. That's why the fallen ones were expelled from heaven. They left their position to experience flesh that wasn't there for them. Can we stop with these questions now? I think you better unfollow that account if it's going to make you like this."

I settle back in my chair, poking at the food on my plate with my fork. Graham is upset, huffing and sniffing indignantly across the table, but I can't worry about that now. I got the information I needed. The information I had suspected for a while but didn't want to admit.

Even then, even at the moment of conception, you didn't really think it was an angel, did you?

It's hard to tell. Who I am now is not who I was a few months ago. Maybe I did believe it. Maybe I needed to believe it. Or maybe it was like everything in my life—a warning that I bypassed because it's what I was trained to do. Why would I ever listen to myself when there were men around to tell me what was needed and how wonderful I was for being at their beck and call?

My true feelings were buried away like lint in the seams of a pocket, unnoticeable unless you turned everything inside out. And anyway, it doesn't matter.

Sweetheart is here, Sweetheart is mine, and I don't care about her parentage. She is my daughter, and I will make sure she grows up safe and happy, whatever the cost.

22

DATE NIGHT ENDS with a fizzle. Graham falls asleep on the couch, stuffed full of trout and the highest number of drinks I've seen him consume in one sitting. He stopped complaining about how the dinner didn't match the wine after his third glass.

In Graham's defense, I threw him off with the fallen angels line of questioning. I don't think he was expecting that.

Checking my phone, I realize Sweetheart is awake; her eyes, black and inverted on the baby monitor, blink at me from the screen. She's clutching the bars of the crib, pulling herself up to a seated position even though everything I've read has said it's far too early for her to be able to do something like that.

I leave my husband slumbering in front of the TV, a sports recap blathering in the background to keep him company while I retreat upstairs.

My chest aches as I tread down the second-floor hallway. It's not even midnight. This is the earliest I've ever seen Sweetheart wake for her nighttime snack, and it worries me. I can't ignore how quickly she's growing and how she is unable to follow any prescribed baby milestones.

But when my daughter's face lights up as I enter the nursery, the tightness in my body melts away. She smacks her lips and babbles at me, a toothy half smile unfolding on her face.

"Aaaaaahhhakk," she burbles, bobbing excitedly.

"Yes, I'm here," I whisper, glancing behind me to make sure I can still hear my husband's car-engine snores before stepping into the nursery and quietly snapping the door shut.

I peel off my orange cardigan and roll up the ribbed midi dress. It's the tightest thing I've worn in a while, and it stays in place as I expose my legs and midsection, pulling the deboning knife and a black garbage bag from their hiding place in a changing table drawer. I lower the adjustable lip of the crib so that Sweetheart's face can peek out, and I step onto the garbage bag.

The nursery smells of baby powder and lavender, with a hint of iron. It's toasty in this room, unlike the rest of the house, and I wonder if it's because Sweetheart's skin always seems heated. She's a tiny furnace, making her own warmth to keep her crib cozy.

I breathe in through my nose, focusing on the smell of the nursery, as I slice off a sliver of my left thigh, offering it to my daughter.

She sniffs, eager, and inhales the flesh, and then looks up expectantly as I step closer. She latches on to the wound, and I sigh as the pain fades with every swallow. Her saliva is anesthetized, and I allow it to carry me away.

Until I realize she's not stopping.

Usually, Sweetheart eats her fill and pulls away when I start to become lightheaded from blood loss. But tonight, she sucks harder, feeds deeper, and when I look, there are trickles of blood running down my thigh. Her milky eyes are closed in ecstasy—her teeth are beginning to work against my leg. I can feel pinpricks through the vague numbness, and my heartbeat speeds.

She is beginning to chew.

I want to give my daughter what she wants, what she needs. But if she takes too much, I will die, and then who will protect her?

"Sweetie, no, that's enough for tonight," I murmur, placing a hand on her soft head, trying to snap her out of whatever blood trance she's in. "Come on."

She ignores me. The wound on my thigh begins to sting and buzz; she's nibbling at it now, as if she can't stop herself. Growls reverberate against my leg like she's a dog with a bone she won't relinquish.

"Sweetheart." My voice is firm and louder now. Mara would call it my "mommy voice." But it doesn't have an effect on my daughter—she opens her pale eyes to glance up at me and then returns to feeding.

She's going to take a chunk out of my leg. There are already small pink patches of skin littered around my thighs and stomach, divots and scarred areas that show where my daughter has been before. I'm almost proud of them, despite needing to hide them from Graham and the rest of the world. They are physical proof of how much I love my child, how much I would do for her.

But as much as I love her, I did not consent to her taking my toes, which have not grown back, and I do not consent to her eating the entirety of my thigh. I need to live to take care of her.

This is going to hurt.

I reach down and grasp Sweetheart around the middle, yanking her away from my leg. Her teeth, sunk into my flesh, tear away, and a wet ripping sound makes my stomach groan in hunger.

Blood flows freely—I let it. I'm too busy watching Sweetheart's mouth, making sure she doesn't lash out and latch on to my arm or hand instead. But now that she's finally detached, she is disinterested in continuing to feed. Her white eyes turn to my face, and there's a soft stirring in her misty gaze that feels *aware* in a way that should disturb me. Sweetheart wiggles in my grip, waving her arms up and down, a little shriek escaping her bloodstained lips.

Arms shaking from holding her, I place her down on the mattress pad, raising the crib side back into its proper place with a click.

"That's enough for tonight," I tell her. "Let's be more careful next time, OK?"

I step a foot away from the crib, breathing heavily, watching the streaks of blood dry on my leg, the wound slowly closing. Red skin spiderwebs across the gash, translucent and netted like tulle. By morning, it will be healed over. But the missing flesh, now a wide, gnawed half circle on my left thigh, is much larger than any of the other feeding spots on my body.

It should repulse me. That would almost be welcome, because my real reaction is worse. I can't deny the growling in my gut, the drool forming in the corners of my mouth. I want to sink my teeth into my own meat. Watching my daughter eat always makes me hungry too. I want to find that blissful state of eyes closed, stomach full.

"Sleep now, baby," I soothe. "Momma needs to get dinner soon as well."

My daughter's eyes are already growing heavy, and she yawns, a shred of skin caught between two of her pinprick teeth.

Sweetheart is getting bigger. She's growing. Which means she's getting hungrier. I suppose it makes sense. Babies transition from liquids to solids in their first year of life, but once again, she's way ahead of schedule. And if tiny bits of flesh and sips of my blood aren't enough anymore, what will she require instead?

Sweetheart rolls onto her back by herself, gurgling sleepily, patting at her face with splayed hands. Red paints her cheeks and palms. I need to clean her, but I don't want to approach her yet. I want to give her a moment to digest. Fall asleep.

I am not scared of my daughter. I love her, always. But after tonight, it's clear I need to at least be wary of her. I also need to finally admit the truth I've been evading for a while. It will allow me to properly plan for our future. I can't keep ignoring the obvious simply because it's a hard pill to swallow.

The fact of the matter is that my beautiful, charming, angelic daughter is not human.

*　*　*

Later that night, after I've woken Graham from his stupor on the couch and guided him to bed, I head outside, slipping away from the house and toward a dark shape lumped in the field.

I'm surprised the wheat hasn't vanished yet. Stalks have fallen, crunching underfoot, but most of them still stand upright, leaning and brittle but maintaining their sea of brown. The perfect place for secrets and hidden meals.

Night is more claustrophobic in November. It sidles in deeper, hunkers down lower, bringing its face to the cold earth and sighing out ice and quiet. Yet despite that, I am unbothered by the darkness and the frost. My coat is the color of crumbling coals and my feet are stuffed in rain boots. I'm not wearing nearly enough layers, but my hunger heats me, sending ribbons of warmth throughout my extremities.

A dead sheep waits for me among the stalks, steaming and fresh.

On the ground next to the animal is a braided mat of wheat, stalks woven together to form a soft protective layer. For my knees, I realize with a start as I lower myself down. The creature must have created this cushion, noticing me wincing after long feeding sessions.

It's unexpected, this thoughtful attentiveness.

I kneel on the wheat mat, digging a hand into the sheep's thick wool, feeling the gnarls of burrs and tiny bits of leaves caught in its fleece. I suspect its neck is broken, like the others', and it must have been killed only minutes ago, because I can taste the life on the air surrounding it. It's the scent of vanilla in a bakery. The hint of spice before it hits your tongue. My taste buds anticipate it; my mouth waters.

It takes a while to tear through the wool and reach the skin beneath. I don't use a tool for this. I shred with teeth and hands.

The waning moon watches. Somewhere, standing among the stalks, the creature watches too.

When I finally get the body open, its skin yielding to my ravenous nails, the flesh parts like a birth, opening up to me the same way I opened up for Sweetheart. Steam rises from the corpse as I bury my face into the rich, loamy meat.

As I consume, I wonder why my daughter cannot join me in these meals. Why she has to take from my body instead. I tried, once, a few days after her first feeding, to offer her the blood and pulp from a dead goat left near the side of the house. She refused it, literally turning up her nose, as disinterested as she had been with the meat from our fridge.

Even as I gorge myself, licking blood from my fingers and peeling away ligaments, I can't help but notice the flavors are fading, as they did with the raw meat from the kitchen. The fresher the meat, the better, but even so, there's something missing. There is a key component lacking in the animals I am forced to feed on night after night, unable to stomach anything else.

Breathing heavily, I finish, having eaten as much as I can without bursting open like a rotten sack of garbage. I sit back on my heels, knees supported by the wheat mat, tipping my face up to the bottomless sky, examining the constellations that speckle the heavens.

My daughter isn't human. So what? Does that mean she's not deserving of love? Does that mean she can't have a good life? My choices created her, and I don't regret them. Not a one. Even if those same choices are changing me too. Gone is my perfectly sculpted body; gone are my steadfast morals and trust in Graham; gone is the life I painstakingly created to look a certain way.

The wheat rustles off to my right, a swaying creak that has nothing to do with the brisk breeze that circles the house, carrying the scent of fir and moonlight. The urge to crawl over to the waving wheat tugs at my chest, but I fight it back.

I may be different, but I am not ready. Not yet.

I rise, wiping my mouth with the back of my hand, glancing down at the remains. I cleaned up the first few meals, the smaller ones I could carry on my own. But with the larger animals, I stopped trying. In the morning, their bones and fur would always be gone, carried away. If I returned to the well, perhaps I would find them all at the unfathomable bottom. If I could ever reach it.

Lifting a hand to the darkness of the wheat field in an effortless acknowledgment, I savor the crisp air before turning back to the house.

Using my tongue, I work a strand of wool free from my molars and wonder how much longer I have before the house of cards I've built around this false life comes tumbling down.

23

THE NEXT MORNING, I dread feeding Sweetheart. I worry about her latching too deeply again and eating more than she should, so I try a different tactic.

Standing over the sink in the kitchen, I make a small but deep incision in my left forearm, squeezing the split flesh together to allow a flow of blood to pour free. Using a baking funnel, I catch the blood, letting the liquid run through the hole so it can pool at the bottom of a baby bottle.

When the bottle is a quarter full, I release the tension on my cut and wrap it up tightly with gauze and tape. This wound hasn't been touched by Sweetheart's mouth, so I have to make sure I'm taking care of it. I roll down the sleeves of my dark sweatshirt, covering the gauze.

Graham widened his eyes at my outfit when I made him breakfast—a sweater the color of stormy skies and black joggers I usually wore only for walks. My hair is hidden under a black beanie, and my pallid skin stands out among the dark colors. He didn't say anything, but I could tell Graham was clocking the lack of effort.

It's Sunday, and my husband is at church. Or, at least, he said he was going to church.

"I agree with your plan," he said this morning when he woke up. "But it looks good to have someone there from our family. And I can stop at the farm on the way back. I noticed we were low on steak. I can grab some more." He paused there, like he was waiting for accolades and praise for taking the initiative and doing something as menial as food shopping.

I didn't commend him, and I also didn't fight him on his insistence on going to church alone. I'm starting to enjoy his time out of the house, leaving me and Sweetheart on our own.

I carry the baby bottle of blood up the stairs and into the nursery, offering it to Sweetheart, who is bouncing on her mattress pad. Earlier this morning, I dressed her in a charming blue floral knot gown that she's nearly too big for already. The matching bow that came with the dress has already been swiped off her head, crumpled in a corner of the crib.

Sweetheart is clearly hungry again, and there's a gleam in her eye that reminds me of my own insistent, feverish craving. The pull in your belly that demands food, that cautions an uncontrollable rage if you can't get it.

Sweetheart stares suspiciously at the bottle at first, the nipple centimeters from her lips, then tentatively suckles at it, white eyes fixed on my face. My heart stretches to see the trust reflected in her expression. I tip the bottle, and blood starts to flow out. Sweetheart drinks more eagerly, but she sucks fast and hard and when she spits the bottle out, the nipple has been gnawed to shreds. Trickles of leftover blood drip out from holes in the rubber; the rest of the bottle is drained dry.

Sweetheart's face twists and milky tears gather in the corners of her eyes as she screws her mouth up and begins to howl.

"Oh, honey, no, please," I beg her, tossing the bottle to the side and, with great effort, scooping her up, gathering her mass to my chest. "I'm sorry. It's not enough. We have to be careful. Do you understand?"

But she *doesn't* understand. She's a hungry baby. Sweetheart is bawling now. Since she rarely cries, I'm unsure of what to do besides comfort her. I rock her in my arms, whispering in her ear, kissing her sweet-smelling head. Her tears unleashed, Sweetheart screams and screams, as if she's been holding in her sobs for her entire short life.

I expect her to realize how close her face is to my warm, pulsing body; I would even allow it, letting her sink her teeth into my skin so she can feed properly. She's so upset, I would do anything to make her feel better. Sweetheart has changed gears, however. She's more focused on sobbing her heart out, wailing and kicking as streams of white-streaked tears race down her cheeks and disappear into her light-blue dress.

I have to sit in the rocking chair after several minutes because she's too heavy. Cradling her, I sing some stupid song that's trending on social media.

After what feels like forever, Sweetheart falls silent. My jaw releases as the deafening screams die out. Her eyes are closed, a gummy white substance clinging to her eyelashes and gluing them together. I delicately brush the goo away, dropping a kiss on her sweaty forehead as she grumbles in her sleep, turning her face toward my breast and heaving out a huge sigh.

I feel like crying myself, but I look bad enough without adding red eyes and blotchy skin to the list. Instead, I gather up my daughter and head downstairs. I rest Sweetheart in her playpen and move it into the kitchen so I can have her close by in case she wakes again.

I need to do something else. Something to get my mind off this turn of events. I'll bake. Make cookies for Graham. Ginger-bread. His favorite, and the right season for it.

As I reach for the ingredients and begin to line them up on the counter, I realize I haven't posted today at all. I've been less interested in taking photos lately. Instead, I stand by the big windows and stare out at the rolling wheat, thinking about dirt and meat and cold rocks.

Usually I would be documenting this, my homemaking: my child sleeping, appearing content and adorable now instead of like a bloodthirsty screaming banshee. I need to keep up appearances. When I wake my phone screen, a new notification catches my eye.

A random account, one that doesn't follow me, has com-mented on a photo of Sweetheart in her crib, fast asleep: *Ew. Her skin looks green. Shrek-ass baby lol.*

Not surprised, another commenter replied underneath. *Baby is prob sick. These tradwives are terrible moms.*

The kitchen shifts under my feet as a rushing sound floods my ears. How . . . how *dare* they? I've had trolls before, but this is the first time anyone has come after Sweetheart. Gnashing my teeth, I delete the offending comments and slam the "Block" button on both profiles.

I'll show them. Whipping open the phone's camera, I frame my daughter in the shot, moving around to find the best light-ing. She looks so sweet, so innocent. I pause with the lens sus-pended over Sweetheart's sleeping face, ready to take another photo that hides her size, her skin, her eyes.

What am I doing?

I'm exposing my daughter to scrutiny. To the world. To people who might realize the truth or say awful things about her without even knowing her. Those comments . . . there will be more. The bigger my page grows, the worse the interactions get.

First there was Melody, then the awful accusation during my live, and now people are spitting venom at my child.

Posting Sweetheart online opens her—and me—up to judgment and aspersions from others. It destroys her privacy before she's even old enough to understand what privacy is. She can't consent to me putting her image on social media—how can I justify doing so if it exposes her to something that might hurt her now or in the future?

I can't do it. Not anymore. I don't care if it hurts my engagement or if it ruins my page's aesthetic.

I delete the photo of Sweetheart the trolls commented on and slam my phone down on the counter. I keep an eye on my sleeping daughter as I mix flour, brown sugar, baking soda, cinnamon, ginger, cloves, and salt in a ceramic mixing bowl. My stomach turns at the spicy-sweet smell, and nausea threatens to overwhelm me, but the distraction is good. My heart rate slows as I go through the familiar movements.

I breathe through my mouth as I add chunks of butter and blend everything until it's a crumbly, soft brown mixture. I look wistfully at the butter—I can no longer snack on it. The texture makes me gag now, and it cannot compare to my midnight meals behind the house.

I think of the sheep I consumed last night as I stir in molasses and milk. I cover the dough in plastic wrap and slide the bowl into the fridge. I have to let it chill for a few hours—that gives me time to figure out what I'm going to do for Sweetheart's next meal.

I put away the ingredients and lay the handmade, one-of-a-kind rolling pin Graham got me for Christmas two years ago on the counter for later. My hands are shaking slightly, leftover fury from the social media comments.

I wipe up dustings of flour and crumbs of sugar, but it's like I'm cleaning a hotel, not my home. It's strange; this house felt more hospitable before, when we first moved in, than it does now. The newness was a hug, but the further I sink into its embrace, the more I struggle to break free from arms that are too constricting for comfort.

I nearly jump out of my skin when the doorbell buzzes.

Glancing over to make sure the bone-jarring sound hasn't woken up Sweetheart, I hurry over to open the frosted-glass door, annoyed but unsurprised to find Renee grinning on the front step. Renee never visits on weekends, yet here she is. She's wearing black leggings and a bright-green sweater that says *Don't wine at Mom.* Judging by her pink cheeks, windswept hair, and white sneakers, she has walked over instead of driving today. Renee is holding a smaller garbage bag this time, and I would bet my entire house that it's full of more baby stuff.

My stomach tenses. Didn't I tell her to stop coming over unannounced? Now I have to worry about her showing up on weekends and running into Graham.

"Hi, so sorry I didn't get a chance to text you! I have plans with my kiddos later, so I won't be long," Renee says, a slight whine in her voice. "I was going through my things, and I found some stuff you absolutely *have* to have for the baby!"

"Isn't it a little cold to be walking around like that?" I ask. I don't budge. I block the entrance to my home, unable to force a smile this time. I'm too shaken from the internet trolls.

"Great walking weather!" Renee insists. "And carrying the bag on my back like Santa helped keep me warm." She laughs. "Plus I was hoping we could talk about doing some jogs together. It's getting colder, but sometimes that's the best weather for a run!"

"Now's not a great time—"

"Oh, it smells amazing in here!" Renee interrupts, leaning forward, pressing against me so she can sniff the air. It's far too personal, and the sour fruit on her breath is masked by some cheap Bath & Body Works ginger-scented spray. "What are you making? It smells like Christmas! Makes me miss my kids even more!"

I pause. "Where are your kids?"

She laughs, too loudly, eyes fixed beyond my shoulder. "Oh, you know. At school. Always off learning something. Or having playdates. Millie's starting Spanish lessons, did I tell you that? She's so smart. Not like me, ha! She must get it from Zach."

Somehow, during her speech, Renee has squeezed past me and now stands in the hallway, the garbage bag crinkling at her side. I want her to leave, but she's clearly not going anywhere until we go through this stupid song and dance of her bestowing ugly used clothes upon me that I never use.

"Sweetheart is sleeping," I say, giving in and leading her to the kitchen. "Please be quiet."

"Certainly," Renee says in a mock whisper, grinning and putting a finger to her large frog mouth. She walks like a wildebeest into the kitchen, nostrils flaring as she sighs. "Gosh, that smell really is nice. Ah, look at the angel!" Renee murmurs, eyes fixing on Sweetheart, who snoozes in her playpen near the cabinets.

"Sorry, I don't have time to hang out right now," I warn her as she drops the bag to the floor.

"Oh wow, look at that!" Renee says, distracted. She hurries over to the counter and caresses the rolling pin, admiring the handcrafted wooden handles, the beautiful marbled pin.

My shoulders sag in disappointment. She isn't listening to me. I need her gone. I have things to do, food to figure out.

"How have you been?" Renee asks, placing the rolling pin back down and turning to face me. "I haven't heard from you in a while." There's a chastising note in her voice: a teacher scolding a child for naughty behavior. Then she softens. "I'm worried about you, Camille. You know I live down the road. Sometimes I sit on the porch. I don't think I've ever seen you drive by. Or walk by. Are you leaving the house? Going on your strolls? Are you getting time for yourself?"

It's not her business, and her nosiness grinds against me. "I've been really busy."

"But Graham is helping you, right?"

The question is loaded; she follows me on social media. She knows what kind of a wife I am. She has to know that I am doing the bulk of the work.

"Yes," I say loyally. "Graham is great. I've just had a lot going on."

"With this darling, no doubt!" Renee swoops over to the playpen and hovers above it, smiling at my sleeping daughter. "Wow, did she get bigger? She looks really large for her age. Good for a growing girl, naturally! But . . . have you checked her out recently? She's lovely. She is. Look at that adorable little dress she's wearing! That's not one of mine, is it?" Renee doesn't wait for me to answer; her mouth is motoring as usual. "But don't you think she's a bit *too* big? And her skin—is it always that color? Does she have a cold?"

The comments I deleted from Sweetheart's photo reappear in my mind's eye, and I grit my teeth. Renee didn't write them, but I want to backhand this woman with all the strength in my newly muscled arms. My gut clenches, and I fight the urge to swipe Renee away from the playpen. "Please don't wake—"

"You know, I've never even held her! Can I please . . . I'll just . . ." Renee doesn't finish her sentence. Before I can stop her, she's scooped up Sweetheart and pulled her toward her chest. "Whoa, heavy!" she chortles.

My blood heats and my stomach bottoms out.

This woman touched my child. She picked her up without even asking. She is *holding* my baby in a way I don't like, with bright, desperate eyes that rove over Sweetheart's body and face. I open my mouth, try to tell her to put my baby down immediately, but I am so violated, so stunned, that nothing comes out. My throat is a desert landscape, and my mouth is parched and gaping.

"My goodness, she's a big one!" Renee grunts, slipping her arms underneath Sweetheart so she can adjust herself. "She certainly sleeps a lot too. Every time I've seen her, she's been fast asleep. Are you sure you shouldn't get her checked out? She's such a cutie, though." She says the last part questioningly too, as if she isn't sure anymore, and it finally breaks me from my shocked trance.

My daughter is cute. My daughter is *beautiful* and perfect. "Please put her down. She's resting," I say tersely.

Sweetheart's nostrils flare, once, twice, and she inhales deeply, just like Renee did at our front door. Her eyes open.

Renee gasps.

Everything inside me ices over. My breath seizes and comes out in short, sputtering bursts. The space on my right foot where my missing toes used to be tingles and itches furiously.

The kitchen is silent for a moment. Sweetheart stares up at Renee, examining her face, slowly realizing the woman holding her is not her mother.

"W-what's wrong with her eyes? Is she . . . is she blind?" I've never heard Renee's voice so groggy and slow.

Like Graham, like my followers online, Renee has never seen Sweetheart's eyes open. She is always sleeping, or perhaps feigning sleep, when Renee comes over to visit. But now my daughter's white eyes are wide open and unblinking, fixating on Renee.

She licks her lips.

"Sweetheart, no—" I start to say.

But before I can stop her, Sweetheart twists her head and latches on to Renee's forearm, sinking her teeth deep into the woman's flesh, easily cutting through the sleeve of Renee's lime-green sweater. It's impossible to tell what Sweetheart's milky-white, pupilless eyes are staring at as they narrow, but her mouth works as she begins to chew.

Renee's screams are delayed by several seconds, as if her brain cannot compute what is happening; the translation from her photoreceptors is working on a time lag. She releases her hold on my daughter, but Sweetheart has locked in, and her tiny hands scrabble for purchase against the green sweater as she hangs from Renee's forearm, teeth buried in the woman's flesh.

"Sweetheart!" I yell, rushing forward. "Don't!"

My daughter is whipping her head back and forth like a dog trying to break a squirrel's neck, clearly frustrated by the excess of fabric she's never had to deal with before. Angry grunting noises come from her mouth, buried in Renee's arm.

"Fuck, fuck, what the fuck!" Renee screams, sounding unlike herself in her hysteria. "Get it off, get it *off*!"

It. My daughter is not an *it*. A flush of heat races through my system as I reach for Sweetheart, my mouth automatically smiling to combat the hot furrows forming on my brow.

Renee spins away from me, screeching, waving her arm, trying to shake Sweetheart off. I dodge Renee's frantic movements, yell at her to stay still so I can help, but she's not listening. The frightened, animal part of her brain has taken over, and she dances around the kitchen, evading me and crying as Sweetheart digs in deeper, blood beginning to stain the green sweater.

"Get off!" Renee begs, swinging her arm wildly. Sweetheart is dangling from Renee's limb like a tick, her heavy body soaring through the kitchen as Renee panics.

I need to stop her. She's going to hurt Sweetheart. If my daughter detaches, she could fly through the air and break her back. She could drop to the floor and land on her head. Fear threads through my bones, making my movements jittery and staccato.

I grab the first thing I can reach—the rolling pin. It's heavy and solid in my hands, and its marble body makes a sick wet crunch as I swing it against the back of Renee's head.

CHAPTER

24

Renee slumps against the counter, arm going slack. The extra weight of my hungry daughter drags Renee's limb down like an anchor. Sweetheart's bare toes hang only a foot above the floor now.

I lift the rolling pin again and bring it down once more on the crown of Renee's head with a sharp, final crack. The woman drops to her knees, and I toss the rolling pin to the side with a clatter, seizing my daughter and holding her tightly as Renee collapses forward, making sure Sweetheart isn't crushed or trapped beneath the falling body.

"Please, darling, let go," I plead with Sweetheart, tugging her gently. Her teeth are fastened and her face is bloody.

Finally, Sweetheart releases Renee, spitting out strips of green fabric and smearing blood all over her lips. She grouses at me, an indignant complaint, as I place her on the floor on her back. Sweetheart shrieks a shrill, high-pitched blast as her pale tongue slides out of her mouth and begins to probe her own bloody lips.

"Let me think," I tell her, my mind a complete whiteout of noise and disbelief.

Reaching over, I press two fingers against Renee's neck. Her skin is sweaty and hot, but I can't find a pulse. Her head is cracked open like an egg, so that shouldn't be surprising. She is bleeding all over my white tile floor, and she's facedown, motionless.

To my left, I catch Sweetheart squirming around on her back, rolling over to her front with a sudden flip, and then scrunching her knees up toward her chest so she can crawl over toward me and Renee's body.

"Are you kidding me?" I breathe. "Crawling? Already?"

Sweetheart is smiling, baring her lizard teeth, white eyes crinkled in joy, as she slaps her palms on the floor, dragging herself over to Renee. Elated screeches echo from the back of her throat, but I block her path.

"I have to think," I repeat. "I have to get her out of this house. Oh, Jesus, Graham could be home any minute."

I grab Renee's feet and begin to drag her to the sliding glass door. A snail trail of blood follows, her head wound still bleeding. I'm grateful we don't have any carpeting on the first floor.

Sweetheart crawls behind us, lapping up the blood that remains, missing streaks to favor the puddles and clumps. I will have to thoroughly clean after this and hope that Graham stays true to habit and doesn't come home for several more hours.

Leaving the sliding glass door open, I pull Renee out of the house and across the backyard, suddenly immensely grateful for the remoteness of our street. Cars rarely go by, and they can't see the back of the house from the road anyway.

Wheezing from the effort, I leave Renee's body several feet inside the wheat field, dying stalks hiding her from view. I'll have to find another plan for her before it gets truly freezing and everything dies, exposing her decomposing corpse.

Or maybe not.

Sweetheart, crawling much faster than I ever could have imagined, is approaching rapidly. Her movements are insect-like and focused—her dress covers her knees and drags against the yellow grass and fallen leaves. I thought my daughter would remain in the house, licking up the blood trail, but she must have sensed her meal leaving the premises.

"Sweetheart, no, you're going to scrape up your hands," I beg, swooping down to grab her.

Sweetheart speeds up, shooting through my arms with unnerving swiftness, white eyes fixated on Renee's body. I follow my daughter, making sure there are no sticks or rocks in her path, watching as she sinks her teeth into Renee's waist. She angrily chews through Renee's thick sweater, spitting out the torn fabric until she can access the flesh underneath.

"Don't make yourself sick," I urge her. "Here, let me help."

Sweetheart growls like a territorial wolf when I approach, but when she notices me pulling Renee's ugly green sweater, tugging it up, she pauses her gnashing and withdraws, allowing me to maneuver Renee's body so that her chest and stomach lay bare. I roll the sweater over Renee's face, hiding it.

I thank God that Renee is wearing a front-clasping bra instead of a sports bra—I unhook it and move it out of the way. I don't want Sweetheart getting any underwire stuck in her throat.

"You don't have to eat it all now," I caution my daughter as she buries her face in Renee's rib cage, large chunks of flesh stripping away from the body faster than I can comprehend.

Poor Sweetheart must have been starving. The pieces of my own flesh and blood weren't enough to sate her anymore, but she was dealing with the hunger because she loves me. It's the only explanation, and my heart sings. I love Sweetheart, but to realize that she loves me too, unconditionally, enough to rein in her own ceaseless appetite, is truly special. It's worth everything.

I didn't want to hurt Renee, but I couldn't have her injuring my daughter. And maybe this is better. Now she can't pry anymore, now she can't tell anyone what she saw. Besides, her death is going to mean something. She's feeding a hungry child. She should be proud of that. Instead of rotting under the ground, covered in bugs, she's allowing a baby to grow up happy and healthy. Isn't that all we can hope for?

"Thank you," I murmur to the body, glad I covered Renee's bloody face with her sweater so I don't have to look at it.

The sky rumbles overhead, clouds darkening. The air is chilled, but there's no breeze, and the ground feels warm under my feet. I look down, my missing toes hidden inside my slippers, thinking about the pink skin stretched over the place where the digits used to be.

The wheat rustles around us, a background lullaby that harmonizes with Sweetheart's ripping and grunting. Viscera and blood smear over my daughter's cheeks and hands—her outfit is definitely ruined, but she seems so content that I'm fine with it. Her little head, fuzzed over with gold, bobs up and down as she digs deeper into Renee's torso.

As I watch my daughter, feeling the first sprinkle of raindrops, my stomach gurgles. The smell—the iron blood, the exposed rib cage, the steaming innards—triggers pulses of hunger. Saliva collects along the corners of my mouth, and I smack my lips.

I take a step closer to the body and my daughter as the rain begins to fall in earnest, chilling my face. I wonder what a strip of Renee's flesh would taste like. I wonder how different raw human meat is from raw animal meat. I imagine it melting on my tongue like the pats of butter I used to eat. I imagine the blood, still warm, dripping down my chin. It must be so much more . . . invigorating to eat something hot and fresh and *human*. The farm animal meat has been lacking lately.

I drop to my knees on the other side of Renee's body, reaching a hand out, fingers trembling.

What the fuck are you doing?

My conscience stops me with a screeching halt, and I tumble backward, landing on my rear in the dirt, which is already starting to get muddy and wet. Stalks of wheat chortle around me, their bones clicking against one another.

"Oh," I whisper. "Oh no."

This is what Sweetheart needs for survival. I can accept that. But it's not what *I* need. I've been fine consuming the meat the creature leaves for me in the yard. I haven't regained my former healthy glow or long locks, but that's probably from a difficult and truncated pregnancy.

The rain patters down harder, and I glance up at the gray sky, water splashing into my face and mouth. My clothes are damp and my bones are cold.

We should get inside soon. I can't have Sweetheart catching anything.

"Finish up, please," I whisper to my daughter as I hunch away from Renee's body. "Don't worry, you can come back later and eat more if you're still hungry."

After a few minutes, Sweetheart pulls away from Renee. Her face is pink, the blood mixing with rain and dribbling down her chubby cheeks. She blinks at me, her white eyes sleepy and milky.

"Done?" I ask, getting to my feet unsteadily, stepping over the husk of Renee to heave my daughter up off the ground.

Sweetheart nuzzles into my collarbone, huffing a contented sigh, face drooping as she starts to fall asleep. I clutch her to my chest, heart racing, as I glance back down at my neighbor. Her stomach and half her chest are gone, eaten away down to the spine. Sweetheart ignored the intestines—they spill over the hollow hole in Renee's body, untouched. But her stomach has been sucked dry, the fascia around her liver shredded like gristle from poultry.

Renee's face remains hidden by the green sweater. I turn away, leaving her in the rain, and walk back to the house, carrying my bloody, sleeping child.

IV

Matrescence

CHAPTER

25

RENEE'S BODY FEEDS Sweetheart for three days. Decomposition is slow with how brisk the nights have gotten lately, and it doesn't seem to bother my daughter anyway. I'm not worried about her getting sick from her food—her stomach is made from stronger stuff than a normal child's.

Every morning, after Graham has left for work, I carry Sweetheart out to the wheat field and place her down beside Renee's rapidly disappearing body. Sometimes there's more missing than I remember. I wonder if something else is feeding on it when we're not around.

Sweetheart is growing faster, invigorated by Renee's body. Blood sustained her for a while, but she's clearly coming into her own now: Her bones elongate, fingers lengthen, mass increases. She is nearly the size of a one-year-old already, and if she keeps going at this rate, I'll have a toddler by the new year.

She'll stop growing eventually, though, right?

Maybe so. Maybe not. My child is not like other children, which is why I must protect her. Nothing I ever studied in school applies to Sweetheart.

Either way, Renee is reduced to a few bare bones and a pile of unwanted organs by the third day, and after putting Sweetheart down for her nap, I bundle the rest of the remains into a garbage bag and trudge through the field, approaching the well. Quickly I shake open the bag, letting the remnants of Renee tumble down the hole into the darkness, the smell of wet soil and crumbling rocks mixing with the bloodstained leftovers.

I don't hear the bones hit the bottom.

My stomach lurches in hunger, and I turn away, pressing the craving down like I've done every single time we've visited the corpse. The creature, perhaps noticing my discomfort around Renee's body and disinterest in the farm animals it brings, has left me different meals these past few nights. Instead of sheep and geese, it has left deer and hawks. The flavor of these wild animals is slightly sharper than that of the others, but there's still something missing.

I crumple up the bag and hurry away from the well, not daring to glance over my shoulder.

Back in the house, everything is quiet. The laundry room isn't whirring; the oven isn't ticking as it heats up; the vacuum remains in the hall closet. Dust has crept into the corners of the living room. The counters in the kitchen are smeared and oily.

After I washed and bleached Renee's blood from the floors, I was unable to summon the energy to do anything else. I've cooked for Graham the past few days, but there's been no heart in it. I've been going through the motions, packing lackluster lunches for him, and yesterday I ordered store-made muffins to the house, which I passed off as my own. I've given up on making folic acid–free food.

Mara would be furious.

I fall to the couch, opening my phone to check on Sweetheart, who is snoozing away in her crib, and then tap over to

Instagram. Mara has a new post—a decadently shot video of her children helping her harvest vegetables from their farm, washing them in her gigantic sink, and organizing them by color as she chops up several veggies for a winter stew. Mara's written a long-winded caption about how this is the season of gratitude and how everyone needs to make sure their children are only eating healthy, natural foods they've grown or raised themselves.

"After all, you are what you eat!" she bleats at the end of the video.

Mara's children are always smiling, but it's a stiff, practiced smile that she must insist on when filming. She has trained her family to expect a camera in their face. They are not on reality TV. They are on social media, exposing their childhood to the world before they even understand what that means.

The phone is hot in my hands as I check Mara's "following" list. My name is still there, and my heart flutters.

I tap over to my own profile, sighing. I haven't posted anything in four days. A new notification catches my eye—someone has mentioned me in a story.

Black background, white text, clearly a continuation of a rant on previous stories: *Not only do women like this perpetuate stereotypes and sexism, I think half of them are faking it! Which blows my mind, like are you that desperate for followers?? This one below blocked my friend when she confronted her about being in a science program (Hi Camille, go ahead and block me too!) and that's sus as hell.*

"Not again," I spit.

This person's profile has far more followers than Melody's and is public. I vaguely recognize the woman in the photos, holding up signs at protests and posting about calling your state representatives: Sophie Tang. She was in CAST too. She was the one who said my prion project was "an ineffective use of time and energy" and that my focus on kuru was "bordering on cultural insensitivity." The critiques from CAST linger in the darkest parts of my brain, unwilling to be forgotten.

My accounts have gotten bloated enough that they've caught the attention of those outside my community. People I haven't seen or heard from in *years*. How does Mara handle stuff like this? She must get negative comments, but I never see them.

Chewing my lip, vibrating from the loose energy winging through my body, I fulfill Sophie's request and block her, then message Mara:

Hi! I've had more and more people coming to my page lately being rude about our lifestyle. I block them, but they come back. Any tips?

Within a few seconds, text appears underneath my message letting me know Mara has seen it. But she doesn't respond. I wait for fifteen minutes, staring at my phone, trying not to blink. Nothing.

Pressure rises in my chest as my breath becomes ragged. I tap back over to my profile, examining it. I stopped posting photos and videos of Sweetheart since my epiphany last weekend. It's not just that she's growing at a rate I can't explain or deny, it's that it feels . . . invasive. She is my child, and I no longer understand how these other women can parade their family on camera for likes and clicks. I don't want to invite the world inside our home to judge or leer.

Sophie Tang is wrong: I'm not faking my lifestyle. Not completely. Do I fully believe in everything Mara and the others say? No, not anymore. But I thought if I tried hard enough, I could. The same way I believe Graham and I will be fine. And that the creature is an angel. You can embrace anything if you commit to it.

I hesitate for a minute, lovingly admiring the high "like" count on my photos of Sweetheart. All the comments. All the reshares.

Who shares a stranger's baby, anyway? Why do they care so much?

I delete all the posts of Sweetheart. I delete the pregnancy announcement video. I delete the story highlight titled "baby" on my profile. Closing Instagram, I tap into TikTok and my other apps as well. In seconds, I have erased my daughter from my social media entirely.

I have to get out of this house. The sun is out. The sky is cloudless. Walk. We need to walk. I shake the urge to chuck my phone at the wall and shrug a coat on over another sweater-sweatpants set instead. The extra fabric covers more, hiding the changes my body continues to go through: the gray tint to my skin, the thick muscles forming in my legs and arms, the scarred and pitted flesh. If Graham and I were having sex, there would be no way to hide it or my missing toes.

But Graham notices nothing because Graham doesn't care to notice.

I tuck a sleeping Sweetheart into her stroller, which we've barely used at all since her birth. I wrap her in a soft gray blanket, pulling the hood of the stroller down to cover her face, and we step outside.

If I walk by Renee's house, I might get a better sense of what's going on over there. If the police have been involved yet. No one has come looking for her even though Renee said she had plans with her kids that day. Her husband must be losing his mind, but maybe he doesn't realize she was visiting me. Maybe he's like Graham and he had no idea what his wife was doing during the day. Maybe all her family knows is that she disappeared three days ago.

I trot down the side of the paved road, along the dusty shoulder. The dying wheat field leaves enough space for me to roll the stroller on the flat dirt, and I smile as I suck in the brisk air.

It takes about fifteen minutes for Renee's house to crest around a slight curve in the paved road. We've passed no other residences; our closest neighbors are up the road in the opposite direction. And no cars have whizzed by either. The cracked road with its painted lines is a silent companion on my right as we slowly approach Renee's property line.

Graham and I have driven by her house only once or twice, since it's in the opposite direction of town. Renee has (*had*) a blue farm-style two-story house like ours, but with red shutters and a disheveled front yard. Hers is on the other side of the road, so the forest doesn't encroach on it the way it does mine.

The house looks more worn down than I remember. The paint on the shutters is chipping and peeling; the front porch is sagging. The wheat field around Renee's house is entirely dead, giving the property an empty look. The building stands out among the flat landscape like a single tooth in a baby's mouth. Renee's car, a beat-up Chevy, is parked in the driveway—she walked over to my house the other day.

There's an off-putting vibe around the property that I can't put my finger on. Glancing both ways down the road, I navigate the stroller on to the pavement and cross, stopping in Renee's driveway.

Quiet, I realize. The house is too quiet.

Where is her family? Why is no one running around, freaking out, looking for Renee?

The house stares back at me, the upstairs windows like wide eyes. There are no curtains, no eyelids, to protect any secrets. The inside of the house is dark.

A faint rushing noise comes from behind me, and I instinctively step closer to Renee's home; a car is coming down the road. I fight off the sudden urge to hide, to grab Sweetheart and burrow into the ground like a mole. But there's nowhere to go besides Renee's house, and Sweetheart's still sleeping, her face hidden by the stroller hood.

I pull out my phone, pretending to scroll as if I'm taking a break from my walk, but the rushing sound slows, replaced by a purring engine, and when I look up, a pickup has stalled on the road in front of the house, directly across from us.

"Howdy," a man says, leaning out from his window.

"Good afternoon," I reply, fighting to stay calm.

"You OK?" he asks. The man is sporting an orange trucker hat and a thick brown beard that is several inches longer than Graham's. Sunglasses cover his eyes, but he lifts the bridge of them so he can look at us.

"Yep. Taking our daily walk." I catch a whiff of the guy in the breeze blowing across the road. He smells like aftershave and sweat. My stomach grumbles.

"Ah, got it." He nods. "You got bear spray on you?"

"Excuse me?"

He cocks a brow. "For protection. A mean ol' bear lives in those woods. We've never seen it on the road, but better safe than sorry."

His tone is slightly teasing, so I shrug. "We'll be fine."

"Hope so. Once they found a human spine outside the forest. Just sitting there. Covered in gristle." He grins at me, wiggles his fingers like he's telling a spooky story. "I'm Bill. I live up the road. You're at 502, right? The new family?"

I shouldn't be surprised. Country living; everyone knows everything. "That's right."

I can't see all of him from here, but he looks big. Like he would have tender, fatty meat that could feed someone for a week. "I'm Camille."

"You visiting Renee Colt?" His brows are raised, and he lifts his sunglasses higher to peer behind me at the house, as if he's not sure he would do the same. His truck's engine chugs, expelling gas out the back.

I don't want to specifically answer this. It's better to be vague. To lie. "We always walk this way. Sometimes we see her kids."

Bill frowns. "Excuse me?"

"You know. Her son and daughter."

Bill shakes his head. "I don't know who you saw, lady. Renee's family doesn't live here anymore. They haven't for quite some time."

My heart drops, and I grip Sweetheart's stroller tighter. I take a step toward the road to make sure I'm not mishearing Bill over the rumble of his truck. "Sorry, what?"

"She home?" Bill hunches lower in his seat to stare at the house. "Her car is in the driveway."

"I think she went for a run," I quickly improvise. "I haven't seen her. What do you mean, her family doesn't live here anymore?"

"Are you friends? Did she not tell you?" Bill asks, sounding more and more skeptical. "Renee's husband divorced her. It was contentious. Big custody thing. Everyone around here heard about it. My wife was friends with Renee for a while before it all went down."

"Are you serious?" I add, "I did—I don't know her well. Maybe I didn't see her kids. Maybe I got confused. I have mommy brain, you know."

"That's gotta be it," Bill says. "Because they haven't been here in a year."

"What happened?" I can't help asking.

Bill scrunches up his nose. "Renee didn't have a job, so the court sided with her ex. There were also some rumors around here that she had a drinking problem, that her ex-husband brought it up in court and accused her of having wine during the day when she was watching the kids. I think Renee has supervised visits on the weekends. But the kids don't come out here. Renee has to go to her ex's new place in the city." Bill seems

to be enjoying himself now, spilling Renee's business to a woman
he's met on the side of the road with a conspiratorial tone.

Locks click into place. This explains Renee's free time, why
she was always eager to see me in the middle of the day during
the week but would rarely pop up on the weekends. It explains
why she appeared so desperate for time around me and my baby.
Her lack of boundaries. The familiar scent I would smell on her
breath and her stained mouth: wine.

"How awful," I say, wondering how many times Renee came
over to my house drunk and how many times I didn't realize it.

"Yeah," Bill answers. "Anyway, I got to get going. It was nice
to meet you. And hey, there are other people on this road. Renee
is . . . intense. If you guys ever want to come over for dinner,
we'd be happy to have you."

My stomach growls again at the word *dinner*, and I smile.
"Thanks, I appreciate that. Nice to meet you."

"You too. Cute kid," Bill says, winking before driving off.
He sticks a hand out his open window in farewell as he rolls
down the road.

When he's gone, I turn back to stare at Renee's empty house.
Eventually, someone will notice she's gone. They will look for
her and find nothing.

I check on Sweetheart, craning my head under the hood of
the stroller. She's awake now, silent and watchful under the
blanket, her white eyes fixed on the home Renee will never
return to.

26

GRAHAM COMPLAINS ABOUT dinner. He says the chicken is dry and the vegetables are undercooked.

We're at the table together, but I don't even pretend to eat. There is no plate in front of me; Graham doesn't notice. But the less-than-perfect food? The line of dust on the counters? *That* he notices.

"Are you feeling OK?" he asks, prodding at his dinner with disinterest. "This is unlike you. And have you washed the floor today? It feels . . . sticky or something." He taps his feet under the table as if to make his point.

I don't answer his questions. I'm *not* feeling OK; I'm stressed. I did *not* wash the floor; I've been too busy trying to figure out where Sweetheart's next meal will come from now that Renee's remains are gone.

"I have to check on our daughter," I say instead, pointedly.

I avoid Graham the rest of the evening, spending time in the nursery with my sleeping child, ignoring his huffs as he walks back and forth in front of the doorway, poking his head in on occasion to coo at Sweetheart and ask me when I plan on tidying up.

"I'll do it later," I say through gritted teeth. "Don't worry. You don't ever need to worry."

When Graham finally goes to bed, miffed and apparently offended by my cold shoulder, I slip downstairs, sneaking outside to gnaw on the deer that was left for me in the same spot Renee's body lay. The creature noticed last time that I ate more of the deer than the previous farm animals; it's obliging me and my preferences in a way Graham never has.

Full and sleepy, I head back into the house, flicking off all the lights and heading upstairs to get ready for bed. I slip into the en suite bathroom, closing myself in as my husband snores in the other room.

I'm wearing my favorite sleep dress—it's heather gray, stretchy and comfortable, falling down past my knees. The long sleeves cover up my thickening arms and the soft fabric hides my scarred body.

My eyes catch on my hairline and scalp in the bathroom mirror. I haven't studied my reflection lately; I'm spending a lot less time looking at myself these days. The selfies on my phone have dwindled down to zero. But now I lean forward, staring. My hair is loose around my shoulders, highlighting the patches that have never grown back. I squint. It looks like black roots are growing in place of my golden locks, but that can't be right. I'm a natural blonde.

I lean in farther, pressing my hands against the cool counter. The bald spots on my head are no longer bald—I tap a nail against the dark roots and touch something hard and slick. The light is unforgiving, shining off the dark oval. I press the pad of my finger against it.

Smooth. Dry. Like a scale.

I pull away from the mirror, clearing the lump in my throat with a cough. Turning the lights off, I continue getting ready for bed in darkness, unable to see myself in the mirror anymore, a faint blue glow coming from the light installed in the toilet bowl.

When I head back into the bedroom, Graham's phone is going off, illuminating his bedside table. The glow blinks in the blackness of the bedroom, beckoning me over. Usually Graham charges his phone downstairs in his office, using me as an alarm clock every morning, knowing I'll gently wake him when breakfast is ready.

But tonight he must have forgotten. He'll be upset tomorrow if he wakes up with a dead phone. I should run it downstairs for him. Plug it in. It's what a good wife would do, and I should try to be one even though it's increasingly hard to care about that.

Quietly, I pick up Graham's phone, waiting for his snores to cut off and his hand to shoot out and stop me. But Graham has proven he can sleep through almost anything, and the cadence of his growling breath doesn't change.

I look down at the screen, which is still lit up from the last notification that came through.

A familiar icon beams up at me.

My stomach empties as my knees start trembling. This can't be right. I'm not seeing this. Graham doesn't *have* Instagram. He's always maintained that he doesn't need it. Yet here is an Instagram message blasting light into the bedroom.

I don't know what the notification is; Graham has his display settings on private so that the text is hidden.

I glance over at Graham again, who is sleeping soundly. Pulling the phone close to my chest, blocking the light, I creep over to the edge of the mattress and quickly flash the front of the phone at my husband's face. Flipping it back around, I smile in grim satisfaction—the phone, recognizing its owner's face, has unlocked.

I slip out of the room, making sure to tap the screen as I go so it doesn't fall asleep and lock me out again.

Once I'm downstairs in the relative safety of the kitchen, the bluish glow from our appliances' digital clocks illuminating the tile floor, I access my husband's secret social media account. The notification turns out to be a direct message from someone named @rosexrose.

How was your day?

I briefly scroll through their messages—there are hundreds of them. Too many to read through in one sitting. Instead, I tap over to the person's page.

The profile picture is of—go figure—a rose. The account has a modest amount of followers, around seven hundred, and only sixty posts, which tells me this isn't someone who's online a lot. Or at least not posting a lot. The photos on her grid are all flowers. No faces, no people. There's no information in the bio besides a name: Rose.

God, she's really branded herself, hasn't she?

I rack my brain, but we don't know anyone named Rose. Or anything close to Rose—no Rosemary or Rosaline. But that doesn't mean anything. Graham could have met her anywhere. The house is my domain. It always has been. The world is Graham's.

Tapping back into Graham's message history with Rose, I scroll. There are no photos, which is interesting, but tons of text DMs. I don't know how far back they go. I'm guessing a while. My eye catches on a cluster of messages from a few days ago.

Rose asked my husband how it feels to be a father.

Do you regret anything? she adds. *Is this what you always wanted?*

Idk, Graham's message reads. *I'm so lucky to have a baby, but sometimes I wish . . .*

What?

I wish sometimes it was with someone else . . . Not with her. You know?

I know.

Maybe one day.

Don't you love her?

C?

No. Your daughter.

Yes. I guess. Idk, it's weird. C has been cagey about the timeline. Idk when we conceived. If we even did. You know it's YOU I'm loyal to. I don't want her. Not anymore.

I know.

And then Graham had the nerve, the absolute, unbearable nerve, to type *Maybe she cheated.*

Oooo. Wow. I would never step out on a man like you.

You're the best, sweetheart.

It's the pet name that makes me scream, a raggedy piercing cry filled with phlegm and nausea. How *dare* he call her our baby's name? How *dare* he?

I pause, panting, waiting for Graham to wake up, desperately *wanting* him to wake up so I can claw out his eyes. But the house is silent. Graham can sleep through anything, even the anguished sound of his wife in pain.

Hands shaking, I tap back over to Graham's burner account, looking at his blank profile. I would have no idea it was Graham behind this page—he's got no photos, no bio. The handle is generic and vague: a string of letters and numbers. He has a handful of followers, mostly bots. He's following only fifteen accounts: sports teams, Instagram models, and a few personal pages, one of which is Rose's. I scroll through his "following" list again, making sure, double-checking.

He's not following me.

This is the final straw. I close out of the app and lock Graham's phone, watching the screen go dark. My chest is severed, the strings of my marriage dangling over my heart's ventricles, no longer tautly connected to the man I thought I'd spend my life with.

I sink to the floor, dropping my head in my hands. Just because it's not a surprise doesn't mean it doesn't hurt.

After I collect my breath, I sit upright. My gut feels like it's been scraped clean by a scalpel. It's raw and weeping, but the empty space means there's room for something else. The parts of myself I've hammered down and made small my entire life. Hunger grows, writhing in my stomach, and this time it's not a physical appetite but an emotional one.

Graham doesn't want me? He doesn't want to save this marriage after everything I've done for him? Very well. I'm not alone anymore; I have Sweetheart. And I can't rely on her for money or security like I did Graham, but *she* relies on *me*, and that's more important.

I stand up, grabbing Graham's phone and taking the stairs two at a time. I'm out of breath again by the time I shuffle back into our bedroom and return my husband's phone to his bedside table. I stare down at him for a moment, watching his eyes roll beneath his lids, despising the suffocating grumble of his snores. No wonder he couldn't hear me scream.

His face is guileless and naked in sleep, reminiscent of the man I met at the farmers market all those years ago. This is the man I gave my virginity to. The man I walked down the aisle for. The man I cooked and cleaned and cared for.

Rolling waves of heat crescendo through my body, and I have to step away from the bed before I pounce on him, eager to feel his skin rip apart underneath my claws.

No. Nails. I don't have claws. Of course I don't have claws.

Swallowing, suddenly cold, I leave the bedroom, heading to the cozy embrace of the nursery. My shoulders relax the minute I enter, my stomach settling and my jaw unclenching. I tiptoe over to Sweetheart's crib and watch her sleep, her skin bathed golden from the night-light.

Her nails—long, tipped white—gleam in the glow.

That's new.

I lean over the sleeping baby and inhale deeply, picking up scents of pine, fresh earth, and talcum powder. Deeper, fainter, is the smell of raw meat. It makes my belly gurgle even though I thought I was full.

I stare at Sweetheart. Will I raise her to be like me, following the whims of every man in her life? Will I teach her to be a wife, a mother, a homemaker? Or will I let her explore what she wants to explore? She could be someone I never got the chance to become. She could learn to live however the hell she wants instead of following a set of rules that keep her in a box.

Maybe I don't want to raise a traditional wife. Maybe I want to raise a feral woman.

CHAPTER

27

Leaving Sweetheart tucked in her crib, taking my phone with me so I can keep an eye on her through the baby monitor app, I slip out of the house again.

I grab my camel-colored overcoat on my way out, and I throw it over my light-gray sleep dress as my black rain boots crunch through the dying grass. I push through the withering stalks of wheat in the backyard, making my way through the darkness by sense alone. It's lightly raining, and my face dampens as I march toward the well, the approaching forest looming in front of me like a squat mountain.

Finally, I arrive, approaching the shape jutting out from the black ground. The forest hums, vibrating beyond my property, a tuneless song that beckons me closer.

I stand by the wishing well, illuminated by the weak moonlight pressing through the clouds. The rain is more like mist, gently scattering itself across my skin, chilling me to the very marrow of my bones. I welcome it, grateful for the raindrops that hide my hot tears.

A twig snaps in the forest, and I move around the well to stare into the gloom, squinting in the low light. The woods beyond the well smell of pine and flesh, like the whole thing is a living, breathing being crouched on the outskirts of the country fields. I wait, but whatever was moving inside the tangle of trees is still.

My skin prickles as if I'm being watched.

The scrape of scales against rock comes from behind me, and I turn in time to see an arm rising from the mouth of the well.

I hesitate to turn my back to the forest, but I do, mesmerized by the creature pulling itself free from the wishing well, unfolding its body so that it stands in front of me, the nubs on its temple backlit by the watery moon. Its wings are pressed tightly against its back, but as it straightens to its full height, they slowly unfurl, as if it's stretching its arms after a long night's sleep.

The creature's white eyes shine in the darkness, threads of black veins creeping around the corners of its unblinking eyelids. I step closer, shortening the distance between us.

I don't know why I came. I don't know what I want. All I know is that there is pain inside me that has been locked in a box for all twenty-four years of my life, and tonight, I finally found the key. Now that I have access to everything I discovered inside, I can't imagine putting things back to how they were. But I also can't imagine moving forward.

I am lost, trapped. Maybe the bottom of a well would feel like freedom to me.

I say nothing. The creature and I stare at each other for a few minutes, the woods humming at my back. Moonlight shines on the raindrops coating the creature's scaly skin, making it look luminous, the reflection of stars on a lake.

As I did on the night we conceived Sweetheart, I reach forward and take the creature's hand. This time, its smooth palm tightens around mine, and it pulls me closer, pressing my chest against its own. I look up, so close to its face: the ridges of its nose, the pattern of scales on its bare head, the dark hole of its mouth, which softly parts and bathes me in the scent of mud and rain-slicked stones.

The creature's free hand drifts to my face, and one clawed finger touches the tender skin under my jaw and tilts my chin up.

It kisses me.

I fall into the embrace, our mouths hot and humid against each other. It's like kissing the earth—wet, spongy, soil filled. The creature drops its hands and wraps its muscled arms around my waist instead, drawing me even tighter against its naked body. My heart pounds as if it's trying to get through my chest and into the creature's, but there are no responding beats from the breast pressed against mine.

It doesn't matter. The heat in our mouths builds until it feels like fire, a blisteringly pleasurable agony that scorches my throat and melts my teeth. I am being consumed, swallowed, and I let it happen; the creature's tongue slips into my mouth with probing interest, dragging across the roof of my soft palate, making the hair on my arms stand up.

Arrector pilis. Again.

Sweetheart's arrival allowed my body to change in fascinating ways; *all* my open wounds have tenderly repaired themselves, including the one that was between my legs.

I let my coat fall to the cold earth, exposing my gray nightdress, which is thin and useless out here in the wintery chill. I don't care; the icy night doesn't bother me. There is warmth in my core and humidity escaping the creature's mouth and skin.

The creature grows against me, pushing into my thigh, and my body responds in kind as a low moan escapes my throat and echoes against its mouth. Spurred, the creature wraps its arms around my lower half and lifts me up, spinning around to sit me on the edge of the wishing well. The uniform rocks press into my bottom as the creature hikes my sleep dress up around my waist, mouth still fastened on mine. I help, tugging down my underwear and casting it to the ground below me.

The creature's claws scrape thrillingly against the bare skin of my thighs as rain gently dampens our bodies, the cold a forgotten component of the night. We are a blazing fireball, burning through each other.

I sense the maw of the wishing well behind me, ready to swallow me up, and my skin becomes even warmer, the space between my inner thighs tingling. The creature pulls back for a moment as if sensing my excitement, examining my flushed face. I stare into its milky eyes, my breath coming fast and hard.

"Please," I whisper.

The creature pushes me down, the edge of my shoulder blades hitting the opposite side of the wishing well, the black hole underneath my torso. My feet dangle off the ground, thighs open and exposed. I am suspended over the void, my arms stretched along the side of the well, holding on to the curve of the rocks, unable to get up on my own. The yawning depth of the well is beneath me, blasting cold air up and into my back. It smells of rotting meat and rancid fur.

The wall of the well is the perfect height—the creature only needs to bend its knees slightly in order to drive itself inside me.

I gasp, and my head drops over the stone lip of the well, upper arms tensing as the creature moves against me, rhythmic, steady. The terror of knowing that at any moment my strength could fail and I could fall, folded in like a greeting card, probably breaking my back and dying a slow, suffocating death, makes me moan.

Pressure grows and the creature pants above me, stroking faster and harder now. My left hand slips against the wet stone and my hip dips down into the mouth of the well before I can reposition myself. The creature makes no move to help, continues to fuck me seamlessly. I stabilize my grip on the well and lift my hips back up, face to the sky, groaning.

One of the creature's hands finds its way to the wetness building between my legs and goes to work, fingers rubbing against my most sensitive area. My skin bursts, unraveling all at once as the creature thrusts deeply, my body splitting apart and sewing itself back together in the span of a few seconds. The same hot liquid I felt months ago burns inside me, and my muscles soften, my body sagging into the mouth of the hole.

I will fall now, smash to bits against the bottom of the well. Though I don't want to leave Sweetheart, maybe this is for the best.

Before I can slip into the opening, the creature seizes me with both arms, lifting me up and over, setting me down on solid ground next to the well. I go boneless and collapse to the wet soil, sniffing. I curl into the fetal position, trying to catch my breath as rippling waves of pleasure and fear crash through me, each one a little less intense than the last.

The creature stands above me, dripping with water, watching. Then it heavily drops to its knees and places a hand on my head. It's warm and comforting, and I relax further, my breath finally evening out.

When I can, I push myself up to a sitting position, the creature's hand easing off my hair and coming to rest on a shoulder instead. We look at each other, my face reflected in the white mirror of its eyes. I am small and messy and soaked. I do not look like Graham's wife. I do not look like a human at all. Hunger grows in my stomach as we stare at each other, steam rising from our skin from the warmth of our bodies.

Which one of us is really the fallen angel? I wonder as I once again imagine what fresh, warm flesh must taste like.

CHAPTER

28

THE NEXT MORNING, Sweetheart is awake when I check on
her, which until now was unheard of.

I make sure to bundle her in blankets, hiding her face and
eyes from Graham as he bustles around the house, getting ready
for work.

I decide not to confront Graham. Not yet, anyway. I need to
figure out my plan, since I have no savings and no job. As a strict
Catholic, Graham has said before that he never wants to divorce.
(Divorce is unthinkable, but cheating is apparently fine.) Besides,
Graham has been planning for the future—the talk of the baptism, visiting his parents, going back to church. It doesn't seem
like he's trying to distance himself permanently, no matter what
he's telling his *Rose*. I'm not sure what Graham's intentions are,
if he will stay with me and continue sneaking around on the
side, but I can't cut him loose before I'm ready.

At least this way, I have a heads-up. I know where I stand. I
can start figuring out a life for Sweetheart that allows her safety.
But it's terrifying—I've never been on my own before, and I'm
not sure that's an option. Neither is moving to Florida and staying with my father.

He's bound to notice Sweetheart's . . . features.

For the first time, I accept how utterly isolated I am. My online friends are just that—online friends. I can't lean on them for support; Mara never answered my DM. And now that Renee is gone, I don't have anyone in my life I see often enough to consider a friend.

I will have to stay here, in this house, with Graham, pretending like everything is normal until I can figure something else out.

The thought makes me itchy with panic; I'm not used to making decisions by myself.

You decided to have sex with a creature that lives in your well, the familiar voice in my head points out. It's moved from the back of my brain to the front in recent weeks. *You made that choice on your own, and you made it fairly fast. Everything will be OK.*

"God will provide," I whisper, and then I laugh.

Whatever God is involved in my life is not the ephemeral and distantly benevolent God I remember from my youth. Maybe it is Graham's God, an immortal being ready to throw brimstone and thunder if you disobey. And I *have* disobeyed. I am no longer a good wife. I haven't been for some time.

"Camille?" Graham calls up the stairs, interrupting my spiraling thoughts. "Camille? Is there any breakfast?"

No, for fuck's sake, there's no breakfast, because I'm up here taking care of our hungry daughter whose eyes you've never seen even though you don't seem to find that strange at all.

I straighten my shoulders and look at Sweetheart gurgling in the crib. "Stay here, honey," I whisper. "Please, no crying right now."

I run from the room, barely glancing at Graham, who stares at me from his position at the foot of the stairs as I brush by him into the kitchen. I yank a bowl from the cabinets, withdraw a box of cereal from the pantry, and listen as the oat rings *ding* into the ceramic. I can feel Graham behind me in the kitchen, watching, as I fling open the fridge and pour the fresh milk we get delivered by bottle into the cereal.

"Here," I say, shoving the bowl into Graham's waiting hands.

He pauses for a moment, gazing at my lips as if expecting to see a smile there. But I don't have one to give him. Not today. Not after last night.

"Are . . . are you serious?" Graham asks, the cereal bowl sagging in his big palms.

"Yes, Graham. I'm busy. Our daughter is awake and hungry, and I've had a late start." I try to massage the irritation from my voice, but the proximity of Graham's eyebrows to each other indicates I'm not being very successful.

"Camille, I think we should—" Graham is cut off by the doorbell buzzing.

For a brief, ludicrous instant, I think it must be Renee at the door, and my hands start sweating thinking about her interacting with Graham. Then I remember.

"Who is that so early?" Graham wonders as he walks the pathetic bowl of cereal over to the counter, leaving it behind as he marches into the hallway.

My stomach twists as I scurry behind him, catching a glimpse of my bleak expression in the hall mirror. I glance down at the baby monitor on my phone—Sweetheart is standing in her crib, completely motionless.

My throat clenches; sweat floods the waistband of the soft pants I wear. My daughter stares directly into the baby monitor camera. Her eyes are wide and empty.

Standing. She's *standing*. Already.

Her fists are clenched around the bars of the crib as if she's a prisoner waiting for her last meal. She is quiet—for now. But I can sense her hunger through the phone screen.

I want to rush upstairs; is this the first time Sweetheart is standing, or has she done this by herself before when I wasn't looking? I should be there for such a milestone, but Graham is opening our frosted-glass front door without even bothering to use the peephole and—

The floor vanishes beneath my feet as a man in a brown uniform wearing a golden badge materializes on our doorstep, nodding at my husband.

Oh, this is bad.

"Good morning, sir," the cop says, spotting me and raising a hand. "Ma'am. I was wondering if you had a moment to speak with me?"

It's hard work to breathe normally; every inhale scrapes the back of my throat, and my chest is an accordion—folded in and crunched. I glance down again at my phone. Sweetheart hasn't moved from her position, but her nostrils flare as she sniffs the air.

"Certainly," Graham says, graciously stepping to the side to allow the police officer to enter. "I'm Graham. Graham Deming. And this is my wife, Camille."

What are you doing? I want to scream at my husband. *Don't let him in!*

"I'm Officer Lipton," the man says. He's shorter than Graham, maybe even shorter than me, and his face is clean-shaven and spotted with beauty marks. Dark hair peeks out from the rim of his hat, and he looks to be in his late thirties. His black boots tread dust and flecks of dirt into the hallway, but I don't care. "Sorry to bother you folks so early, but I have a bit of a situation I was hoping you could help me with."

"Sure," Graham says, pausing in front of the staircase. "Sorry for the mess. We have a newborn. My wife is trying to find her balance."

I grit my teeth against the unnecessary barb, focusing instead on my relief that Graham is not leading the cop deeper into our house. Until, right on cue, Sweetheart's pterodactyl screech comes from upstairs, short and high-pitched.

"Newborn, huh?" Officer Lipton says, offering me a wan smile. "I know how it goes. My oldest just turned seventeen. They scream a lot at that age too. Do you need to go get your baby?"

"No!" It comes out more panicked than I would like, and I plaster on a smile. "I mean, no, she's OK for now. Please, continue." I want this done—fast. Sweetheart's scream means her hunger is growing.

"Well," Lipton says, glancing around the house in a way I'm sure he thinks is surreptitious. He's trying to take stock of us through our tastefully decorated home. "I'm looking for a neighbor of yours who has been reported missing. Renee Colt? I'm trying to figure out the last time anyone saw or spoke to Ms. Colt."

I straighten, watching Lipton's droopy eyes as my heart hammers. Graham shifts next to me, and I resist the urge to whip around and fly up the stairs to barricade myself in the nursery with Sweetheart.

"Uh, yeah," Graham says before I can answer. He smiles at the cop but drops it when he sees it's not being reciprocated. "Renee. She lives down the road. We know her. She's *missing*?"

"Her ex-husband said she didn't show up for visitation with her children on Sunday afternoon," Lipton explains, locking eyes on Graham as if he's forgotten I'm here. "Apparently, she can be flaky. Mr. Colt didn't worry right away, but when he tried to contact her earlier this week and never heard back, he got concerned. When he drove out to the house to check on her, no one was home."

"Hang on," Graham says. "Visitation? With her own kids? And did you say her *ex*-husband?"

I want to elbow my husband, step on his foot to make him shut up, but Lipton would notice and I'm starting to suspect

Graham might be too dense to catch on to my meaning anyway.

Lipton nods, raising a brow. "That's right. They are divorced. Didn't you know that?"

"No," Graham gasps, and it's not because Renee is missing— it's the *d* word that has freaked him out. Graham has a low opinion of people who divorce. He turns to me. "She didn't tell you, Camille? She never said anything to you?"

I had averted my eyes, but now I clench my back teeth, thrown off-kilter by being put on the spot. Clearing my throat, I glance up at Graham, then Lipton. "No, she never mentioned it."

Lipton doesn't look surprised by this. "Well, her ex-husband said she was having a bit of trouble accepting it. Might not have wanted to talk about it. How close were you?"

"We weren't actually that close," I say at the same time Graham announces, "She was our midwife."

Perturbed silence falls over the hallway. Lipton slowly reaches into his front pocket and pulls out a small notepad and a pen, flicking the cover of the pad open.

He clears his throat. "So which was it? You weren't close or she was your midwife?"

Graham looks at me, frowning, and I swallow down the cast-iron lump in my throat. "Both," I lie. "I haven't seen her in a while. She helped me when I was pregnant. And in giving birth."

"I find that interesting," Lipton says. "Because Renee Colt isn't known to have any midwifery training." He looks up from his notepad, zeroing in on me this time.

I see which way this will go, and I'm powerless to stop it. The tower I've built is starting to come down.

"Camille?" Graham asks. "What's going on?"

"I don't know what to say," I tell Lipton. "She told me she had training, and she knew what she was doing. Obviously. I'm alive, aren't I? But like I said, I really didn't know her that well. And I haven't seen her in a while."

Graham is looking at me, beard twitching as his lips work, like I'm a zoo animal he's unfamiliar with. He's never heard me be contrarian like this before, especially not to another man.

"How long?" Lipton asks, pen hovering above his notepad. His face is impassive. "How long since you've seen Ms. Colt?"

From upstairs, Sweetheart screams again, a blast of sound, and I chance another look at the video monitor on my phone, using it as an excuse to break eye contact with the cop.

Sweetheart has moved to the edge of the crib closest to the door of the nursery, and her head is tilted up, as if she's a hound trying to catch a scent.

Seeing her steadies my heartbeat.

"I'm not really sure," I say, improvising. "I've had such bad mommy brain lately. Not a lot of sleep. *You* know. But"—I lower my voice—"the last few times I saw her, after my birth, she smelled like wine."

Graham is frowning; could he make our disconnect any more obvious? I want to smack him and erase the perplexity from his face.

Get on the same page as me, I want to shout. But maybe we've never been united on anything and I'm only realizing it now.

"Got it," Lipton says, but his expression doesn't change. If Renee's ex-husband Zach told the cop about his former wife's drinking when he called in the missing-persons report, my story will align nicely with that narrative. "Well, I don't blame you for not knowing the exact date you saw her last. My wife's sleep schedule was a mess for a year. Can be hard to remember."

"Sorry, Officer, I hate to rush you," Graham interrupts. "But I really do have to get to work."

"Oh, I can stay and chat with your wife a bit, then," Lipton says, and my heart clenches.

But Graham finally does something helpful. He shakes his head, stepping in front of me. "I don't think that's a good idea. She has a lot to do. You can hear our daughter upstairs, I'm sure!" Graham softens his words with another boyish grin. "And the house needs some work today. We're in a bit of a state. Maybe you can come back another time?"

My goodwill toward Graham evaporates as he once again finds a way to get in a jab—he must still be pissed about the bowl of cereal.

"I understand," Lipton says, smoothly flipping closed his notepad and returning both it and his pen to his pocket. "Another time. I'd love to chat soon, though. We're trying to contact Ms. Colt, and I'd love to return to her family and tell them there's nothing to worry about."

"I'm sure that's true," Graham replies. "Maybe she went off for a vacation."

"Maybe," Lipton says, shrugging in a way that feels too casual. He is piqued—he will be back. "All right, folks. Thanks for your time. Hope you get some sleep, Mrs. Deming."

I nod at him, my mouth glued shut. Graham walks the cop to the front door, and Sweetheart screams again from upstairs, as if she can smell them moving farther away. But I don't dare go to her; not yet.

"Have a nice day, Officer," Graham says, and we watch Lipton head back to his cruiser, which is parked on the side of the road. No wonder we didn't hear him in the driveway.

When the cop pulls away, Graham slams the frosted door shut and whips around. "What the hell is going on, Camille?"

He's serious—Graham never uses the word *hell* like that.

"Nothing!" I protest.

"Nothing?" he repeats incredulously. "Why is that cop saying Renee has no midwife training? And what do you mean, you weren't that close? I thought she comes over here all the time!"

"You're never home, so how would you know?" I retaliate, our voices rising notch by notch to match each other.

"Camille, you better tell me what this is all about," Graham warns. "Something is wrong. It has been for a long time."

"I couldn't agree more." My voice drops, and I stare baldly at my husband, layering truths I can't yet speak into my words.

Graham freezes, catching my weighted tone but apparently deciding not to push. "You need to take some time. Think about this. Let me know what's really going on. And maybe I can get my wife back, yeah? The woman who loves her hobbies and dresses to impress every day and who effortlessly cares for the people around her."

"Oh, do you mean the woman who cooks and clean for *you*, wears impractical dresses for *you*, and effortlessly cares for *you*?" I bite.

Graham takes a step back, eyes wide. "Camille! You know it's not about that. What has gotten into you lately?"

Meat. Lots and lots of meat.

I almost cackle at the thought, my composure slipping again, my face hot and tight like a plaster-cast mask. "Nothing," I whisper. "Nothing has gotten into me at all."

"Look, I'm gonna be late for work if I waste any more time with this," Graham says. "We'll talk when I get home."

A memory, unearthed like rotten roots in the soil of my mind, sprawls forth at my husband's words—my father, a decade ago, finding a human anatomy book hidden in my bedroom.

"What is this, Camille?" he growled. "Why do you have this? Do you know what kind of photos are in here? I flipped through it. This isn't a school textbook." He held up the book, which had a whole chapter on sexual organs, and shook it threateningly. "Girls your age shouldn't be reading smut like this."

I was wildly confused. I'd wanted to learn more about why my vagina was bleeding every month, what was happening inside my body that could cause something so surprising. My mother was long dead by then. We didn't live near any female relatives, and there was no one at school I trusted enough to ask.

"I wanted to learn," I said weakly, and my father's face loomed above me, dark shadows nestling in creases I didn't know he had.

"School is for learning. This"—he waved the book around again—"is not learning. Unless you're taking notes on sexual positions and STDs? Something you need to tell me?"

I flushed hot, and tears formed. "No! No. I'm sorry, Father. I'll get rid of it."

"To hell you will." His voice was like a storm. "I'm throwing this away myself. I'm going to work, but we'll talk more when I get home."

My father—Graham is talking to me now like my father talked to me when I was fourteen, trying to discover the truth about my own body. My guts cramp as I acknowledge what I've politely ignored for four years: I traded in one domineering man for another.

But Graham talking to me like a child doesn't make me want to cower and apologize like I did with my father. Instead, my stomach gurgles and my head throbs. The scaled pieces of skin on my hairline itch under my beanie; the spot on my foot where my toes used to be burns.

I am not a little girl anymore. And Graham is *not* my father.

"I have to go," he says, moving toward the garage door, staring back at me with mistrust. "I'm really disappointed in you," he adds.

I don't fight the frown this time. I allow it to slowly settle on my features with weighted silence as I meet Graham's eyes from the hallway. I pair the frown with the simpering, wheedling voice Graham is used to hearing from me: "I'm so sorry to hear that, babe."

It's worth it to see his face before he slams the garage door.

I breathe in the silence of the house after he's gone, wondering how I've managed to lie to myself for so long.

The truth is a ghost: hovering at your peripheral vision, disappearing when you turn to catch it. It's easy to ignore a ghost that does not want to be revealed. A cabinet opens on its own. A door creaks. But it's all easily explained away, and the ghost remains at the fringe of your awareness until you can step back, see enough of the house to realize what it is that you're looking at.

I can't return this haunting now. I cannot put it back into the outskirts of my perspective. The truth is mine, and I will kill it before I pretend I haven't seen it.

CHAPTER

29

I RACE UPSTAIRS WHEN I'm sure I'm alone again, nearly falling into the nursery.

Sweetheart is upright, facing the door, chunky legs supporting her entire considerable weight while she bounces on the balls of her feet.

"Hi, baby," I cluck as I approach the crib. "Look at you, my love. Standing all on your own like a big girl!"

Sweetheart opens her mouth as I draw closer and screeches, a protestation that echoes in my eardrums.

"I'm sorry," I whisper. "I'm working on it. I'll figure something out. Should we try the bottle again?"

But when I reopen the same cut on my arm, filling up a new bottle with my blood and presenting it to her, she doesn't bother to latch on. She bites into the nipple, ripping it free, and claws at the bottle as I help her tip it into her mouth. She swishes the blood for a moment and then spits it out, howling.

It's as I feared. Blood is not enough anymore. She needs meat.

"You want real food, don't you?" I say to her as I dab at the bloodstains on her two-piece outfit with a wet wipe, trying to calm her.

"Food," she babbles.

My heart nearly stops. "W-what did you say? Did you say . . ."

"Food," Sweetheart demands again.

"Oh, baby," I croon. "Your first word! Oh, how lovely!"

Out of habit, I pull out my phone as if to document this moment. A few weeks ago, I would have recorded Sweetheart, getting creative with the camera angle and lighting so no one online would be able to see her unnatural eyes and long finger-nails and mouthful of barracuda teeth.

Not anymore. I lower the phone. Now I am content to have this special moment shared between the two of us. It's not like I can tell Graham; even if we were getting along, it's too early for Sweetheart to be talking. And Graham is "disappointed" in me. He's also a liar. He doesn't deserve to be a part of this.

The phone buzzes in my hand, and I glance down at the notifications stacking up on my home screen. The latest one catches my eye:

Why did you delete all your baby photos??

Hissing, I open the app. I haven't posted in a while, but there are comments and messages cluttering my page anyway:

What happened to the baby stuff? Did something happen?

Where's Sweetheart??

I heard ur not a real tradwife. Our culture is not a costume!!!!

There's more, but nothing from Mara. She never replied to my plea for help. When I tap over to her page, checking her list, my stomach drops.

Mara isn't following me anymore.

Maybe my DM notified her of the CAST drama. Maybe she saw I deleted my posts and didn't approve. Maybe she found a new influencer to follow she liked more. It doesn't matter. She's abandoned me.

"Food," Sweetheart reminds me. Her tears have ceased. Her ethereal gaze settles on my face.

"Yes," I say, returning to her, shaking. She is the only thing that matters now. "Yes, OK. But you have to be careful. You can't take too much." I don't think she can understand me, but it's soothing to speak to her this way. It makes me feel better about what I'm about to do. Even if the worst happens, dying to feed your child isn't such a bad way to go. "And let's go downstairs. Cleanup is easier on the kitchen tiles."

Sweetheart reaches her arms up as if she agrees with my plan, and I gently turn her around and pick her up, lifting with my newly muscled legs. Carrying Sweetheart with her back against my chest, one hand under her rear and the other across her torso, I start to sweat again as we head down the stairs. Sweetheart is like a barrel of cement, compact and concentrated in one small space.

We don't make it to the kitchen. At the foot of the stairs, a soft knock comes from the front door. No doorbell this time.

I startle, glancing over at the dark shape behind the frosted glass. The shadow is drifting back and forth like a cloud, and my heart leaps.

"Is it you?" My voice comes out hushed and hopeful.

I hurry over to the entryway, forgetting to check the peephole, shifting Sweetheart so I can free a hand to unlock the door, throwing it open before I can second-guess myself.

Lipton is back, hovering on our front step.

"Hi," he says, rubbing the nape of his neck and giving me a sheepish smile. "I'm sorry to bother you again. But I seem to have misplaced my pen, and it's the only one I have. Mind if I check? I think I might have dropped it in your hallway. Oh— ah, I think I see it."

He makes a show of peering behind me, staring at the floor. I turn as well, eyes landing on the same pen I could have sworn I saw Lipton return to his pocket earlier. It's resting on the floor, near the baseboard, tucked out of the way so that it won't be stepped on.

Alarm bells go off in my head. Sweetheart dangles heavily in my arms; Lipton is so busy with his playacting he hasn't noticed her sudden stillness, her wide, white eyes. But I do; my daughter's body grows stiff, and deep, sharp inhales of breath whistle through her nose.

"I think you should leave," I say, my voice muffled and scratchy as if coming through a wool blanket. "My husband said—"

"I'll just grab my pen real quick, OK?" Lipton says, nodding as if I've agreed with him and entering the house, slipping past me into the hallway so he can bend down and scoop up his "lost" pen.

I hesitate for the briefest of moments, then close the front door. The lock clicks, my fingers caressing the smooth latch before I return my hand to my daughter's body, supporting her. I move toward the cop, Sweetheart silent and calm in my arms.

"Since I'm here, I thought we could talk for a bit," Lipton starts to say. "It kind of felt like you didn't get a chance to tell me the full story earlier. When your husband was here. He tends to do the talking, doesn't he?"

"I have nothing else to say."

"Well, I think—" Lipton finally notices Sweetheart, does a double take when he realizes what he's looking at. "Is . . . is this your daughter?"

"Yes." Sweetheart and I stare at the cop. I take a step closer. His back is to the staircase, and the pen is in his hand. I peek at his gun in its holster. "This is Sweetheart."

"She's, ah, she's . . . Pardon my question, but is she *OK*?" Lipton's dark brows are twitching, and he steps forward in spite of himself to get a better look.

"She's hungry," I say.

"Didn't you say she was a newborn?" Lipton asks, eyes darting up to my face. I am the one cool and aloof now, a direct switch from our earlier dynamic. "She is . . . big. And those eyes . . ."

"She's fine," I insist.

"Right." Lipton shakes himself as if he doesn't want to be rude. "Let's get back to Renee Colt."

"Sure," I say, stepping closer again. Sweetheart goes even more rigid in my arms, and a dribble of hot drool splashes on my hand under her chest. "We can talk. But Sweetheart needs to eat first." And because he's only trying to do his job, I add, "Sorry."

"I don't—"

I move too fast. Slipping both my hands under Sweetheart's arms, I swoop her forward as if I'm going to shoot her at Lipton's face. He reacts, dropping the pen for real this time, both arms coming up to catch my baby even though I have no intention of actually throwing her.

Sweetheart passes through Lipton's open arms as I thrust her at his neck, and warm blood splatters against my cheeks as my daughter fastens her teeth into the man's trachea. He doesn't get a chance to scream; blood chokes him, his face turns white. Lipton's constellation of beauty marks stand out on his skin as he pales and convulses.

Sweetheart snarls against the man's throat and then jerks her face violently to the left, ripping his trachea out. Lipton's legs give way, and he slumps to the hallway floor, twitching and gurgling.

The red flesh and jellylike plasma from Lipton's neck disappear into my daughter's mouth, her teeth working furiously.

Blood paints us; my sweater set is dark with spots and the floor is collecting a puddle of crimson under Lipton's shuddering body.

Sweetheart screeches up at me, and I sigh. "Relax, I'm putting you down!"

I place Sweetheart next to Lipton. On her hands and knees, she crawls over and attacks his throat again, pulling at his exposed esophagus with her needle teeth. A glimpse of his larynx pops out from the top of his throat, and my stomach groans in hunger.

Sweetheart digs in, gnawing on Lipton's neck until his feet stop trembling and his hands go limp. I stand over them both, protectively, watching for a moment until drool begins to spill from the side of my mouth.

When Sweetheart starts to move downward, I kneel by her side. "Be careful," I tell her. "I don't think you should eat through the clothes. Hold on one moment, and I'll help you."

I'm not sure if she's listening, but she does pause, chewing something thick and slimy, giving me enough time to unbutton the brown uniform and wrestle the top half of the cop free from his shirt.

The cop.

I fumble around, taking Lipton's belt, his holster, and the contents of his pockets. When I find what I'm looking for, I pat Sweetheart's head, trying to ignore the growing ache in my belly.

"Stay here. Eat up. I have to do something really quick."

She doesn't acknowledge me; she's too busy feasting on Lipton's clavicle, strings of flesh dangling from her chin, smacking wetly against her lips. I leave her in the hallway, sitting in a pool of blood, and slip out of the house through the front door.

A different mother would be concerned about leaving her child home alone, especially while eating, but I'm no longer worried about Sweetheart's fragility. I am raising a strong daughter. She will be fine.

Lipton's car is once again parked on the shoulder of the road. His keys jangle in my hand as I trot across the yard. I keep my head on a swivel, checking the road, but it's late morning and it's a weekday. No one is around to see my bloody face.

The withering wheat fields rustle; frostbitten air nips at my cheeks as I hurry to the squad car. It's brown, matching Lipton's uniform, and the paint is chipped near the treads. In the reflection of the passenger side window, the house rears up behind me, framing my head like a standing ruff, as if I am royalty.

I kick up puffs of dirt as I skirt around the vehicle, once again making sure no one is around. Grateful there is no blood on the back side of my body to stain the seats, I unlock the car, slither inside, and cut a sharp U-turn.

It takes less than ten minutes to drive to Renee's house. I park the cop car in her yard, next to her sedan, and use fistfuls of the inside of my sweater to wipe the steering wheel and door handle. I pocket the keys; I'll toss them into the well later. I'm sure the creature won't mind.

I walk home, praying, and my luck holds; no one drives by.

By the time I make it back to the house, Sweetheart has hollowed out Lipton's stomach. The yellowed, ridged vertebrae of his lumbar spine are visible through the remaining viscera floating like soup in the bowl that used to contain the man's inner organs.

My daughter is sucking on her thumb, her other fingers already licked clean. The oatmeal-colored outfit I put her in this morning is thoroughly destroyed—blood is drying on her pants and sticking her to the hallway floor. But her face is glowing. She is smiling and chattering gibberish to herself as she wriggles her feet, toes squirming like excited maggots.

"All done?" I ask as I kneel down next to her.

Sweetheart smacks her lips and continues her babbling, adding dainty handclaps now that she's finished slurping gore off her fingers. My heart inflates to see her so content, but I am quickly distracted by the meat in front of me.

The smell of Lipton's cracked-open body makes my mouth water again. Hot blood, exposed bones, tattered flesh. I lean over him, inhaling deeply, eyes tearing with overwhelming need. The hunger grows so great inside me I fear it will turn my stomach inside out, heaving its way out of the internal and into reality with devastating assuredness.

Groaning, I dip a quivering fingertip into the puddle of blood resting in a socket of pockmarked flesh near what used to be Lipton's waist. I drag a line of red sludge across the flayed flesh and imagine what it would be like to mimic my daughter and suck the ichor from my finger. A blast of unrealized flavor surges through my mouth, and drool rolls down my chin, sopping the front of my sweater.

I am going to do it. I am leaning forward, letting the heat overwhelm me, allowing the urge to take over, when I notice my daughter. Done eating her fill of Lipton, Sweetheart's beautiful milky eyes have narrowed, and she waves unsteadily like a kitten who is simply too sleepy to bother getting comfortable. With great effort, I tear myself away from Lipton's remains and catch Sweetheart before she falls backward, already dropping off into a deep sleep.

She's a mess. I will have to unstick her from the drying crop circle of blood she sits in and clean her up, toss away her clothes, return her to the crib upstairs so she can rest. And I must drag the rest of Lipton's body outside, hide him in the field like I did Renee. I have to remove the remainder of his clothes and throw all evidence of him into the well. I have to clean the blood seeping into the floor.

I will not lick the blood up like a dehydrated animal. I cannot. That would be . . . preposterous.

I can't be distracted by anything right now. I need to erase all evidence of this occurrence from the entryway of our home.

Hoisting my daughter up, I get to work, imagining what tips my ex-friend Mara Shoemaker might have for getting bloodstains out of hardwood floors.

CHAPTER

30

THE CLEANUP TAKES much longer than I anticipated.
Lipton is heavier than Renee, even without his midsection, and harder to drag into the field. The afternoon slides away as I scrub the floor, pour baking soda, blot bleach, using every method at my disposal to remove the evidence of what happened this morning from our hallway.

Sweating profusely despite the house's interminable chill, I finally remember to return to the field and remove the rest of Lipton's clothing, carrying the bloody bundle deeper into the wheat until I reach the well and the fringe of the forest. The trees hum beyond the dusty field, a low vibration that sits on my bones. The wind murmurs through the pines, carrying the scent of leathery skin and fresh soil.

A hook in my chest tugs toward the woods, but I ignore it. Instead, I approach the wishing well, neck growing hot when I think about the last time I was here, spread-eagle over the dark hole, gasping into the night.

Peering over the edge, I whisper, "Look out below," and shove Lipton's clothing, gun, and car keys into the void. The keys ring out against the walls, bouncing off hard rock, but the sounds eventually fade into oblivion. Like with the penny and Renee's bones, there is no finality—no faint thud or clatter to indicate there's a bottom.

Next, I yank the framed photo I grabbed from the craft room out of my coat pocket. Mara smirks up at me. Our faces, edited together, look garish and mismatched in broad daylight. Lifting the frame over my head like an axe, I smash it against the rim of the well. It crimps and glass shatters, sprinkling into the opening. Ripping the photo I created from the remnants of the frame, I tear at Mara's face with my teeth, shredding my own image in the process. Then I throw it all into the well too.

I wait for a minute, even though I'm tight on time. I haven't checked my phone much today, but in between my scrubbing Graham texted me—he will be home for dinner, and he wants to "talk about what happened earlier."

Gone are the days I prayed to have him home at a normal hour. Now I wish he would go stay with Rose and give me more time to finish up here.

"Are you down there?" I murmur into the well. "Can you hear me?"

The abyss of darkness is silent and unmoving, but the stench that comes from the mouth of it is familiar in a way that shivers my heart and curls my toes. There's a gravity to the hushed well that makes me think it's listening.

"I'm not sure I can do this anymore," I say, lowering my lips to the hole as if I can kiss the darkness itself. From far below comes the shifting of stiff wings, the soft carving of claws against stone. "Not *this* this," I clarify. "This as in the house. This with Graham. How much longer can I hide? How much longer can I keep up this charade?"

A warm sigh of air wafts from the well, coating my face like exhaust. I imagine a clawed hand under my chin—bare, smooth palms holding my tired, gray-tinged cheeks. There are no words. But I hear it all the same—a subdued declaration of finality.

This will end soon.

It's what I need. Placing my hands on the cold rock rim of the well, I straighten, glancing over at the matted forest eating away at the dying edges of the wheat field. Its presence felt ominous months ago. Intimidating and massive. An unknown entity that would keenly swallow me up without a second thought. But that feeling has dispersed; now the forest is full of curiosity and barbed promises. Still an unknown, but one that winks cheekily in the darkness—an invitation to explore, if you dare.

I don't. Not today. I have to get back to my tasks.

Turning from the forest, I reluctantly remove my hand from the lip of the well even though I want to stay, chopping off bits of myself so I too can fall down into the black.

*   *   *

Graham comes home to a cold kitchen.

I didn't have the time to cook dinner. I barely finished everything else I had to do after Lipton's unexpected return. Part of me wants to apologize, but then I remind myself of Graham's secret social media account, and atonement dies on my lips.

"What's going on?" Graham says, blinking around at the kitchen like a cow. "Didn't you get my text? I said I'd be here for dinner."

I'm standing at the fridge, doors wide open, shelves bereft and wanting, when he walks in. I was trying to figure out what I could prepare him, but I drifted off into thought instead, remembering the metallic scent of Lipton's split body.

Graham steps farther into the room, shoes squeaking on the floor. I mopped the kitchen vigorously, not wanting it to be obvious that the front hallway was the only surface I cleaned. "Whoa, it smells weird in here."

I scrubbed with vinegar, which I tried to cover up with a five-wick cinnamon-scented candle. It didn't work. Now it smells like rancid cinnamon rolls.

"I thought you wanted me to clean?" I say mulishly, letting the fridge doors slap shut.

Graham crosses his arms, and the temperature, already too low despite my efforts to wrestle with the thermostat, drops another several degrees. "You never had a problem managing cleaning *and* cooking before."

"We didn't have a baby before," I point out. What is he not understanding? Just because his life hasn't changed doesn't mean mine hasn't.

Graham sighs, his arms loosening as he comes closer, leaning against the fridge so he can meet my eye. His voice, when he speaks again, is softer, affectionate. "Seriously, Camille, what's going on with you? Are you sick or something? Because we can get you help . . ."

He smells like cologne and blood. I can sense it, the river of red pounding beneath the surface of his skin. I've never been so acutely aware of someone else's heartbeat before. Graham reaches out to brush a hand against the fringe of hair visible underneath the beanie I'm wearing. He lurches back when his fingers touch brittle strands and slick dead ends.

"I'm not sick," I snap, and I fight against adjusting my tone. My knee-jerk reaction is to defer to him. Apologize profusely and pretend that everything that has happened over the past month was a dream. We could go back to normal. It would be like muscle memory—slipping into our old dynamic and sinking into the anesthetizing banality of the routine I grew so comfortable with. But when I continue, the tenor of my voice is exactly the same. "I feel fine."

Graham's sympathy reaches its limit. "Really? Have you checked a mirror lately? Your skin looks gray or something."

I'm slightly surprised he's mentioned my skin—I haven't cared to do my usual face full of makeup, and Graham didn't seem to notice. But now I'm realizing he did; he kept it as ammunition until he was ready to use it.

What he hasn't noticed, however, are the dark spots on my charcoal outfit and the dried blood under my fingernails.

Graham adds, "Your hair . . . it's slimy. Looks dead."

I smile at him. "Technically, all hair is dead. The follicles have blood vessels to keep it growing, but once the hair breaches the scalp, the cells aren't alive anymore."

Graham stares at me like I've declared myself an atheist. "Camille, I'm concerned, OK? You are *different*. God forgive me, but it's like even the shape of your face has changed." He glances up and down my body. "But you've also gained some weight?"

"I just had a *baby*," I hiss. Yes, I've gained weight. I have muscles now where I didn't before. I am no longer slender and easily lifted, and he doesn't like that.

"This isn't you. This isn't *us*," Graham says, pushing closer to me. He sniffs the air, winces. Then eyes me. Sniffs again. "We never fight. And now it's all we do."

"I know."

Graham inhales again, and his face erupts in disgust when he attributes whatever he's smelling to me, his wife. I wonder what it is. I haven't showered yet today and I did a lot of manual labor, but I'm so comfortable in my stained sweatpants and dark knit hat that I can't identify my own scent. All I can detect is the alluring aroma of Graham's warm body.

"Camille," Graham says, and his voice is low and even more subdued. "We need to discuss this morning. That cop."

A thrill runs up my spine at the thought of Lipton's naked body hidden in a nest of wheat fifty yards from our house. My mouth waters. I haven't eaten yet today. I can't wait to gorge myself on whatever fresh meat the creature leaves for me tonight.

"I don't know what he was talking about," I say to Graham, swallowing the excess of saliva collecting on my tongue.

"Why did he say Renee isn't a midwife?" Graham's words are urgent, rushed, and this is the crux—the question he's been wanting to ask all day. He's lingered on it, mulling it over in his mind. He knows I'm lying, but he doesn't believe it. Not his little wife. She would never. She *could* never.

"He must have been confused," I say. "Got bad information."

"He also said she's divorced," Graham reminds me. "And *you*. You said she smelled like wine? You let a drunk woman inside our home? Near the baby?"

He's talking too fast, and his words are vipers striking my chest and making me step back, farther and farther away from the man I thought I'd love forever.

"Why did you say you haven't seen her in a while?" he continues, stalking forward, tracking my retreat, my eyes wide and beseeching. "Didn't you say you saw her all the time? What's going on, Camille?" Graham pauses, his throat bobbing as he swallows. "Who delivered that baby?"

It's the way he says it. *That baby.* As if she's a stranger. A friend's pet he's allowed in his house who has betrayed him by peeing on his favorite shoes.

Sweetheart is not Graham's daughter. The messages I read prove that Graham is suspicious of that anyway. But now I hear it in his voice—he's actively working to disentangle himself from the ties of fatherhood. Not *our baby*. Not *my daughter*.

That baby.

"It's true," I lie again, feeling no remorse about it this time. "Renee was my midwife. I don't know what else to say to you."

"The truth," he demands.

I am suddenly shouting. "Would you reciprocate? If I tell you the truth, will you finally do the same?"

Everything that has been submerged inside the beating ocean of blind love breaks free from the surface, rearing ugly sea monster heads, ecstatic to be above the waves at last. I want to rein in the beasts baring their teeth who will make it impossible for me to continue on as if I have no clue. I am not ready for reality. I am not ready for life without a husband. But the writhing sea snakes have blotted out the sun, and I can't contain the rage bashing against the shore anymore.

"What are you talking—"

I cut him off. "I know, Graham," I thunder. Then I drop my voice, words hollow and hushed. "I know about Rose."

His face pinches as if someone has squeezed his cheeks, bulging out his eyes and whitening his forehead. His mouth opens, flaps for a moment, searching for oxygen, and then closes. Graham's expression goes slack, and he shakes his head. "I don't know what you're talking about."

"I saw the messages, Graham," I spit. "Stop lying."

"What messages?"

"On your Instagram. The one you said you didn't have."

He shakes his head again, as if he's sad for me and my stupid little lady brain. "You're mistaken. You know I don't have social media, Camille. See, this is why I'm concerned about you. Something is wrong."

"Yes, you! *You* are wrong!" My head is spinning; I can't fathom why he would try to keep up the farce. What are we doing here? What is he getting from this?

Graham taps at his phone, unlocking it and turning it around so I can see his home screen. Without even looking, he swipes through his limited apps. "See? Nothing there."

I snatch the phone from his hands and investigate, but he's right. The warm ombré colors of the Instagram icon aren't present on his device. My brain snaps apart, sinewy gray matter holding it together by stretched threads.

Did I imagine the whole thing? Have I gotten everything wrong?

I thought I was seeing things months ago, before Sweetheart was born. Maybe the reason Graham hasn't noticed anything about our daughter is because there is nothing wrong. Perhaps the truth is that the insanity I feared all those weeks ago has fully rooted now, warping my existence and planting lies in my mind.

The messages seemed so real. I recall the glow from Graham's phone on the bedside table, the bang of my heartbeat, the scent of Holy Peony. Despair skids grooved marks into my heart as I bite my lip, questioning everything.

Then I remember: The glow from Graham's phone was from a message. A message I opened, barely reading it as I scrolled back through their communication. A message not marked as unread after I snooped. I returned the phone to its rightful place by its owner and went out into the night to fuck a monster.

If my husband woke the next day and checked his account, expecting a message from Rose or wanting to contact her, he could have realized there was a read message that he hadn't opened. He probably deleted the app from his phone, knowing this accusation was coming, prepared to manipulate me into believing his lies.

That absolute *prick*.

"You knew," I whisper. "You knew I saw your messages. And now you're trying to cover your tracks."

"You're mistaken," Graham insists. "You're tired, I can see that now."

I throw his phone at him, and Graham scrambles to catch it before it smashes to the kitchen floor. "Nice try," I say, allowing a snarl to crumple the edges of my voice. "I know what I saw. You're cheating."

Graham's mouth parts for a moment, as if shocked that I didn't go for his scheme, and then he quickly knits his brows together in a mimicry of pity. "Oh, babe. This is going nowhere. I can't talk to you when you're like this. You're not *you* when you're like this."

He doesn't know who I am. Neither did I until Sweetheart's birth a few months ago. The shattered remains of our marriage surround us, littering our new house with jagged ends. The finality hangs over our heads, but I can't bring myself to say it. Not even now.

And apparently neither can he.

Graham shifts from foot to foot, waiting, before breaking the exhausted silence by saying, "So . . . dinner?"

CHAPTER

31

THE NEXT MORNING, Graham astounds me.

"I decided to take the day off," he says when we wake up on opposite sides of the bed. In our sleep, we've naturally rolled as far away from each other as we can get without falling over the side of the mattress.

This is not ideal. I didn't plan for this.

I'm exhausted from sneaking out of the house at one in the morning to suck on boar bones and chew gristle, long after Graham went to bed with a belly full of mashed potatoes and grilled chicken. I ended up making him dinner last night for reasons I still can't understand. It's like the movements of wifehood have been tattooed on me and I need to find new ink to cover them up.

I felt better after eating my own dinner—I'm not sure where the creature even *found* a wild boar, but who knows what lurks in the forest. The creature left the boar closer to the house, away from Lipton's body, a gesture of consideration I appreciated. It's hard enough finding pleasure in animal meat these days without the alluring aroma of Lipton's flesh nearby.

"Oh," I reply finally, struggling to find a response. Graham and I are verbally tiptoeing around each other, neither of us willing to restoke the fires from last night. "I see."

I don't want Graham here. I will have to feed Sweetheart, and I'm unsure of how to do that with him lingering around the house. But in his next sentence, Graham saves me the trouble of stressing.

"I'm going to church," he informs me as he rolls out of bed, cracking his neck and groaning, rubbing a hand across his beard. "They have a late-morning Friday mass."

"Uh, OK," I say. "Sounds good."

I watch him go into the bathroom, bare legs poking from his boxers. My stomach grumbles, and I hastily get up, rushing to the nursery next door, not bothering to change out of my long, flannel pajamas.

I check on Sweetheart, tying a bandanna around my head to hide the growing scales on my scalp. My daughter is alert and grousing, but she perks up when I enter, turning her satiny eyes toward me.

She has yet again grown overnight—there is no amazement left inside me. Sweetheart is busting out of the onesie she's in; I only bought clothes for babies who are zero to six months, and Sweetheart is well past that size now. I lean over the crib to help her out of the too-tight outfit. She rolls around her mattress happily, naked save for her cloth diaper, holding her feet in her hands, gurgling at me. Her white eyes are crinkled. Sharp teeth and nails glint in the morning light.

"Food," she babbles.

She can't be hungry again already, can she? She ate nearly half of Lipton yesterday.

"Food," Sweetheart confirms.

But Graham is still in the other room. "Soon," I whisper to her. "He's leaving soon. Then we—*you* can eat."

She blows a bubble of spit and giggles when it pops, spraying her face. I don't know if she understands, but Sweetheart rolls to her side and begins to crawl around the crib, sniffing the air.

I make sure to shut the nursery door tight when I leave, telling Graham she's asleep when he emerges from the bathroom.

"I'll be back later," Graham says. "Hopefully with a clear head."

"That'd be lovely."

He gives me a look and clomps down the stairs, allowing me to get dressed in private. He leaves an ominous trail in the house, a presentiment I don't want to acknowledge. The garage door slams, and I wonder about the magnitude of Graham taking off work to go to church alone. He didn't even bother to invite me or see Sweetheart.

Opening my closet, I make to reach for yet another pair of joggers, neatly folded on the top shelf above my many dresses, but my eyes catch on a streak of darkness among my beige and neutral-toned belongings.

Two years ago, Graham's uncle passed away. We traveled out west for the funeral. Black isn't my color, but I purchased a pleated ebony long-sleeved dress with a sash around the middle for the occasion. It calls to me now.

I haven't worn a dress in weeks, but I slip out of the flannel pajamas and pull the vintage-style garment off the hanger and over my head. I tie the sash tight around my waist, fix the cuffs at the ends of the billowing sleeves that cover my scarred arm. The fabric falls down to my ankles like a heavy curtain.

I yank off the bandanna and let my oil-slicked locks spill down my shoulders. The scales on my head are itchy, and I scratch absently, noting that there are more of them today. A clump of hair comes out in my hand, and I toss it on the floor, unbothered.

Reaching for tights, thinking of also adding black socks to hide my missing toes, I pause. I push the closet door closed. Today I will go barefoot.

I return to the nursery, feeling like a bat stirring from its cave, cloaked in black.

"Food!" Sweetheart is screeching now and standing completely upright once again.

"All right. Let's get a quick breakfast, then," I tell her. "And then we can nap? You're always sleepy afterwards."

She gurgles her acceptance of this plan, and I heft her onto my hip to take her downstairs and out back. She's definitely bigger. Her weight on my waist causes me to slouch over to the side. Sweetheart tries to nibble on my shoulder as we walk toward the field, and I kiss her forehead and hush her even though she's not making any sounds.

"Soon," I promise.

When we reach Lipton, I watch her eat, winded, tasting the gore on my soft palate, inspired by her voraciousness. I stop her after she finishes Lipton's right thigh. This is a cruel torment, one I can't take any longer.

"That's enough for now," I whisper, even though Sweetheart protests and reaches back over my shoulder for her cache as I carry her away.

Back upstairs, I place her in the crib, relieved she's heavy lidded and yawning despite having her feeding cut short. I could use a nap too. It's too difficult to be awake right now, throbbing with want and hunger.

My phone hasn't left my bedside table all morning. I haven't checked my social media since Mara's betrayal. There's nothing for me there anymore, that much is clear.

I leave Sweetheart in the nursery and plod next door, throwing myself on our bed, swathed in the black gown. I slam a pillow over my head, shutting my eyes. My chest is full and bursting, like an overripe apricot. It takes a while for my breath to steady, but when it does, my body goes limp, strings cut.

Time blinks, and I dream.

The eye on my ceiling is no longer one giant eye. Instead, it's thousands and thousands of tiny ones, all blinking and rattling together, a collage of pupils and eyelashes and wet gazes. The wings surrounding the mosaic are tipped in black this time, as if they have been dunked in ink, and sticky feathers drift down to land on my frozen body, gently kissing my bare skin; I am naked, and the bed is empty. The room is a dark cavern.

The voice ripples from the ceiling, landing on my face like warm rain: *When you are ready, we are ready.*

The tiny eyes above me clack together as they all blink in unison, lashes like silver spears clanging against each other. Slowly they change, white sclerae expanding, spreading like moldy rot, morphing together. The wings flap and a slightly sour breeze ushers in a deep exhale from my body.

One giant white eye stares down at me. *Allow me to fix it. Fix everything.*

No, I think urgently. *It's my life. I have to do this myself.*

Are you sure? So quick. So easy.

My chin moves an infinitesimal amount from side to side as I launch my thoughts toward the familiar white eye: *It's my responsibility. I must do it for me.*

The voice repeats *When you are ready, we are ready.* A pause, then, again, *We are ready.*

I lick my lips. Part my mouth. And this time, finally, I can speak. "I am ready."

The white eye begins to fade, the wings start to disappear. Only the voice remains, echoing around the room: *Ready. Ready. Ready.*

I jolt awake.

Graham is sitting on the bed, watching me.

CHAPTER

32

THE LIGHT IN the room is low—streaks of sunset bleed through the gauzy curtains.

"Jesus," I say, jumping. "Why are you doing that? How long have you been there?"

"Taking the Lord's name in vain, Camille, really?" Graham snaps.

I didn't even notice. "Oh, sorry. It's . . . I was napping. Sweetheart's napping too, in the nursery. I thought you were at church."

"I was," Graham says tersely. "It's over. I'm back now. The sun is setting. How long have you been asleep?"

"How long have you been gone?" I retort to cover up my disorientation. I slept the whole day? Graham was *gone* the whole day? The sun sets earlier now, but it's hard to believe I lost all that time.

"Camille?" Graham tries to get my attention. "What are you wearing? Is that the dress you wore to Uncle Freddy's funeral?"

I sit up, lunging for my phone, which is still connected to the charging port on the bedside table, since I haven't used it yet today. Ignoring Graham, I flick open the baby monitor app. Sweetheart is awake. She's once again standing in the crib, holding the bars, staring directly at the monitor. Not a noise comes from the nursery. It's like she's listening, even though I'm sure she can't hear us next door.

"Camille."

"Yes, husband?" I reply, and Graham frowns. My lips flatten grimly as I realize he must have heard the note of sarcasm in my voice. I can't help it. I can't pretend with him anymore; slips of resentment are making it through the cracks in my veneer.

"Get up," he orders, and I despise the way he talks to me. Like I'm a pet or a child he needs to condescend to. Will he speak to Sweetheart like this when she gets older? "I'll meet you downstairs. We need to talk."

Graham rises with an air of gravitas, like he's done something incredibly noble and brave, and sweeps from the room.

I kick the blankets off, revealing my bare feet. My missing toes throb. I don't know exactly what Graham wants to talk about, but I know what he wants to see when I come downstairs. Contrite, demure Camille. Graham wants the woman dusted in flour and kissed by the sun. I could still save this. I could give him what he wants—I could beg for his forgiveness. It would work; he would benevolently pardon me and continue quietly seeing Rose on the side.

I know exactly what to do to smooth it all over.

But when I walk downstairs, I haven't changed out of the black dress. I leave my feet unadorned. The scaly scabs on my scalp are shining in the artificial lights. I catch a glimpse of my reflection in the hall mirror as I pass by; there's an unmistakable greenish tint to my skin, as if I'm standing over a brackish pond lit by sunlight. My cheeks are hollow, but my body is broader, more muscled than ever before.

I am different. I am strong. I am *hungry*.

I find Graham in the dining area, sitting at the table, fingers steepled together. At the sight of me, his expression darkens and his eyes crease; I've confirmed something for him.

"Lord," he breathes.

"How was church?" I ask, smiling. My teeth are pointier than they used to be. I noticed them this morning, tapered and silvery. I must be too far away for Graham to see, because he doesn't react.

"It was good. Illuminating," Graham replies. "I went to confession. Talked to the priest. Thought a lot. And I know what I need to do now."

"Sure," I say, drawing out the word, noticing a dawning heaviness in the house.

"Take a seat, Camille." Graham's voice is dry and empty like a grave. "I'm sorry it has to come to this, but I think we're at that point now."

I don't want to "take a seat"; foreboding creeps over my flesh, but I obey because part of me is curious. Whatever Graham is going to say can't be worse than what he's already done, right? My handsome, lying, cheating husband.

There's a small piece of white lint balanced on the tip of Graham's right ear. I focus on it, wondering how it hasn't fallen off yet.

"I love you very much, Camille," Graham starts, and my heart skips a beat, because there's an unmistakable note of farewell in his voice. "I want you to be happy. But you've changed a lot since we moved here. You're no longer taking care of the house. You're not even taking care of yourself. I mean, what's on your head? Are you gluing stuff to your hair now?" He adjusts the volume of his voice, clearing his throat and calming himself

down. "You aren't the woman I married. You don't seem interested in me anymore. And besides all that, my commute is too
difficult to keep doing. You and Sweetheart are amazing, but . . .
I don't want to be with you anymore. Not in a romantic way. Do
you understand?"

There's a throbbing sound in my head, wet and thunderous.
I wonder if there's blood pooling behind my eardrums, filling my
ear canals and sloshing around with every rapid beat of my heart.

I'm not "interested" in Graham? He's right, but he doesn't
mean sexually or emotionally. He means I've stopped catering to
his every need. I'm no longer his perfect wife, and he can't abide
that.

"What are you saying, Graham?" I ask, my voice coming
from far away. "Spit it out. I don't need a rehearsed speech."

He takes a deep breath. "This is over. *We* are over."

My heart isn't breaking—it broke a long time ago, perhaps
in my childhood—but it *is* shaking, rattling around in my chest.
Delusion, aggressive and hungry, tries to rise and envelop my
brain: *It will all be OK; he'll change his mind; he doesn't mean it;
he loves you; he is a good husband.*

I squash it, allowing room for rage instead. "I thought
divorce was against your beliefs," I say, my lips numb.

"I'll be seeking an annulment," Graham says.

This moron.

"Under what grounds?" The words march out of my mouth
wearing heavy boots.

"Misrepresentation. You . . . you aren't the person I thought
I was marrying. Where is that sweet, innocent girl whose greatest dream was to have a family?"

"I misrepresented myself?" I snarl.

Maybe he's right. I misrepresented the truth to myself too. I
buried away my interests; I ate what I was told to eat; I exercised

the way I was told to exercise; I posted what I was expected to post online. I was born in a small container, so I remained there, not realizing that perhaps I could fill more than the confining walls established by the men in my life.

All I ever wanted was to be loved. But the love I sought had conditions attached: my father, Graham, the fickle community on social media. I was only loved when I was doing what they expected, what they wanted.

Until the creature. Until Sweetheart.

Graham complains, "Camille, you've been irritable, you haven't let me touch you since the birth, and look at the house!" From the violent anger in his voice, I suspect he's remembering the one time he tried to have sex with me, so recently after Sweetheart's birth, and the refusal I laid at his doorstep. He rejected me for months, but when I do it once, the sky falls down. "This house is a mess, Camille. What have you even been doing here?"

"Taking care of our daughter," I hiss, jerking my head up, in the direction of the nursery. I yank out my phone, pull up the live feed from the baby monitor. I shove the screen toward Graham's face, shaking it. "I do everything myself. You haven't helped out once. I'm tired and overworked, but I've been a kind, considerate wife. Yet *I'm* the one who misrepresented themselves in this relationship?" I give him a meaningful look, then drop my voice. "If your precious church finds out what you've done, it's *you* who will be disgraced." I close the video feed and put my phone away, slipping it into the pockets of my dress, raising my eyebrows at my husband.

The lint on Graham's ear wobbles as his voice rises. "You don't know what the hell you're talking about, Camille. And you have no proof of any . . . indiscretions you think I might have engaged in. Which I didn't."

A liar until the very end. I can almost respect it. Though I pity the past version of myself who would have eaten that up, believed every festering word out of this man's mouth because that was easier than admitting something wasn't perfect. Before Sweetheart, I thought Graham's increasing distance and disinterest were due to my shortcomings. My failure to live up to the expectations of being the adulated homesteading wife I saw online. Now I can see Graham's detachment is because he's a coward.

He shrugs to release some of the anger in his voice. He fiddles with his wedding ring, like he can't wait to rip it off. "Listen, it's been decided. I'm pursuing an annulment. I'll help out with Sweetheart when needed. I'll be fair. I'll send money. You can keep the house, even. But it's over."

It's almost amusing how confident he sounds. None of it is cemented yet, but because he's made his choice, he believes it so.

Renee lost everything after her divorce. Her husband got custody, she barely saw her children, and no one even noticed she was missing until it was too late. I don't like the parallels between her situation and mine. Graham has a job, a support system. I do not. Right now, he's saying he'll provide for us and assist with Sweetheart, but what if he changes his mind? What if he decides he wants custody? Or a paternity test? What if he takes me to court and the same thing that happened to Renee happens to me? He could ruin everything.

Graham wants to throw us away, but at any moment, he could change his mind and take my daughter. I can't live on his allowance, his pity, relying on the weakness of hope that he will stick to his word. Most of all, I can't risk Sweetheart being exposed to the wider world and being labeled a monster by real ones.

Graham is already living in a future without me, outlining it with a faux gracious attitude; he can't imagine things playing out a different way.

But I can.

"There's something you need to know about your daughter first," I say, interrupting the silence we are sitting in. I don't smile. My frown settles in as if it has bags and intends to stay for a while. That's fine; I'm owed a few frowns.

Graham looks suspicious. "What?"

I get up. "Come on."

He shakes his head. "What's going on, Camille? Did you hear what I said? It's over."

He wants me to beg and scream and cry and plead for him to stay. It's what he's hoping for, and perhaps if I do it, he really will reconsider. He's leaving not because of the other woman or the stress of being a new father but because I have changed, and that scares him. He didn't think, after four years, I was capable of changing. He liked the cardboard-cutout version of me that he could carry around and set up where he wanted. It must be shocking for him—as if a store mannequin suddenly came to life and called you a dick.

"I heard you," I say. I will not ask him to stay. The delusion has faded. "Please. Come upstairs. I need to show you some-thing. Then you can leave. I won't fight you on anything. I'll agree to your annulment."

Graham's eyes widen. "Really?"

"I promise."

He gets to his feet and follows me up the dark staircase, down the upstairs hallway, and into Sweetheart's nursery. The night-light casts a yellow hue on the walls as the orange sunset creeps in through the cracks in the curtains. Sweetheart twitches in her crib, waiting.

"Come closer to the crib," I say.

He does, but stops a few feet away, jaw dipping open.

Sweetheart's white eyes shine in the dim lighting, and her head turns, taking in Graham. Her fingers clutch the railing of the crib as she stands on thick legs, watchful.

"What the fuck, Camille," Graham croaks. "What happened? What's wrong with her eyes? What did you *do*?"

"I didn't do anything," I snap. "She's always been like this. You never noticed."

"She's standing . . ." he whispers. "She's *big*. That's not . . . She can't . . ."

"You would have known if you were around. You barely interacted with your daughter." I stress the last word so that Graham can't help but notice.

He glances at me over his shoulder. "What do you mean?"

I smile at him, baring my teeth. This time, he notices—he flinches, gawking at the row of fangs that weren't there yesterday. Giving him a good look, I say, "She's not yours. See?" I point at Sweetheart, and Graham reluctantly turns back to her as if he has no control over his body.

I glance over at the lamp on the dresser. Its wrought-iron base is pale green, designed to look like a vine reaching upward to house the bulb and wicker shade. The night-light makes the lamp's stand look like it's glowing in photosynthesis.

"Go on," I say again, sliding away from Graham as he takes another shuffle toward the crib, drawn into Sweetheart's hoary stare like a moth to a bonfire.

A gagging sound comes from Graham's throat, and my stomach lurches, aching with hunger.

His voice radiates around the nursery, laced with vehemence. "She's not . . . she's not human. This is . . . unholy. This is evil. And your *teeth* . . . Good Lord in heaven, Camille, what did you—"

Graham's words are interrupted by the base of the lamp smashing into the back of his head with a wet *crunch*.

The lamp is heavy in my hands—I left the shade on the dresser, quietly unplugging the cord while Graham examined Sweetheart, and now I swing again, bringing it down on the top of Graham's head.

Sweetheart shrieks gleefully as Graham flops to the ground in front of the crib, slapping her hands against the bars. Hot blood sprays our faces, and I lick a drop that lands on my bottom lip. Flavor surges through my mouth, alighting on my tongue, spreading through my body until I am burning, a wild, ceaseless fire that begs to be released.

Dropping to my knees, I turn Graham over, lovingly undressing him the way I used to do on the nights he approached me with clumsy hands and starving eyes. But this time, when I brush my lips against his chest, I do not stop there. My jaw clicks, hinging wide, wider than I thought possible, and I sink my teeth into my husband's body.

I'm not sure he's dead yet.

The first bite sends me into utter ecstasy. Electric trembles vibrate my spine; drool spins across the floor as I become a frenzied tornado of sharp nails and snapping fangs. My abdomen clenches in pleasure as I inhale the steaming meat, the freshest blood I've ever tasted. I find the heart, gently quivering, and squelch it between my canines.

I lose myself in the feast, disappearing into the rampant flavors that decorate my mouth, traveling down to my patient stomach.

I am vaguely aware of Sweetheart chattering above me, but I cannot stop. Not now that I've started. Blood blotches my face like sludgy honey, and nothing has ever tasted this good; not the butter pats, not the dead animals, not a single thing that has ever passed my lips.

At some point I remember the baby monitor, pointed directly at the crib, and I look up, innards dribbling down my chin, staring right into the camera.

I lift a hand, coated in a glove of red, and wave, then return to my meal.

33

I EAT ALMOST ALL of him.

After filling myself enough to be woozy, I pull back, surveying the mess.

I rip the remains of a forearm free, using my teeth to sever the tendons that struggle to keep the limb connected to the elbow. There are hunks of unmarred flesh on the forearm, and I reach over the top of the crib, giving the appendage to my daughter. She grumps, offended I've taken this long to remember her, and plops down on the mattress pad to work at the arm like it's corn on the cob.

I lick blood from my hands, suck the shredded muscle glued to the diamonds on my wedding ring. When I finish, my heart rate is steady and slow.

Retrieving my phone from my stained skirts, I open the baby monitor app. It records all footage, deleting it after twenty-four hours. I tap through the recent recording, rewinding, watching myself feed. What a beautiful bonding moment for this family: a fabulous feast, provided by the husband. Look how much we love each other.

I download the video to my device, trimming and cropping it. My body, black and white and covered in gore, fills the screen, waving a hand.

Baring my teeth, I upload the video to my social media.

I tap out a caption. Hit post. Drop the phone so it lands upright near the ravaged, inhuman form smeared on the floor. The phone screen winks at me as the video appears at the top of my feed.

Reaching over the crib, I help Sweetheart clamber out. She's gnawing on the ulna, cracking it open to get to the marrow within, but she drops it and clings to my chest instead. Clutching her tightly, I glance down, barely able to read the single line of text I typed under the video, which is automatically playing:

Fuck you, Mara Shoemaker. #tradwife

We head out of the nursery and turn right, stepping into the bedroom I used to share with my husband. Sweetheart protests on my hip; she wants to go outside.

"One minute," I whisper. "I need to get something."

Stopping at my bedside table, I open the drawer and suck the wedding ring off my finger, spitting it free. The big center diamond clatters against the wooden surface as the ring bounces down to the floor. Ignoring it, I dip a hand into the open drawer and pull out the penny.

"OK," I whisper to my daughter as I slip the penny into my dress pocket. "Let's go."

On the way downstairs, I catch a glimpse of myself in the hall mirror and pause.

I have perfect vision. I can see everything in crystal clarity. That hasn't changed. But something else has. My eyes have always been brown. The color of freshly baked goods.

"Look," I whisper to my daughter, shifting so she can see herself in the mirror too. Our faces look good together. Strong. Alluring. "We are the same."

My sclerae have swallowed up my brown irises and black pupils. The eyes that blink back at me in the mirror are completely white.

34

WE FIND THE creature in the backyard, waiting at the border of the wheat field. Its face doesn't change at our approach, but I sense a tug from it that I gravitate to.

My black skirts drag along the ground, stirring up dust and dead grass.

The sun slips behind the horizon as the indigo light of dusk blankets the wide, empty field. When we reach the creature, I place Sweetheart down, and she sways on her feet, chirping at her father like a bird.

"I am ready," I say.

The creature doesn't move, only looks at me with that fathomless white gaze. Its wings are unfurled, ushering in the creeping night.

"You know," I remark, noticing how difficult it is to talk with all my new teeth. "I think I knew all along. I think it was easier for me to pretend. To hide behind my naivety. I did what I needed to do. I thought I was saving my marriage. I didn't think I'd feel this way about you."

The creature doesn't say anything. It doesn't need to. Soon I won't need to either.

The wheat rustles around us, stalks rattling and sighing in harmony. The air smells of stars and soil.

The creature reaches out to me, and I fall into its ropy arms, turning my face up so that it—*he*—can place his lips on my own. Blistering heat travels down my chest, and a sudden absence of sound echoes through my body. I can't place it at first.

The creature deepens the kiss, and our teeth click together, diamond daggers wrapped in our soft mouths.

"Ma!"

I pull back from the creature, looking down.

Sweetheart, completely naked, standing fully on her own, huffs up at the two of us, locked in embrace.

"Food," Sweetheart says, as if she's reminding us of restaurant reservations.

And then she takes a step toward us.

"Oh!" I cry. "Oh, you're walking!"

The creature twists his head at my voice, and we break free from each other, arms still entwined, watching as the beautiful baby we made hobbles toward us, stepping carefully but surely. I kneel down to meet her when she approaches, my eyes watering, milky-white streaks blurring my line of sight.

"Food," Sweetheart insists. She didn't eat enough of her surrogate father. I suppose I was a bit greedy, but in my defense, I was starving.

"Yes," I say, glancing back up at the creature, smiling at his placid, remarkable face. "Let's get you a real meal."

Lipton's remains are nearby, and Sweetheart knows it—her nostrils are flaring again.

The creature helps me to my feet, slips an arm around my black-clad shoulders, and stoops to take Sweetheart's hand in his own.

The three of us slowly walk over to the decomposing human, kneeling in front of it to have our first meal together as a family.

35

SATIATED AND SLEEPY, we amble through the wheat field. The sun has left bruised colors in the sky, and we admire them as we reach the old well. I rub a finger across the mossy stones and stop, reaching into my pocket and pulling the penny free.

"Goodbye," I murmur against the copper coin.

Holding a hand out over the well, I let the penny fall, not bothering to watch it disappear into the maw of darkness. I trail after the others, heading to the trees knotting the path ahead.

The creature is holding Sweetheart's hand, and they pull ahead of me, stepping lightly toward the crush of foliage before us. I drink them up, watching the easy way they move together, the wordless current that flows between them. Soon that will be me too. Soon I will abandon anything else that tethers me to Camille.

I will be as beautifully unholy as the rest of my family.

My daughter and her father step into the forest, welcomed by black branches and snarled lichen. The scent of ancient, rotting pines and damp fungi brushes my face; soaking stones and the faint lullaby of mildew hover farther inside the embrace of the woods. The approaching night promises to be freezing and unforgiving, but my chest is warm, my extremities gloved with heat.

My dress is tattered and torn. I help along its destruction, slicing through the rips with my clawed hands, slashing it from my body. I leave the black fabric in a pile on the ground in front of the woods, stepping out of my undergarments, relishing the wind against my scored, scaled skin.

I glance over my shoulder once to look at the shadow of our former house, outlined in blue dusk and the first peeps of a half-moon over the wheat field.

The forest hums, bringing me back, and now it sounds like a song, haunting and welcoming. Facing the woods, I place a hand over my naked breast. It is a tomb, holding the remnants of what used to be there.

Enjoying the absence of my heartbeat, I follow my family into the trees.

ACKNOWLEDGEMENTS

T HE RISE OF tradwives is a symptom of society's larger, more persistent issues. Capitalism, racism, sexism, etc., have created a culture that can twist things as simple as aesthetics and farm living into something far more insidious. Zen Buddhists say the only way out is through. I believe the only way out is to *devour*. Let's consume, transform, and in that way, resist. Maybe that's how we give ourselves a new start. (To be clear, I'm not advocating you go eat your neighbor. This is a metaphorical feeding.)

I had a lot fun writing *Trad Wife*, and I hope you had fun reading it, even though it touches upon some dark stuff. If any part of Camille's story resonated with you, I hope this book was cathartic to consume. And, if you, like me, escaped a toxic situation, I hope you let your hunger guide you to what you truly deserve.

As always, a huge thank you to my fearless lion of an agent Amy Giuffrida, who upon reading the toe scene for the first time messaged me in all caps saying, "WHO ARE YOU??" I'm very glad to have you and your expertise in my corner.

To my editor Rebecca Nelson—who was immediately just as passionate about this deranged book as I was—thank you for helping me polish this story until it shined like monster teeth.

Thank you to the whole Crooked Lane Books team, including Dulce Botello and the marketing department, Stephanie Manova and the subsidiary rights department, Thaisheemarie Fantauzzi Perez, and all the other team members who worked on this project in some capacity. Thank you to Meghan Deist for the creep-tastic cover!

Thank you to my early readers for their undeniable enthusiasm and helpful notes. Brooke Dorsch, I thoroughly appreciated you saying this was "beautiful and disgusting." Eren Simpson—thank you so much for matrescence. It's perfect.

To the A Team and Boozeless Book Club—I still can't believe how lucky I am to have such positive and wholesome communities of writers and readers in my life.

Cricket and Sloopy, thanks for being by my side (or literally *on* my side) during drafting, and thank you to Reg and Blake for screaming at me to take breaks during pass pages.

Mark, thank you once again for taking my headshots and barely blinking when I described the premise of this book. I promise not to eat you. (Unless you suddenly turn into Graham. And then all bets are off.)

To Bella, my forever first reader—thank you for not knowing what tradwives are and making me explain them to you. I got the idea for this book mid-text and immediately pitched it to you, upon which you said, "Sounds like I will read it." And you did. *Trad Wife* literally would not exist without you. I love you and our nontraditional ways.

Thank you, Mom and Dad, for raising us to question, consider, and forge our own paths. I'm lucky our little unit is on the same page, and consistently grateful to have parents like you.

To all the readers, bookstores, libraries, social media reviewers and authors who have taken a chance on my work, thank you so very much. I couldn't do this without your support.

Last, and most certainly the least, to the men who thought they would never have to face the consequences—how do my teeth feel?

Saratoga Schaefer has a background in marketing, content creation, film and art and has been writing stories about murder for as long as they can remember. In addition to telling stories and acting as an alcohol-free ambassador, Saratoga climbs rocks, teaches yoga and hikes mountains. Originally from Brooklyn, Saratoga now lives in upstate NY with an anxious dog and a very possessive cat.